DEATH AMONG THE DAFFODILS

De Lacey and Squires Mysteries
Book 2

AVIVA ORR

ARE YOU SIGNED UP FOR DRAGONBLADE'S BLOG?

You'll get the latest news and information on exclusive giveaways, exclusive excerpts, coming releases, sales, free books, cover reveals and more.

Check out our complete list of authors, too!

No spam, no junk. That's a promise!

Sign Up Here

www.dragonbladepublishing.com

Dearest Reader;

Thank you for your support of a small press. At Dragonblade Publishing, we strive to bring you the highest quality Historical Romance from some of the best authors in the business. Without your support, there is no 'us', so we sincerely hope you adore these stories and find some new favorite authors along the way.

Happy Reading!

CEO, Dragonblade Publishing

Additional Dragonblade Books by Author Aviva Orr

De Lacey and Squires Mysteries
Death at Villa De Lacey (Book 1)
Death Among the Daffodils (Book 2)

Love and Literature Series
Love and Literature (Book 1)
Love and Vengeance (Book 2)
Love and Liberty (Book 3)

The Lyon's Den Series
The Lyon and The Rose of Mayfair
The Imperfect Lyon

I wandered lonely as a cloud
That floats on high o'er vales and hills,
When all at once I saw a crowd,
A host, of golden daffodils;
Beside the lake, beneath the trees,
Fluttering and dancing in the breeze.

Continuous as the stars that shine
And twinkle on the milky way,
They stretched in never-ending line
Along the margin of a bay:
Ten thousand saw I at a glance,
Tossing their heads in sprightly dance.

The waves beside them danced; but they
Out-did the sparkling waves in glee:
A poet could not but be gay,
In such a jocund company:
I gazed—and gazed—but little thought
What wealth the show to me had brought:

For oft, when on my couch I lie
In vacant or in pensive mood,
They flash upon that inward eye
Which is the bliss of solitude;
And then my heart with pleasure fills,
And dances with the daffodils.

William Wordsworth, 1802

CHAPTER ONE

Westmorland, England
Spring 1821

PLANTING THE DAFFODILS had been Bridget's idea, and what a good idea it was, she told herself as she stepped outside and inhaled the crisp early morning air. The sea of yellow that now dominated the front edge of Villa De Lacey's Garden looked spectacular against the backdrop of Lake Windermere's sparkling blue waters and lush green fells. They were the perfect greeting for all who entered the gates of Villa De Lacey. After all, this was the land of the lakes, home to William Wordsworth, and what could better honor Westmorland's greatest poet—and greatest poem—than a field of daffodils?

But it wasn't only the daffodils' beauty and symbolism that had made them attractive to Bridget—they also served a purpose. The flowers were a distraction from the villa's notorious Venus fountain and adjacent rose beds, tucked away to the far right of the garden. The area had been the scene of one of two crimes that had taken place at Villa De Lacey during the previous summer. And rather than repelling potential customers to her luxurious inn on the shores of Lake Windermere, the murders had drawn a host of curious guests, eager to stay at what had now become known as the infamous "murder inn."

Bridget shook the morbid memory from her mind and smiled at the small white terrier who trotted by her side. An orange butterfly fluttered past his face, skimming the tip of his little black nose. He responded by barking and chasing after it, his tail wagging as he romped across the grass. She laughed at her pup and took a deep breath, enjoying the fresh, sweet scents of spring. The smell of blossoming flowers and new grass filled her nostrils. Bridget smiled to herself. Just like the world emerging from winter, bursting with new life and color, her future was filled with renewed promise—a stark contrast to her world just one year earlier when she'd experienced the darkest day of her life.

That was the day she had received news of her papa's death—and worst of all—been told that he'd died by his own hand. That day, her world had turned as black as the treacherous storm clouds she'd feared as a child. She'd not only become an orphan, her mama having died when she was a little girl, but she had almost lost the home she'd shared with her papa and aunt. Her papa had gambled their beloved Villa De Lacey in a card game, losing it to a wealthy earl, and he had not been able to cope with that catastrophe—a catastrophe that had been building for years, due to a secret gambling habit that Bridget had known nothing about. Her papa had been devoted to her and her aunt, and she imagined the shame of what he had done was too much for him to bear. So, he'd chosen the worst option possible, leaving this world and all his problems behind him. Bridget had tried to reconcile why her devoted father would leave her and her aunt to fend for themselves. And she knew in her heart it was because he believed she would find a husband to provide for them.

But Bridget had refused to give up and leave the only place she had ever called home. Villa De Lacey had been built by her French grandfather, who'd fallen in love with the remote Lake District while visiting the area. Wanting to live out his days in the exquisite region but still missing his home country, he'd built himself a three-story, eighteen-room French villa from Parisian Lutetian stone. Trimmed with pale blue shutters, a matching two-paneled double door, and a fleur-de-lis railing that wrapped around the raised portico, it was a piece of home in a new land.

Villa De Lacey was the only home Bridget had ever known,

and she loved it with all her heart. She'd dreaded facing its new owner—the man who'd not only taken her home but her father's dignity and, ultimately, his life. But things are not always what they seem. The Earl of Westerly had won Villa De Lacey, but he'd forced it upon his wayward brother, Nathaniel Squires, in a bid to banish him from London. And just two months after her papa's death, Nate had arrived to claim his new home. But Nate was nothing like the ogre she had imagined the new owner to be. He was charming, kind-hearted, and determined to gain independence from his controlling older brother, who'd banished him from London and forced him to Westmorland. So, Bridget developed a plan that allowed her to stay in her home and gave Nate the independence he craved.

It so happened that Nate's arrival at Villa De Lacey coincided with the publication of Wordsworth's new guidebook to the region, which had sent wealthy visitors flocking to Westmorland. An exclusive inn was precisely what Westmorland needed, and Villa De Lacey, sitting on the shores of the magnificent Lake Windermere, was the perfect location. Nate had agreed to try Bridget's plan and appointed her hostess of their new inn.

That had been a mere eight months ago, and the transition of her ancestral home into an inn had not been smooth. Scandalous behavior, theft, and murder had plagued them soon after they opened their doors to the public, forcing Bridget and Nate to become investigators in their own home. But all those troubles now seemed far behind them. Although she ached for her papa every day, Villa De Lacey was thriving, and her future seemed to hold promise once again.

Bijou's high-pitched bark caught Bridget's attention, and she shielded her face with her hand as she scanned the garden for her terrier. Shock seized her heart when she spotted him standing at the very edge of the massive field of daffodils.

"Come, boy!" Bridget ran toward Bijou, her heart racing. He knew not to go near the daffodils—indeed, he had avoided them like the plague ever since a recent foray into the sea of flowers had made him sick. On that day, he'd chewed on a flower petal and suffered for it. That was the day Bridget had discovered a sinister side to the beautiful spring flowers. She had not known the pretty yellow daffodils could harm her dog, and neither had Thomas, her gardener. After the incident, she'd considered asking Thomas to rip them from the ground, but it turned out to be unnecessary because Bijou had learned his lesson and kept his distance from the flowers. *So, what is drawing him there now?*

Bijou continued to bark, but stayed at the edge of the daffodil field, not daring to venture inside.

"What is it, boy? What have you found?" Bridget said as she neared the daffodils. *It's likely another field vole.* Bridget shuddered, remembering the last terrified little creature Bijou had dropped at her feet. The poor thing had been paralyzed with fear. But luckily, Bijou had not injured it. He was a hunter but not a killer. She'd scooped the furry little creature up in the palm of her hand and carried it back to the thicket that surrounded the garden, where it had disappeared among the grass and trees as soon as she'd set it down.

Bridget hoisted Bijou off the ground, tucking him safely under her arm, and then peered into the sea of flowers. Bijou whined. "Shh," she said soothingly. Then she saw something that made her momentarily freeze.

A person lay among the daffodils.

Bridget could see the form of a man's body and his thick blond hair, cascading in waves at the back of his head. Recognizing the lush, yellow hair, she relaxed and smiled. "It's George," she said, planting a kiss on Bijou's snout. "Just silly old George."

She skipped through the daffodils toward the young poet, who'd become a frequent visitor and entertainer at Villa De Lacey. *What wonders is George dreaming up among those daffodils whilst contemplating the clouds?* she thought happily. But as she neared her friend, she stopped abruptly. Something was wrong.

George's thick, yellow hair was matted with what looked like wet soil or dirt. His arm lay stretched out behind his head, and his stiff hand grasped at the air.

"George?" she said, inching forward. Then she gasped out loud. George's white shirt had been ripped open, and his chest was smeared with dried blood—or something that resembled blood. Bridget covered her mouth with her hand and turned abruptly away from the body, her heart beating wildly.

This is one of his tricks. It must be. The young poet was known for his dramatic flair and grand gestures in the name of art. Was this some form of grim artistic expression? Had he staged his own gruesome death for the sake of his writing? Was George making a point about his body being one with nature? Or was this inspiration for a masterpiece that was currently forming in his mind?

"George!" she said sternly, her back still to the poet. "You know I support your art, but this will scare our guests." *Or perhaps it will delight them,* she thought cynically. When no answer came, she turned and took a cautious step toward the body, her mind doubting her eyes and her heart racing. "George!" she snapped.

Just then, two black crows swooped in front of Bridget's face, causing her to stumble backward. She tried to shoo them away, but the birds, seemingly unflustered by her frantic hand waving and Bijou's barking, landed on George and started pecking at what looked like a cavity in his chest.

Bridget put her hand to her throat as a wave of nausea hit her. The ground swayed beneath her feet as she raced out of the daffodil field. This was no act. George was dead!

NATE SAW BRIDGET go down from his bedroom window.

Drawing open the curtains and stretching in front of the exquisite view whilst taking in the sun's rays had become part of Nate's early morning routine since he'd moved to Westmorland. And when he did so this morning, he saw Bridget running through the field of daffodils with Bijou under her arm. Then he watched her fall. Bijou flew out of her arms and rolled, then he turned and rushed back to Bridget, barking madly. One minute she'd been standing on her own two feet, and the next she was on the ground. Had she fainted?

The fact that he was in a state of undress did not stop Nate from rushing outside to her aid. He threw on his trousers and shirt, stuffed his feet into his shoes, and ordered his startled valet, who'd just brought in his morning tea, to fetch the smelling salts before he raced outside.

Bijou circled Bridget, pawing at her body and whining.

"I'm coming," Nate called. "Don't worry. I'm here now," he said as he approached Bridget and Bijou, but a murder of crows in the daffodils momentarily distracted him. *What is going on there?*

He glanced at Bridget, and seeing the rise and fall of her chest, breathed a sigh of relief. Then he strode forward into the daffodils, and what he saw there set the ground swaying beneath his own feet. A dead man lay among the flowers. Crows swarmed his chest, pecking and pulling at what looked to be his insides. The gruesome sight almost sent Nate to the ground alongside Bridget. He'd seen dead bodies before, but none as grim as this.

When Nate saw Bennett race toward him with the smelling salts, he sprinted forward and intercepted the man, not wanting him to witness the horrific sight. "Run and send for Magistrate Hunt. Then, bring me a sheet."

"A sheet, sir?" Bennett craned his neck to see behind Nate.

"Yes, a sheet. No! Make that two sheets—thick ones," he said, snatching the smelling salts from his valet's hand.

"Is the young lady—"

"She'll be fine! Go now!" Nate barked, giving Bennett a light push. "The magistrate and the sheets—run!"

"Yes, sir." Bennett's brown eyes grew wide. Then he turned and raced toward the villa.

Nate went to Bridget's side and placed the smelling salts under her pert nose. Her nostrils flared, and then her eyes opened. As always, Nate was taken aback by their pale blue loveliness. He felt a pleasurable flutter in his stomach, followed by an immediate sense of relief.

"Nate!" She blinked. "Oh, thank heavens! I…" She sat up and turned to look at the body in the daffodils. "Good grief, he's still there." She pressed a hand to her chest. "I wasn't imagining things! It's so horrible. Oh, Nate. Over there." She pointed to the daffodils now swarming with crows. "George is dead!"

George Otis. The poet? So that's who lies in the field. "I know," Nate said, shielding Bridget from the horror with his body. "Don't look again. It's too terrible. I've sent for Magistrate Hunt."

𝒫

"THE KILLER TOOK his heart." Magistrate Hunt knelt next to Otis's body and inspected the wound as Nate watched. Although sickened by the sight, he found he could not turn away. *Who would do such a thing to another human being? He looks like a butchered animal.* Nate dared not say the words out loud for Bridget's sake. She stood with her back to the body, cradling Bijou. Nate ached for her. She'd suffered tremendous losses already, and she'd been fond of the young poet. He hated that she hurt.

"But that's not what killed him." Magistrate Hunt lifted Otis's head slightly, and Nate saw the blood matted in his hair at the back of his head. "Someone hit him with something hard—possibly a rock." Magistrate Hunt gently placed Otis's head back onto the ground and scanned the area. "Here, what's this?" He reached forward and picked up a medium-sized rock that lay nearby. As he turned it over, Nate saw that the rock was stained with blood. "This is what ended him. It's not heavy, mind you. But with enough force, it could be lethal. I'd say the killer smashed his skull with this rock and took his heart after that."

Bizarrely, Nate felt some sort of relief at hearing that. He loathed to think that Otis—or any living creature—would have to endure having his heart torn from his chest while still conscious. Then again, it made sense that he had not been alive. Young and strong, Otis would likely have fought hard to save his life had he seen his assailant coming for him. But he'd been hit from behind—taken by surprise—and so had no chance to fight for his life. Whoever murdered Otis was a vicious killer. Someone extremely dangerous was on the loose—someone who'd been on their front lawn mere hours before.

🔍

"IT'S A BAD business." Magistrate Hunt pulled the sheets back over the victim, concealing the ugly wound in his chest cavity. "Never seen anything like it before—such brutality. I thought I'd seen it all last summer with those two murders, but it appears this place of yours attracts death. It's beginning to feel as if Mr. De Lacey cursed us with his act of self-murder. He brought darkness upon us with that act."

"That's preposterous!" Nate snapped, outraged on Bridget's behalf. He worried for Bridget and hated that people harbored superstitions about her father's actions. Self-murder was tragic, but Nate did not believe it to be an eternal sin. In this case, it had been the final act of a desperate man, one rendered hopeless by Nate's heartless brother.

"Don't get me wrong." Magistrate Hunt stood and brushed the soil from his trousers. "I respected Mr. De Lacey. He was an honest man and a friend. I want to uphold his reputation and that of his home. But all this death makes one wonder…"

"Mr. Otis wasn't even a guest here," Nate said. "His murder had nothing to do with Villa De Lacey."

"But he died on your land. And we can't rule out the possibility of another killer lurking behind your walls."

Bridget shuddered and pressed her face into Bijou's fur. Nate ached to comfort her, but he refrained from doing so. They'd only known each other a year, and she was still mourning her papa. She was essentially under his care, and she was vulnerable. As a gentleman, he would not take advantage of that.

Bridget turned and faced Otis's now-concealed body. "Whoever is responsible must be caught. It's a truly monstrous act, taking a man's heart," she said mournfully.

Nate knew she was thinking of her papa, who'd cruelly had a stake driven through his heart after dying by his own hand. Self-murder, according to the law, was murder. And that was how those who took their own lives were dealt with after death. But what terrible thing could Otis have done to deserve such a fate? "One can only wonder why," he murmured out loud.

"A jealous lover, perhaps?" Magistrate Hunt scratched his gray beard. "Jealousy is a powerful motive for murder. It's my understanding you were close to the victim, Miss De Lacey. How much did you know about his life?"

"Not much. As Nate has said, he wasn't a guest here, but he was a frequent visitor. He and his friends are poets—admirers of Wordsworth. They live in a small cottage about half a mile from here, between the lake and the village. But George…Mr. Otis…often spent time at Villa De Lacey, entertaining our guests."

"How so?" the magistrate asked. "Did he recite poetry to them?"

"Oh yes, oftentimes. He was charming and witty. People liked being in his company. He was the type of person who was favored by everyone."

Not everyone. Nate had seen the young man as more of a fop than a humble poet, but he refrained from expressing as much out of respect for Bridget's feelings.

"Charming, you say?" Magistrate Hunt arched his bushy eyebrows. "Would you say he was more popular with the ladies than the gentlemen?"

"I don't believe so. As I said, he was liked by everyone. All the guests seemed to enjoy his company. I know I did."

Nate's jaw tightened. The comment irked him. He'd been wary of Bridget's friendship with Otis. He hadn't entirely trusted the man. He had been, in Nate's opinion, a rake disguised as a poet. Otis had taken advantage of Bridget's good nature, and he'd often supped for free at the villa as though he were a paying guest. Bridget had reasoned that the guests adored the poet and that he'd kept them entertained. Nate knew that was only partially true. Some of the guests loved him. Others were irritated by him. But none, as far as he knew, had a motive to murder him.

"Was that what you observed too, Mr. Squires?" the magistrate asked as if reading Nate's thoughts.

"If you ask me, he flattered the ladies, and they enjoyed the attention," Nate said, unable to hold back any longer.

"Was there any lady in particular he favored?"

Bridget's forehead creased. "Well, I don't quite know. He spent a lot of time with Lady Matheson. She's a widow, and I think he made her feel a little less lonely."

Nate scoffed. Lady Matheson might be a widow of middle age, but he doubted she'd ever wanted for attention. She was, to put it mildly, a beautiful woman. Tall and lean with a swan-like neck, high cheekbones, almond-shaped amber eyes, and a head of light-brown curls. She never failed to capture the attention of men.

"Did this Lady Matheson have any other admirers?" Magistrate Hunt asked. "A wealthy widow is quite a prize."

"Wealthy and beautiful," Nate said before he could stop himself.

"Interesting." Magistrate Hunt drummed his fingers on the back of his hand. "Did you notice any tension or rivalry between your gentlemen guests and Mr. Otis?"

"No," Bridget said. "As I've already stated, Mr. Otis was well-liked. Everyone enjoyed his company. That's why he was a frequent guest. I—we—would not have allowed a troublemaker to infiltrate our villa and mingle with our guests."

"What about the ladies? Perhaps, one of them thought he was giving too much attention to Lady Matheson."

"I doubt that. Mr. Otis was generous with his time. He spent time talking to all of us, including me. Even Miss Jennings seemed to open up to him," Bridget said.

"Miss Jennings?" Magistrate Hunt lifted his brows in question.

"She's Lady Armstrong's companion," Bridget said.

"A spinster, in her late twenties, I'd say," Nate added. "She's a shy, quiet woman—petite, too. I doubt she would kill a fly, let alone a man."

"Hmm, yes. A young lady certainly would not have the strength or the stomach to remove a human heart. As I said before, a jealous husband or lover is far more likely our killer. Did he spend time with any other women in the house?"

"Only Mrs. Harley. You remember her from the summer. She and Mr. Harley decided to stay on as long-term guests."

"Was she close with Mr. Otis?"

"I believe they were friends," Bridget said.

"And Mr. Harley did not object to this friendship?"

"I don't believe so."

"Harley's not the jealous sort," Nate agreed. Though he was kind to his wife, Harley's marriage had not been a love match. It wasn't the sort of marriage Nate envisioned for himself.

"So, no enemies for Mr. Otis, then?"

"None that I know of. He was well-liked." Bridget continued to defend the poet. "I've said it many times because it's the truth."

"And this is your opinion too, Mr. Squires?"

"I am unaware of anyone in particular who disliked him," Nate said casually. *Aside from myself, of course.*

"Well, clearly someone disliked him." Magistrate Hunt glanced at the body. "Now, we just have to find out who and why."

CHAPTER TWO

TWO MEN PASSED through the front gates of Villa De Lacey on foot and walked toward them. From their lanky, slim frames, Nate could tell they were Otis's poet companions, who'd shared a cottage with him.

Bridget must have caught sight of them too because she held her free hand up to her forehead and peered into the distance. "Oh dear," she said. "It's Rupert and Charlie."

"They must be looking for Otis." Nate sighed. The two young men were brothers who always went by their Christian names, possibly to avoid confusion. Nate did not even know their surname.

"Dear me, how are we going to tell them?" Bridget covered her mouth with her hand, and Nate saw tears pool in her lovely eyes.

He moved closer to her and said gently, "I'll take care of it."

"You won't have to tell them anything." Magistrate Hunt stepped forward. "That's my job." He strode toward the men, clearly wanting to stop them from nearing the daffodils and Otis's corpse. Nate and Bridget followed him.

The two young men stopped as the magistrate approached them, just a few feet away from their dead friend's concealed body. They'd been more like Otis's followers than peers. He'd been the ringleader, exuding charm and confidence. Nate preferred these two. They were quiet thinkers, far more serious about their work, he suspected, than Otis had been.

"Gentlemen." Magistrate Hunt folded his hands together. "I assume you're here in search of your friend, Mr. George Otis."

"That's right," Rupert, a thin, pale young man with a sharp nose and protruding Adam's apple, said. "He didn't come home last night. And he wasn't at the lake this morning."

"You had plans to meet at the lake this morning?"

"We take a walk along the lake together every morning. We typically go after breakfast, but since George didn't come home last night, we thought he might be waiting for us there. When we didn't find him, we came up here." Rupert shrugged. "So here we are."

"When was the last time you saw your friend?" Magistrate Hunt asked.

"Yesterday at supper," Rupert said. "We worked together on our poetry all afternoon. Then we supped at The Black Horse."

Magistrate Hunt frowned. "What do you mean by 'worked together'?"

"We write individually but then read our work aloud to each other, and then we give our opinions, tell each other how to improve, that type of thing."

"Did Mr. Otis say anything to upset either of you—about your poetry, perhaps?"

"He could be a harsh critic, but that never upset us. We welcomed it."

"And how did Mr. Otis react to your criticisms of his work?"

"They aren't criticisms. They are suggestions to make the writing better. Stronger." Rupert shook his head as if to stave off his frustration. "Look, what's this all about? Has something happened?"

"You stated Mr. Otis didn't come home last night? When did he go out?"

"As I said, we supped together at The Black Horse and then stayed to enjoy a few jugs of ale. As the night wore on, the men who had supped at home started piling in, and it grew a little rowdy. George decided to leave, but we stayed."

"And that was the last time you saw him? Before he left The Black Horse?" Magistrate Hunt asked.

"Correct." Rupert nodded. "When we got home, he wasn't in his bed."

"And that didn't worry you?" Magistrate Hunt said.

"George is a grown man. He doesn't have a curfew. We were both exhausted from too much ale and fell to bed right away. When we awoke this morning, George was not in his bed. So, we assumed he'd risen early and gone to the lake. It was not unusual for him to do so."

Rupert looked from the magistrate to Nate, who stood side by side, blocking the view of Otis's concealed corpse. "Look here," Rupert said, "are you going to tell us why you're asking all these questions?" He turned to Bridget without waiting for an answer from the magistrate. "Miss De Lacey? What's happened? Is George in trouble?"

"I'm so sorry." Bridget bit her trembling lip.

"I'm afraid Mr. Otis is dead," Magistrate Hunt said.

"Dead!" Rupert exclaimed.

His brother, Charlie, turned a degree paler. Like Rupert, he was exceedingly thin with dark hair and large soulful eyes. Nate wondered if their appetite for poetry substituted for an appetite for food and drink. It certainly hadn't in Otis's case.

"How?" Rupert demanded. "How is he dead?"

"He was murdered." Magistrate Hunt turned and gestured to the wrapped corpse in the daffodils. "It happened last night—or in the early morning hours. We aren't certain of the time."

"Murdered!" both men exclaimed in unison. It was the first utterance Nate had heard Charlie make. He was a man of few words, and when he did speak, it was usually in a whisper.

"I don't believe it." Rupert started forward, but Magistrate Hunt put out his hand to stop him.

"No one is allowed near the corpse. It's evidence. There will be an inquisition, and my men must take it to Dr. Elias for further examination."

"But…" Rupert said. "What you say is not possible. It must be a case of mistaken identity. We knew him best. We should be the ones to identify his body."

"You don't want to see him," Nate said. "That much I promise you."

"He's right," Bridget said, her eyes moist with tears. "It's too awful. I'm the one who found the body. And I can assure you that it is George."

"Dear Lord." Rupert rubbed his face with both hands as if he could wipe away the reality that confronted him. "How is this possible? How is it that he ended up murdered on your property?" He looked accusingly at Nate.

"That's what we'd like to know." Nate met Rupert's accusing stare with one of his own. He wasn't about to take on any culpability for this murder. He didn't know why Otis had been on his property late at night, but whatever the reason, it certainly wasn't his or Bridget's responsibility.

Nate's forcefulness seemed to work, and Rupert's stance slackened. He shook his head, and his face turned scarlet—either with grief or anger.

"I simply don't understand it," Bridget said. "Who would want to harm George? Everyone loved him."

"That's not true," Charlie spoke in an even fainter whisper than usual. "There's that butcher in Braithwaite. He was making threats against George just last night at The Black Horse."

"Last night?" Magistrate Hunt repeated.

Rupert straightened. "That's right. Mr. Groby. He was drunk and screaming all sorts. I don't think anyone took him seriously, though. I know I didn't."

"Mr. Groby is a respectable member of our community." Magistrate Hunt puffed out his chest. "What did Mr. Otis do to provoke him?"

"He was giving Groby's wife reading lessons—at her request," Rupert said. "The butcher was jealous. He ordered his wife to stop the lessons, but she refused. I warned George that it was dangerous to come between a man and his wife, but he wouldn't listen. He only saw the good in people. That was his flaw."

It's more like he enjoyed provoking them, Nate thought. He had seen in Otis what others had not—the man had been conceited. He'd admired himself in a true Narcissus fashion, and the irony of Otis being murdered in a field of flowers named after the demigod was not lost on Nate. He had known plenty of men like Otis among his peers in London. They were irritating to be sure, but that wasn't a reason to murder someone and cut out his heart. Jealousy, however, was a more powerful motive. John Groby was on his third marriage—his first two wives having died in childbirth. And the current Mrs. Groby was considerably younger than the butcher. She was also a beautiful woman.

"That can't be right. I've never known Mr. Groby to be mean-spirited," Bridget said. "He was Papa's friend, and he has always treated me and my aunt with the utmost respect. He wouldn't hurt anyone. I'm sure you must be wrong."

"We're not wrong," Rupert said. "We heard him say he would carve George up and feed him to his pigs."

Nate's breath caught in his throat, and he heard Bridget gasp audibly.

"When did you hear him say this?" Magistrate Hunt asked.

"Last night at The Black Horse. Everyone heard him."

Nate glanced at Bridget, who paled considerably. The magistrate had not revealed that Otis's heart had been cut out, so Rupert had to be telling the truth.

"Carve him up, did you say?" Magistrate Hunt repeated.

"That's right," Rupert said.

"And you heard this too?" Magistrate Hunt turned to Charlie.

The young man nodded. "I did."

"You heard a man threaten to kill your friend, yet you showed no concern when he failed to come home?"

"No one took Groby's threats seriously. He was badly intoxicated and raging like a bull. We were all laughing at him."

"So, you didn't take the butcher at his word, then?"

"Of course not. I never thought Groby would seriously harm George. I imagined that if George continued to spend time with Mrs. Groby, he'd likely receive a beating from Groby. But murder? I never thought he'd actually do such a thing."

Magistrate Hunt straightened his shoulders. "Well, as you can see, that is exactly what's happened." He sighed. "It's a disturbing turn of events, but I'd say that it looks like we've got our man."

$$\mathcal{Q}$$

"I DON'T BELIEVE it!" Bridget said. "Mr. Groby has been part of our community since he was a child. He's a decent man with a kind nature. Why, I've seen him give free scraps of meat to the poor so they can make soup. And Mrs. Groby has never complained about her husband's behavior. They seem perfectly happy together. I had no idea he was capable of—to think he'd even make such a threat, let alone act on it." She swallowed, feeling nausea rising in her throat.

"I think we've both learned that things aren't always what they seem," Nate said dryly.

Bridget knew he was referring to the murders last summer. She squeezed her eyes shut. She could not think about that. It was all too raw. She could not reconcile the horror of it in her mind. And to think it should happen again—that someone she trusted and thought she knew was, in fact, someone else entirely. *No! It cannot be. Is anything what it seems?* Still cradling Bijou, she pressed one hand against her stomach to stave off the nausea.

"I know you're right," she told Nate as she watched the magistrate's men lift George's wrapped body onto a stretcher, ready to transport it to Dr. Elias for examination. "But to cut a man's heart out. It's unimaginable."

"It seems quite plausible to me," Magistrate Hunt said. "As much as I hate to think Mr. Groby capable of murder, the man is a butcher. He has the tools and the know-how to do it. And I imagine you become desensitized to blood and organs and such in that profession."

"What are you saying?" Rupert, who'd been focused on the men preparing to cart George's body away, suddenly turned to face the magistrate. "Are you saying that butcher carved George up like a piece of meat—cut out his heart and fed it to his pigs?" The young man's face was ashen, and his dark eyes widened with horror.

Charlie stood beside him and looked as though he might swoon. He was a sensitive young man with a boy's face. Bridget's heart went out to him.

"Unfortunately, that is the case," Magistrate Hunt said gravely. "Your friend was murdered, and his body desecrated most savagely."

"Good God!" Rupert stumbled backward. "That brute! That monster!"

"I'm so sorry," Bridget said, feeling wretched that the young poets had heard the gory details of their friend's brutal murder because of her carelessness in speaking about it out loud—and while she was trying to defend the potential killer! "It's awful. It truly is, but you mustn't jump to conclusions. Mr. Groby must be given a chance to explain himself—"

"Don't say that man's name to me," Rupert growled. "I won't rest until I see him hanged by the neck."

Bridget took no offense to Rupert's harsh tone and words. She knew exactly how he felt. The agony of knowing her papa's body had been violated and buried at a crossroads in London, far out of her reach, was something from which she'd never recover.

"Now, let's all stay calm, shall we?" Nate said. "Why don't we go inside and have a strong drink?" he offered the men. "It's early yet, but I know I can use one." He turned to Magistrate Hunt. "You too, Magistrate. I imagine you'll want to question our guests. We can all have a drink and calm down a bit, and then, once the guests have breakfasted, I'll tell them to gather in the drawing room. That way, you can address everyone at once."

"I'm not sure we'll get that chance." Bridget looked toward the villa and saw Colonel Kendall striding toward them. "It's the colonel."

The colonel was a stout man with a curvy gray mustache and bright eyes who had come to Westmorland for a bit of relaxation after retirement. But Bridget was convinced that he'd chosen Villa De Lacey on purpose because he hated relaxation and wanted to retain a bit of excitement in his life. He was one of those guests who'd heard about the "murder inn" and secretly hoped there'd be another murder during their visit. And now—unbelievable as it seemed—there had been.

"Good Lord! He's the last person we need," Nate said, taking a step forward to go and intercept the man and stop him from approaching, but Bridget's warning came too late. The colonel had spotted the corpse on the stretcher and headed toward it.

"I say, what's going on?" Colonel Kendall pointed his walking stick at the magistrate's retreating men, each of whom held one end of a makeshift stretcher. "Stop!" Colonel Kendall bellowed. "That's an order, do you hear?"

Bijou lifted his head in the direction of the commotion and growled softly. Bridget could feel his little heart beating wildly as though he sensed danger.

Unbelievably, the men did as they were told, causing Magistrate Hunt to snarl under his breath, "Keep moving, lads!"

The colonel marched toward the men and pointed his walking stick at the blood-stained sheet concealing George's body. "Good God, has there been a murder?"

The magistrate's men stood frozen as though unsure of this new authority figure and whether or not he was someone they ought to take seriously.

"Oh dear," Bridget said as they watched the scene unfold from a few feet away.

Nate groaned. "We had better get him inside and put a brandy or two in his hand. We don't need him spreading hysteria among the guests by telling everyone there's been another suspicious death."

"Why don't we all go inside together and let the magistrate finish his work here?" Bridget gave Charlie and Rupert a sympathetic smile and then turned to Magistrate Hunt. "You will join us when your tasks out here are complete, won't you, sir?"

"I shouldn't think so," Rupert interjected before the magistrate could respond. "He needs to get over to Braithwaite and arrest Groby."

"Arrest?" Bridget could not believe her ears.

"Now, wait a minute," Nate said, taking his eyes off the colonel and turning to Rupert. "Isn't that a bit rash? There must be a proper investigation."

"What for? We all heard what Groby said at The Black Horse," Rupert exclaimed.

"He's right," Magistrate Hunt said. "I see no need for an investigation when I have two witnesses here who heard the man admit that he planned on carving up Mr. Otis with his knife."

In that moment, the colonel left the magistrate's men to their task and strode toward them. "I say, what's going on? I just saw a dead man being carted away on a stretcher."

"That's right, Colonel," Rupert said. "Our friend George Otis was murdered—slaughtered most savagely with his heart ripped from his chest."

"I knew it!" Colonel Kendall said in a triumphant tone. "Those insubordinates refused to tell me anything, but I'm no fool. Heart ripped from his chest, you say? How ghastly! Who would do such a thing?"

"Come with me, and I'll tell you all about it over a glass of brandy." Nate interjected, placing a gentle hand on the colonel's back and steering him away before Rupert could reply.

"Well, it's a little early, but I don't mind if I do—considering the circumstance, I mean," Bridget heard the colonel say as he walked off with Nate.

"Please, gentlemen," Bridget said when Nate and the colonel

were out of earshot. "We mustn't jump to conclusions. Mr. Groby was inebriated. People say all sorts when they've had too much. It's not proof." She tried to reason with the men.

"It's proof enough for me," Rupert said. "I know he murdered George."

"I agree," Magistrate Hunt said. "With all due respect, Miss De Lacey, the events of last summer do not make you a magistrate. You must leave the investigating and the arresting to me."

"May we come back to the village with you?" Rupert asked the magistrate. "We owe it to George to see that brute arrested and locked away."

Magistrate Hunt nodded. "Very well. I suppose you deserve that much. Now, Miss De Lacey, if you'll excuse me, I have things to attend to." He gave a slight bow and then strode into the field of daffodils, where he bent to pick up the rock that had been used to kill George, tucking it under his arm.

Charlie stepped forward to follow the magistrate, but Rupert pulled him back. "When the magistrate is in with Dr. Elias, we'll spread the word about what Groby has done. I wager the whole town will want to see him locked up after they find out what he did to George. I'll not let that butcher escape."

"No!" Bridget cried, alarmed. "Mr. Groby has little ones. You'll frighten them and his wife to death."

But Rupert and Charlie paid her no heed and raced after the magistrate.

Good heavens! Bridget's chest tightened as her panic rose. *I need to get to Braithwaite and warn Alice Groby that a mob is about to descend on her home.*

"Is it true?" Mrs. Jane Harley almost collided with Bridget as she intercepted her flight to the kitchen. She wanted to place Bijou safely with Cook before she went to Braithwaite. "Has there been another murder?"

Bridget paused to catch her breath. Jane had come to Villa De Lacey in the summer with her husband and, despite having witnessed the terrible summer murders, had elected to stay for an extended period rather than return to London, where they had lived with her husband's bully of an aunt, Lady Darby. Jane had changed immensely in the months she'd been at Villa De Lacey. She'd arrived as an exceedingly pale, frail, and downtrodden woman who'd been driven to desperate measures by the vile aunt. But she'd since transformed into a more robust woman with a much healthier complexion and a zest for life. Her light brown curls were shinier, and her downturned blue eyes brighter. Despite a rocky start to their relationship, Jane and Bridget had become fast friends.

"Well?" Jane said. "Has there been another murder?"

Bridget chewed her lower lip. Nate had said to inform all the guests at the same time. She glanced at the villa. *But where is Nate? And who'd told Jane about the murder?* "What makes you say that?" she asked, trying to play it safe.

"Colonel Kendall. He burst into the breakfast room and announced it to everyone. He said a man lay dead among the daffodils with his heart ripped out of his chest. I thought perhaps it was some type of gruesome game. He's that sort, you know. The kind who dreams of becoming embroiled in a real-life murder. He's up there now, trying to convince everyone to follow him outside."

Bridget's stomach dropped. Nate must have let the colonel out of his sight—or lost control of him somehow. No, that wasn't possible. Nate was too clever and capable for that. Something must have distracted him—something more important than the colonel. But what?

"Bridget!" Jane's tone grew urgent. "You're starting to scare me. Is someone dead? If so, who is it?"

Bridget swallowed. She loathed to speak the truth out loud because it all still seemed like a terrible dream that she hoped would disappear. She eyed Jane's cheerful peach-colored spring dress and felt her chest tighten. If only she could wake up and realize all was right at Villa De Lacey again.

Just then, a group of guests led by the colonel exited the villa. Jane's husband, Mr. Harley, was among them. His bright copper hair made him easy to spot.

"Oh no!" Bridget said. "This cannot happen. Nate was supposed to contain him."

"No one can contain the colonel," Jane said.

Mr. Harley spotted them and broke from the crowd. He came to them and said, "What on earth is going on? The colonel says someone has been murdered."

The guests streamed past Bridget, Jane, and Mr. Harley as they followed Colonel Kendall, his walking stick raised like he was once again leading a platoon of soldiers. Bijou squirmed in her arms and gave a bark. He wanted to join in the excitement. Bridget petted him to be quiet.

"The magistrate's men carted the body away, but there's still a lot of blood," the colonel announced with an air of importance.

"But who is it? Who has died?" someone asked.

Don't tell them! Bridget pleaded with the colonel inside her head. *Please, not like this.*

The colonel stopped and turned to face the crowd with a somber expression on his face. "They say it's that young poet everyone is so fond of—what's his name—Otis George."

"George Otis!" the beautiful Lady Matheson shrieked. "That can't be. No, I don't believe it." She clutched her chest and almost sank to the ground before grasping onto Miss Jennings and righting herself. Rather than assisting the woman, the reserved Miss Jennings flinched as though she'd been struck.

Jane gasped, and Bridget felt her throat constrict. Jane had been as fond of George as she'd been. "No!" she said. "It can't be true."

"Well, I'll be..." Mr. Harley said.

"Oh, dear." Bridget clasped her hands together. "This is going to cause a lot of distress. I'd best go and talk to them."

Just then, Bridget's aunt exited the villa and strode toward her with forceful, giant steps. "Good gracious, Bridget. They say someone has died!" she said when she reached her niece. "Tell me it's not true. There cannot be another murder at Villa De Lacey. I won't stand for it."

"I'm afraid I can't do that, Aunt. There has been a murder, and a brutal one at that." Bridget glanced worriedly at the guests who were approaching the daffodils where George's blood still stained the yellow petals.

"Oh, my! This cannot be happening again."

Bridget's heart hammered as she watched Colonel Kendall use his walking stick to point at the location of the murder. She saw Lady Matheson put a hand over her mouth as if to conceal a scream. And Miss Jennings swayed on her feet as if she might swoon. The only person who looked unperturbed was Mr. Angert. He was an artist from Germany who'd come to paint the sublime beauty of the lakes. He studied the scene before him intently, as though committing it to canvas in his mind.

Where is Nate? Bridget glanced anxiously at the villa, partly annoyed and partly bewildered. How could he let the colonel run loose and behave as though he were a ringmaster in a circus? It wasn't like him at all to lose control of a situation. Something must have distracted him. But what could be more important than containing the colonel?

"You should go find Mr. Squires," Aunt Marianne said as if reading Bridget's thoughts. "He needs to rein this in before it gets out of hand."

Before? Bridget glanced again at the villa. *It's far too late for that.* For a moment, she was torn between finding Nate and rushing to Braithwaite. Then she made her decision. Nate must have had a good reason for letting the colonel out of his sight, just as she had a good reason for leaving the guests now.

"You'll need to go and find him," Bridget said to her aunt. "I must make haste."

"Make haste?" Aunt Marianne said. "What for? You can't leave now. I forbid it."

"I'm sorry, Aunt," Bridget said, "but I must leave things in your capable hands." Then she turned and hurried toward the servants' entrance at the back of the villa. She needed to get to Braithwaite before Rupert sent a mob to the butcher's farm, and if Nate knew where she was headed, he'd try to stop her from going. She entered the servants' quarters and dashed into the kitchen where the scullery maid was hard at work scrubbing dishes, and Cook was sitting down with a cup of tea. The stout woman stood immediately when she saw Bridget.

"There you are, Miss Bridget."

"Were you waiting for me?" Bridget asked.

Cook furrowed her brow. "James says there's been another murder. He says the victim is the poet, George Otis, and that his body lies in the daffodils. But Mr. Squires forbade us servants from going upstairs. So, you must tell me—is it true? Is the poet dead?"

"Mr. Squires?" Bridget said. "You saw him?" Bijou struggled to free himself from her arms. The kitchen floor was his favorite place to hunt for scraps and crumbs. Bridget suspected that most of them were left on purpose by Cook and the staff.

"Aye, he came down here in a hurry, gave us our warnings, and then left. It seemed as if he were in a great rush."

Bridget bit her lip. Could Nate have had the same idea as she? Had he cantered off to help Mr. Groby?

"Well, miss?" Cook urged.

"I'm afraid it's true." Bridget put the squirming Bijou on the floor. He immediately ran to Cook's side and looked pleadingly up at her. "George Otis has been murdered."

"Good grief, miss! Another murder!"

Bijou barked, clearly frustrated by the lack of attention he was receiving from Cook. She looked down at him. "What you be wanting?" she said. "Looking for scraps, are you?"

Bijou wagged his tail and barked again.

"None of that barking or you'll get nowt!" Cook waggled her finger at him, and Bijou barked again. She put her hands on her hips and said, "I'll get you some scraps after your mistress tells me about this murder."

"I can't stay," Bridget said. "I must get to town before…"

"Before what?" Cook eyed her.

"Something important. Trust me when I tell you that if I don't leave this minute, there will be dire consequences."

"Dire consequences?" Cook's forehead creased into a frown. "For who?"

"For a potentially innocent man," Bridget said.

CHAPTER THREE

WHEN BRIDGET ARRIVED at Groby's slaughterhouse on the outskirts of the small village, the mob, led by Rupert, was already there. It appeared that Rupert had gathered as many men and women as he could find, obviously spreading the word that Groby had acted on his promise to 'carve up George.' What the same crowd might have laughed at the previous night, they now reacted to with horror. Despite having been his friends and neighbors for years, the enraged mob accosted the butcher in his slaughterhouse—a large shed attached to his cottage—and demanded justice for George.

As Bridget squeezed her way through the throng, she heard Rupert shout, "You slaughtered my friend like a swine, and now you're going to pay for it."

"What are you on about?" Mr. Groby scanned the room of familiar faces and laughed. "Is this summat of a joke?"

"It's no joke," Rupert cried. "George Otis is dead, and you killed him. We all heard you say you'd carve him to pieces and feed him to your pigs, and now you've gone and done it."

"Aye!" his neighbors chanted angrily. "We all heard it!"

"Gone and done it?" Mr. Groby seemed bewildered. "I've done nowt! You can't take what a man says when he's full of ale for the truth." He looked around the shed and laughed, as though he could not quite grasp the fact that his friends and neighbors had turned on him.

"Don't play innocent," Rupert spoke again. "This morning,

George Otis was found butchered like an animal, and we all know why. He'd turned you into a cuckold, so you killed him just like you said you would." Rupert pointed his finger at Groby and took a threatening step forward. "You killed my friend, and now you will pay for it."

The horde moved forward with George, attempting to corner the butcher. Bridget felt the squeeze from the crowd. "Wait!" She cried in desperation as the mob closed around her and pushed her forward. Panic rose in her throat. If she didn't move with them, she'd likely get trampled.

"Stay back. I'm warning you!" Groby grabbed two butcher knives he'd been using to chop chunks of flesh and pointed them at the crowd.

The sight of the bloody flesh and bits of fat hanging from the blades—one heavy and square and the other long and skinny, culminating in a menacing curve—momentarily stilled everyone. Bridget clasped her pulsing throat as she stood transfixed by what was unfolding before her. Mr. Groby's face looked as red as the bloodstains on his apron, and his expression mimicked that of a thundercloud. His thick, dark eyebrows came together in a furious frown under his angry black eyes. The normally genial man had transformed into someone frightfully unrecognizable. Someone capable of murder.

"I'm no cuckold, and anyone who says different will meet the sharp end of my blade!" He jabbed one of the knives into the air, and a collective gasp emanated across the room. People instinctively stepped back, and Bridget took the opportunity to move closer to Groby, hoping that a friendly face might calm him.

"Your knives won't save you now, Groby," Rupert shouted. "George will have his justice. We're coming for you."

"Stand aside!" Magistrate Hunt's voice thundered, and Bridget breathed a sigh of relief as the people parted. Then, she saw the magistrate enter the fray with Nate by his side. So, Nate had gone to alert the magistrate! He must have realized the same thing she had. But what had taken him so long? *What does it matter? He's here now.* Her earlier annoyance melted away, and she felt like running up to him and throwing her arms around him.

"Put down the knives, Groby." Magistrate Hunt stood with Nate in the center of the parted crowd. "You need to come with me."

"I'm not going anywhere! You'll have to get past me knives first," the butcher growled.

"You don't want to do that, Mr. Groby," Nate said. "Magistrate Hunt only wishes to talk to you. You'll have a chance to explain what happened."

"There's nothing to explain," Rupert shouted. "We all heard him say he'd carve George up and feed him to his pigs."

"Aye! That we did!" Hornby cried. "I heard you say you'd take the man's heart!"

"As did I," Mr. Morris shouted. "He's guilty! Arrest him now!"

"Arrest him. Arrest him," the people jeered.

"Stop!" Mrs. Groby's voice tore across the room, and Bridget turned to see her standing in the doorway of the slaughterhouse with her babe in her arms and her small son clinging to her skirt. "You can't take him. He's innocent. He were here with me all last night. Once he returned from the tavern."

The crowd jeered again, but this time it was less forceful.

Mr. Groby stared at his family, and his snarl transformed into a look of anguish. After a minute, he dropped the knives. A mixture of relief and agony tore through Bridget. She'd been right. Mr. Groby was a good man. He cared about his wife and children. And such a man wouldn't butcher someone and leave him for dead. That much she was certain of.

"You can take me away if it pleases you," Mr. Groby said to the magistrate. "But I didn't kill that damned poet." He looked around the room. "I kill swine for you to eat. I don't butcher men!"

"You deserve to hang!" Rupert shouted, but the people did not cheer him on. They seemed to have been subdued by the presence of Mrs. Groby and her children. It was as if they suddenly remembered that Mr. Groby was a family man who had been their trusted neighbor and friend for as long as they'd lived in Westmorland.

Groby untied his bloodied apron and threw it onto his workbench. Then, he walked placidly toward the magistrate. Everyone remained silent as Magistrate Hunt led him through the crowd.

"I won't rest until I see you hanged!" Rupert shouted as Groby exited his slaughterhouse with the magistrate.

"Get out! All of you!" The butcher's wife stepped forward and scolded her neighbors. "You're frightening my children."

Nate grabbed Rupert by the arm and whispered something to him. Then, he led him toward the door, and the rest followed. He made eye contact with Bridget as he came toward her and frowned. "You shouldn't have come on your own," he said, letting go of Rupert. "Things are getting dangerous."

"That's exactly why I came," Bridget said. "And I'm staying to have a word with Mrs. Groby. She's going to need my support."

"You're right," Nate said. "That's a good idea. I'll wait for you outside."

"No, you should go home. The colonel is on the loose, creating chaos as we speak, and poor Aunt Marianne isn't too pleased."

Nate hesitated, pressing his lips together as if contemplating what to do. "I'm sorry about that. I was worried about this exact scenario, that's why I left in a hurry. I thought a few brandies would be enough to subdue the colonel. He usually falls asleep after a glass or two."

"But what took you so long to get here?" Bridget asked.

"The magistrate was deep in conversation with Dr. Elias about Otis's wounds and wasn't to be rushed. He seemed far less concerned than I about a mob gathering at Groby's slaughterhouse. Still, the damage at home is already done, and I hesitate to leave you now."

"Go on," Bridget said. "I've got my mare with me to ride safely home. And you're needed at the villa. I'll be there as soon as I'm finished here."

"Very well," Nate said reluctantly and went outside. Bridget watched as the rest of the men filed out, their bent heads reassuring her that all was not lost in her little village.

Once they were gone, she approached Mrs. Groby—a young, slim woman of one-and-twenty with chestnut ringlets and large green eyes—and put a comforting hand on the woman's shoulder. Alice Groby had been a figure of interest in Braithwaite since she'd married Groby a little over three years ago. People speculated that she'd been forced to marry the gruff butcher, who was much older than she. But Bridget wasn't so sure. Mr. Groby had a substantial farm and a solid business. And, for as long as Bridget had known him, despite his boorish appearance, he'd always been a genial man who was generous to others.

The babe in Mrs. Groby's arms, a sweet-faced little girl of twelve months with tufts of blond hair, gave Bridget a toothy grin. Thankfully, she was too young to understand what had just taken place, but unfortunately, the Groby's three-year-old son would not come out unscathed. Bridget had always known Edmund to be a cheerful and rambunctious child. But today, he clung desperately to his mother's skirt, his large blue eyes filled with fear, and his round face ashen. Her heart ached for him. She knew what it was like to lose a beloved parent, and she recognized the child's fear. More than that, she'd learned the hard way how to stomach slander and shame for an accused family member. Because her papa had died of self-murder, he'd been branded a sinner and had been buried alongside traitors and murderers. He'd been denied a Christian burial, and his memory and his good nature had been blighted for eternity. The pain of such cruelty was overwhelming and frightening. No one understood that better than she did.

Bridget turned and scanned the now-empty slaughterhouse and shuddered. She could still hear the shouts and cries for Groby to hang ringing in her ears. She had to get Mrs. Groby and her children away from here and safely inside their cottage. She knew that what they needed now more than anything was a bit of kindness and comfort from someone who understood their plight.

♀

THE BUTCHER'S COTTAGE was modest yet comfortable and well-stocked. Mr. Groby was a hard worker, and he'd provided well for his family. The kitchen pantry was loaded with dried meats, potatoes, wheat, flour, eggs, and other staples. Also, his farm spanned out behind the cottage and housed a herd of cattle, sheep, pigs, and chickens. Mrs. Groby and her children would certainly not starve for now, but if nothing could be done to save their papa, then their lives could take a serious turn for the worse. Bridget assumed it would be difficult for Mrs. Groby to maintain the farm, butchery, and children on her own.

As they entered the house, Mrs. Groby said faintly, "I was just making John his morning tea. But he won't be needing it now."

"Sit down while I make it for us," Bridget said. "I'm sure the children could use a bite." Bridget guided Mrs. Groby to the rocking chair by the fire in the front parlor. "Then we can talk about what needs to happen next."

Still holding her babe, the woman sank into the chair, and the child snuggled against her mother's breast.

"Perhaps Edmund would like to help me?" Bridget smiled at the little boy. "Do you want to show me where Mummy keeps the tea?" The child shook his head and scooted closer to his mother's chair. Bridget could not blame him. He'd just watched his neighbors turn on his papa while the magistrate escorted him from his home. It was no wonder he didn't want to let his mama out of his sight. "How does Mummy like her tea? Does she take cream and sugar?" she asked, trying again to engage the child. He turned his face and buried it in his mother's skirt.

"Black for me," Mrs. Groby said flatly.

In the kitchen, Bridget found the pot of tea Mrs. Groby had prepared for her husband, along with a jug of milk. She poured a glass for Edmund. And after locating some biscuits, she prepared a tray and took it to the front parlor. Edmund turned to his mother and waited for her nod of approval before he accepted the cup of milk and a biscuit. Bridget then placed the tea tray on the small table beside Mrs. Groby's rocker and poured two cups of tea, but the woman made no effort to touch hers.

Bridget pulled up a stool and sat next to the young mother. "Drink," she said. "It will make you feel better."

Mrs. Groby lifted her cup, but her hand trembled so much that she had to place it back in the saucer. "Mr. Otis is dead," she said. "Murdered! And John will hang for it! How will my children hold their heads up in this village with a father who hanged for murder?"

"They won't hang him. I won't let them—at least not without a proper investigation."

"Investigation? They don't care about the truth. I've seen it before. It happened once at the market in Harrogate. They accused a man of stealing, and a mob set upon him. He were taken and hanged a week later. Mr. Oliver, he were called. A farmer and a good man, known to all. I saw them turn on him like rabid dogs. Then a month later, the true thief were uncovered."

"That's not going to happen," Bridget said, although fear of the very same fate for the butcher had filled the pit of her stomach. This wasn't a mere case of theft, which was serious enough in itself. This was murder, and no ordinary murder at that. George Otis had been mercilessly and brutally butchered. And even though George had been new to Westmorland, he had been well-liked. And Rupert had whipped the good people of Westmorland into a frenzy. They'd felt the injustice of a young life lost keenly, and they would want justice, precisely because they were good, honest people.

"Everyone is against us," Mrs. Groby said, breaking into

Bridget's thoughts. "Only you can help us now."

"Me?" Bridget asked.

The babe in Mrs. Groby's arms began to fuss and stuffed her small fist into her mouth. Bridget handed her one of the hard biscuits. The child clutched it with her tiny fist and began to suck furiously on it.

"You are clever. You solved two murders last year. You're the only person who can save my John."

"Mama, where have they taken Papa?" Edmund looked up at his mother, his blue eyes wide.

Bridget's heart twisted, but she did not want to give false hope. "I—that's not something I can promise." Things did not look good for John Groby. Not only the people but the magistrate believed him to be guilty, and she didn't have a clue as to who could have committed this murder.

"But say you'll try. Please. If John hangs, we will suffer his shame forever." She gestured to her little boy at her feet. He'd barely touched his milk and biscuits. "Your papa had a murderer's burial. You know what this will mean for my children."

Bridget swallowed the pain that rose in her throat and threatened to choke her. She had known the butcher her whole life and desperately wanted to believe in his innocence, but she'd recently learned that no matter how well you thought you knew someone, you could never know all their dark secrets. Still, she had to try.

"I'll do all I can to help, but you must be honest with me. I will need to ask you some difficult questions."

"What do you mean?" Mrs. Groby frowned. "I have nowt to hide."

"Very well, then. Tell me, what happened between you and Mr. Otis that made your husband so upset?" she asked. "Why would Mr. Groby threaten to carve up George and feed him to his pigs?"

"Nowt happened!" A blue vein pulsed under the pale skin on Mrs. Groby's neck.

"Rupert said you were taking lessons from Mr. Otis," Bridget nudged the woman.

"He were teaching me to read. But John didn't like it. He said he needed me to cook and care for our little ones, not read all day. But you see, I wanted to learn so I could teach my children one day. It might seem like a grand notion, but I thought it could help give them a better chance. People who can read have the respect of others. It makes them—well, you can read. You understand."

Bridget nodded. "I think it's wonderful you want to learn how to read and teach your children. Did Mr. Groby force you to stop learning?"

"He didn't forbid it—at first. But then he refused to let me pay for the lessons, and when Mr. Otis said he'd give me lessons for free, John became cross. He said men didn't do acts of charity out of generosity, and eventually George would want another sort of payment from me."

"I see." Bridget frowned. *Why would Mr. Groby say something like that? George had always behaved like a perfect gentleman.*

"I told him I could take care of myself. But John wouldn't listen. He said he knows men like George Otis. And that's when he ordered me to stop the lessons."

Bridget worried her bottom lip. *So, Mr. Groby had been jealous, but had he been jealous enough to murder?*

"But I didn't want to stop my lessons. I thought John were wrong, and I don't like being told what to do. So, I refused. And now, someone has killed him, and my John will hang for nowt!"

Bridget glanced at Edmund, who looked fearfully up at his mother. She wished Mrs. Groby would stop talking about hanging in front of the child. He was young yet, but children were accustomed to seeing public hangings in town just like adults were. Thankfully, young Edmund Groby may have been spared as much, living in Westmorland, where crime was minimal—at least it had been until last year.

"And you believe Mr. Groby to be innocent, despite his suspicions and threats?" Bridget asked.

"John wouldn't do a thing like that—he wouldn't kill anyone." Mrs. Groby pulled her daughter close. "He says silly things sometimes when he's had a little too much to drink, but he wouldn't actually…no, he couldn't have."

Bridget bit her lip. Mrs. Groby didn't sound too confident that her husband was innocent. "Was he home with you all of last night?" she asked.

"He were at The Black Horse, and I were asleep when he came home."

"So, you don't know when he returned home?" Bridget asked, her heart sinking.

"I can't think what we will do now," Mrs. Groby said, ignoring the question.

"Do you have any family? Someone who can come and stay with you and help with the children, at least."

"I have nowt. Even young Miss Evans, who were helping me in the house and watching the children when I took my lessons, has abandoned me now. I saw her papa in the crowd today. He will never let her return." She gazed at her daughter who still sucked contentedly on the hard biscuit. "How could they?" she said, her voice a whisper. "How could they turn on him—our neighbors and friends? John were good to everyone. He were always helping those in need, letting them pay when they could. He never wanted people to go hungry."

"Do a lot of people owe him money?" Bridget asked.

"A few people, I think. But most are good about paying."

"Well, you should be able to collect what's owed to you while Mr. Groby is…away."

Just then, a knock sounded at the door, and Mrs. Groby straightened in her chair, looking startled.

"What is it? Are you expecting someone?"

The woman shook her head.

"Stay here." Bridget patted the woman's arm. "I'll go. It's likely Mr. Squires." She stood, walked to the door, and opened it a crack. "Mr. Collins," Bridget said in surprise upon seeing the young man. He was a tall, fair-haired, well-spoken gentleman who was new to Westmorland, and he lived in a rented cottage not five minutes from the Groby's farm and slaughterhouse.

"Miss De Lacey," he too sounded surprised to see her. "I came to see how Mrs. Groby and the children are faring."

"How kind of you," Bridget said, glancing back in the direction of the parlor. "But I'm not sure she's ready for company just yet."

"Of course. I understand. I am new to town, so I don't know much about how things work here, but I thought what happened today in front of Mrs. Groby and her children seemed terribly cruel. I imagined they might be feeling rather friendless; that's why I came to lend a kind word. But now that I see you are here, I feel quite relieved. Perhaps you can send her my regards."

"Of course," Bridget said. "It was very kind of you to—"

"Let him in," Mrs. Groby said, coming up behind Bridget. "The children will be happy to see a friendly face."

Bridget looked back, startled. Mrs. Groby was smiling at Mr. Collins. Bridget quickly moved aside to let the gentleman step into the cottage.

"Thank you for coming," Mrs. Groby said. "I thought everyone had abandoned us."

"I imagine you did," Collins replied. "But I would never abandon a neighbor in need. Still, I don't mean to intrude. I didn't know you already had company." He glanced at Bridget.

"I've just prepared some tea," Bridget said, suddenly feeling uncomfortable, yet she couldn't put her finger on why. "Shall I fetch you a cup?"

"Oh, I don't want to be a bother. I only wanted to see that Mrs. Groby was being looked after, and now that I know you are here…"

"It's no bother," Mrs. Groby said. "Stay. We are in need of all the friends we can hold on to."

"You will always have a friend in me." Mr. Collins bowed his head slightly, and his blond hair flopped forward into his blue eyes. He swept it back with his hand and smiled at Mrs. Groby. A silence fell over the room, and for a minute, Bridget felt as though she was an intruder.

"I'll just go and fetch that cup of tea for you," she said and edged toward the kitchen. She returned a minute later with a teacup and a plate of biscuits, only to find Mrs. Groby and Mr. Collins engaged in a whispered conversation.

Bridget's chest tightened, and she cleared her throat to alert them of her presence. They sprang apart. Something was afoot. Perhaps there was more to Mrs. Groby than a distraught wife and worried mother.

CHAPTER FOUR

B Y THE TIME Nate arrived at the villa, it was mid-morning, and the damage had already been done. Colonel Kendall had declared himself an authority on the murder and had taken it upon himself to give a tour of the murder site to the guests.

Aunt Marianne, who'd anxiously been awaiting his return, marched out to the stables and confronted him as soon as he dismounted his horse. She was beside herself after having been bombarded with questions from both the guests and the servants regarding a murder she knew nothing about, so she'd directed them to "put their questions to Mr. Squires upon his return." And that is exactly what they did.

"It cannot be true." Lady Matheson was the first to accost him as he poured himself a much-needed brandy in the drawing room. "Oh, Mr. Squires, tell me the colonel is wrong. The man who has been killed isn't George Otis."

"I'm not wrong." The colonel strode into the drawing room. "I saw the body with my own two eyes. I might be retired, but my eyesight is still as sharp as a hawk's, as are my senses."

"You saw a body enclosed in sheets." Lady Matheson wrapped her arms around herself. "It might have been anyone."

"I know what I saw, and I know what I heard. That young

Rupert was shouting up a storm about how his friend had been carved up by some lunatic with a knife." The colonel's silver mustache quivered with apparent indignation.

"Oh, do stop!" Lady Matheson put her hands over her ears. "I cannot take any more."

Nate turned to give the colonel a look that he hoped would convey the words *shut up*, but it seemed to have no effect. The colonel had no self-awareness. Nate's only solution would be to get rid of the man. "Perhaps you should gather everyone and ask them to come to the drawing room. I don't want to answer the same questions repeatedly. What do you say, Colonel?"

"Righty O," the colonel said. "I'll be back with the lot in a jiffy." He raised his cane, turned, and marched out of the drawing room like a man on an important mission.

Nate gave a sigh of relief. The colonel's insensitivity hadn't helped the situation at all.

"Oh dear. I'm afraid my nerves cannot tolerate this." Lady Matheson sank onto the settee once the colonel had left the room.

"Shall I pour you a glass of port, or something stronger, perhaps?"

"Yes, do. Please. A little brandy to steady my nerves."

"Certainly, I think we can all use a bit of that." Nate turned back to the drinks cabinet and poured a second brandy, which he then took to Lady Matheson. "There you go. It's a good, strong cognac, and just the thing to help calm you."

Lady Matheson accepted the glass with a shaking hand. Then, much to Nate's surprise, she swallowed its contents in one gulp. "Oh yes," she said, putting a hand to her throat. "That's lovely and warm. I think I'll have another."

Nate hesitated. She'd just drained a quarter glass of potent cognac without so much as a splutter or a tearing eye. The only other woman he'd seen drink like that had been his former betrothed, Helen Morley—now the Countess of Luxton—and she'd turned out to be a heartless creature. Like Lady Matheson,

Helen was an exceptionally beautiful woman, and she'd used her beauty to climb the social ladder. Starting with himself, she'd wormed her way into society, and then, she'd discarded him for someone old enough to be her grandfather, but that had not mattered to her, as the gentleman was richer than Croesus. And that begged the question, what had a wealthy society widow wanted with a poor poet? If Lady Matheson were lonely, surely, she would have no problem finding a new husband.

"Mr. Squires"—Lady Matheson stood and held out her glass—"shall I pour the brandy myself?"

"No, of course not." Nate snapped out of his reverie and took the glass from the lady with a smile. When he returned it to her, he wondered if she would swallow the brandy in one gulp again, but she did not. Instead, she wrapped her gloved hands around the glass as if it were her lifeline and stared into it.

"Why don't you sit down again, Lady Matheson?" Nate said.

She looked up at him. Her exquisite amber eyes mirrored the color of the liquid in her glass. "It cannot be him," she said. "Say it's not George." Then her knees buckled, and Nate lunged forward, catching her by her arm before she fell. Luckily, she managed to hold onto her glass, but brandy splashed onto her navy-blue dress. She didn't seem to notice. Nate helped her into a chair. She sank into the plush, pale blue armchair and cradled her forehead as if she were too weary to lift her head.

Nate left her to her thoughts and went to fetch his own brandy. He stood by the decanter and sipped his drink, thinking he would need to pour a few more when the others arrived, and checked the contents of the decanter to ascertain if there would be enough.

He glanced at Lady Matheson, who had not moved. He wondered if she was truly upset or if she was being melodramatic. Helen had always been melodramatic, either for attention or to fool those around her. Her feelings were seldom honest. Was Lady Matheson the same?

It irked him that Helen's dishonesty had made him skeptical

of most everyone he met. She'd distorted his reality. He would put her right out of his mind if it weren't for their son. His heart contracted. He still couldn't believe he had a son—a boy Helen had sworn he'd never see again. She liked to punish those who refused to do her bidding or rejected her demands.

Nate inhaled, but the heaviness in his chest did not subside. Helen had cut out his heart just as truly as the murderer had done to Otis. Whoever killed Otis wanted to make a point. They wanted to hurt him or someone dear to him—someone who'd loved him. Nate's mind immediately jumped to Bridget. She'd had great affection for the poet, though she'd only known him for two months. He moved to the window and peered out at the garden. Perhaps, he should have waited in the village for her. If there was a vengeful lunatic on the loose, no one associated with Otis was safe.

"I've given them all five minutes to gather in the drawing room," the colonel's voice sounded behind Nate as the man marched into the drawing room. "But I daresay they might be here sooner. They seem quite eager for details about the death."

Nate turned away from the window, and Lady Matheson stood up again. He noticed that her glass was empty once more. "Oh, please don't make me wait for the others. I must know now. How did George die? Is it as the colonel said? Did someone…did the killer cut out his…heart?" she heaved rather than spoke the last word.

"I'm afraid the colonel is correct," Nate said gently.

"Of course I'm correct," the colonel snapped. "I am never wrong."

Lady Matheson's cheeks paled, and she slumped back onto her chair as if she had no more strength left in her body. "No, it cannot be. I simply cannot believe it. It's a mistake, I tell you. Why, I saw him just last night."

"Did you?" Nate swallowed. There'd be no distancing Villa De Lacey from this murder now. He went and sat across from the woman. "What time was that?"

The corners of Lady Matheson's lips curved into a dreamy smile. "It was rather late. The moon was out, so we walked by the lake." She circled the rim of her empty glass with her gloved finger, the slight smile still on her lips as though she was relishing the memory of her evening with Mr. Otis. "It's beautiful under the moonlight, you know."

"Yes, I do," Nate said.

"And the stars. Oh, my goodness, the stars! George loved to gaze at the stars."

"Are you saying that you and Mr. Otis were out alone in the middle of the night?" the colonel asked.

"And why shouldn't we have been?" Lady Matheson straightened her back. "He wrote me the most beautiful poem."

"It hardly seems appropriate," the colonel sputtered. "A lady of your standing mingling with that…"

"Continue," Lady Matheson said coldly.

"Ruffian," Colonel Kendall said.

"How dare you!" Lady Matheson snarled. "Mr. Otis was a talented young gentleman, well versed in the classics. And he had a gentle soul. You should know better than to speak ill of a man who is no longer here to defend his person."

The colonel shifted in his seat. "Perhaps you're right. It was a bad choice of words. I only meant to say that he was not of your class. He has no place writing poems for society ladies, and one old enough to be his mother at that."

"I beg your pardon!" Lady Matheson straightened her shoulders. The insult had worked to reignite her energy.

Embarrassed for the colonel, Nate dropped his gaze. It was utterly unacceptable to refer to a lady's age in that way. Colonel Kendall had been abominably rude. But that was the colonel's nature. He often spoke out of turn and without thinking.

"I was only stating the obvious," Colonel Kendall said, proving Nate's thoughts by being seemingly oblivious to the *faux pas*.

"I think the more important point here," Nate interjected, "is that Lady Matheson may have been the last person to see Mr.

Otis alive."

"Oh, my." Lady Matheson seemed to wilt like a dying flower. "I hadn't thought of that."

"Aside from the killer, of course," Colonel Kendall said.

"Oh, poor George. My poor, sweet, kind George. To think that I was the last friendly face he saw before…it's too horrible." She lifted her glass and attempted to take a sip before realizing it was empty.

Nate refrained from offering her another.

"Did Mr. Otis walk you back to the villa?" Nate asked.

"Why yes. Of course, he did. He was a gentleman."

"So, you went inside, and Mr. Otis left to go—where?"

"He was going home. It was quite late, and he was tired."

"He wasn't meeting anyone else?"

"Not as far as I know." Lady Matheson picked up her glass again and gave it a forlorn look.

"The killer must have been lying in wait for him then," Nate mused. "He must have been spying on the two of you and waiting patiently for Mr. Otis to escort you back to the villa before accosting him."

"Oh, stop!" Lady Matheson slammed her glass down and covered her ears. "It's too horrible!"

Nate cleared his throat and picked up Lady Matheson's glass. Perhaps a touch more brandy was warranted. He went and poured two splashes into it and then raised the decanter in the direction of the colonel. "Cognac, Colonel?"

"I don't mind if I do," the colonel said.

Nate poured the colonel's brandy and took the two glasses, handing the larger to the colonel and the smaller to Lady Matheson.

"Would you mind showing me the poem Mr. Otis wrote for you?" Nate asked after Lady Matheson had swallowed her brandy.

"Oh, he didn't write it down. He recited it to me as we walked by the lake. It was something about the stars and the moon and…" her cheeks pinked. "Well, it was simply charming."

Nate sighed. He'd thought the poem might have contained some clues.

"Impudent little bugger," the colonel snorted. "He had no business courting a woman such as yourself."

"Oh, don't be ridiculous! He wasn't courting me." Lady Matheson's mouth trembled. "He was simply a friend, a dear, dear friend."

The colonel gave another loud snort, indicating his disbelief and disapproval. "I'd say it was your money he was after."

"I'd agree with that," Lady Armstrong said as she entered the drawing room and walked to the settee whilst leaning on her cane. Her companion, Miss Jennings, trailed reluctantly behind her.

"And I'd say it's none of your business." Lady Matheson turned her nose in the air.

"Well, it doesn't matter now that the man is dead," Lady Armstrong said, and Miss Jennings came forward to assist her as she lowered herself onto the settee. "If you ask me, it's a good thing that the poet will no longer be lurking around here. He spent far too much time chin-wagging about poetry and the mysteries of the world. What utter rot! He filled my companion's head with such fancy notions! His talk was enough to excite a young woman into madness." Lady Armstrong eyed Miss Jennings who sat timidly beside her.

"Did he, indeed?" Lady Matheson looked at the lady's companion and gave her a tight smile. "George was a wonderfully charitable person, and so generous with his time—even to those most others would simply ignore."

Miss Jennings's cheeks colored, and she dropped her gaze to inspect her black leather house boots.

"My word," Lady Armstrong chided her companion, "if you continue with this mournful expression, I shall have to send you back home to your mama. I rescued you from shame and spinsterhood to be my companion because your attentiveness and quiet disposition suited me. But your wallowing of late simply does not suit!"

"I'm sorry, my lady." Miss Jennings lifted her head, but her voice came out in a whisper, and her body trembled.

"Really!" Lady Armstrong gave her companion a sharp poke between the shoulder blades. "Get a hold of yourself and straighten your shoulders."

Nate could stand no more of the woman's bullying. Stepping forward, he said kindly, "Perhaps you'd like a drink of brandy, Miss Jennings? It's been quite a shocking day for all of us."

"She'll have no such thing," Lady Armstrong interjected before the woman could answer. "Tea will suffice."

"Yes, my lady," Miss Jennings said meekly, but Nate noticed the briefest flash of anger in her eyes as she glanced at Lady Armstrong.

Good, Nate thought. *There is a fighting spirit within her—however slight. Heaven knows, I could not hold my tongue as well as she.*

"I'll ring for the tea." Nate turned and went to pull the bell cord.

"Not for me," Lady Armstrong said. "Miss Jennings can prepare mine later. I'm very particular."

Nate sighed and let go of the cord.

"Where is Bridget?" Mrs. Harley asked as she entered the drawing room with her husband and Aunt Marianne. "She rushed off this morning, and I haven't seen her since."

"She's in Braithwaite with Mrs. Groby." A tug of worry pulled at Nate's chest. "But she should be here shortly."

"Mrs. Groby? Why?" Aunt Marianne said.

"The magistrate has arrested the local butcher, Mr. Groby, for the killing," Nate said.

Aunt Marianne gasped. "Mr. Groby, the butcher? There must be a mistake."

"We hope so, but as of now, the magistrate thinks he is the killer."

"The killer?" Lady Matheson squeaked as though saying the word 'killer' had the effect of throttling her. "So, they've caught the monster who did it?"

"A butcher. But how perfect!" Mr. Angert said in his distinct German accent, giving Nate a start. He hadn't seen the artist enter the living room, which was strange considering the man was as tall as a giraffe.

"Nothing has been proven yet," Nate said hastily. "The man has been accused, but there has not yet been an inquest, nor has he been tried. We shouldn't be so quick to condemn him."

"Not condemn him!" Lady Matheson glared at Nate. "If the butcher was innocent, the magistrate would not have arrested him." She stood up. "That monster took George's heart, and I, for one, will be glad to watch him hang for his crime."

Nate sighed inwardly. This was exactly what he was afraid of. It didn't matter whether Groby had yet to be proven guilty—the public had already condemned him.

"I saw a man hang once in Berlin." Mr. Angert ran two of his long, thin fingers down his neck. "A thief—I believe that was his crime. It wasn't a quick death. He struggled for quite some time, slowly choking until he turned a deep shade of blue. His tongue—"

"Thank you, Mr. Angert," Nate said sternly. "Please try to remember that there are ladies present."

The artist had clearly been enjoying the memory, and his smile faded. "My apologies, Dames." He gave them a low bow.

Nate frowned. He couldn't quite decide if Mr. Angert was half-mad or simply eccentric.

Colonel Kendall drummed his fingers against his knee as if agitated by something. "It's too bad. A good murder to solve was exactly what I was hoping for. This one was over too quickly. We shall have to hope for a second one. And if that fails, then at least there will be the trial to look forward to."

"I must ask you to stop with those callous comments, Colonel," Nate said. "We are talking about a man's life and not some type of mystery game."

"Oh, I am well aware," the colonel said. "This is far more exciting than a game. This is a real murder." He clasped his neck. "And real justice must be served."

Nate turned away from the man, disgusted by his insensitive display, and walked to the window, tugging at his cravat. The room had grown unbearably warm and stuffy with so many people occupying it. He gazed out at the garden, hoping to see Bridget ride up the winding carriageway on her horse, but all was quiet. A niggling worry settled in his stomach. *What is keeping Bridget? If something has happened to her, I'll never forgive myself.*

CHAPTER FIVE

W HEN BRIDGET ARRIVED home, she was met by the gardener, Thomas, and his apprentice, Fred Smythe—a quiet but strong young man of about seventeen who'd come from Cockermouth and was a distant relative of Thomas's.

"Miss De Lacey." Thomas removed his cap, and Fred followed suit. Bridget smiled at the men. Thomas had been serving Villa De Lacey for years, well before Bridget's birth. He'd known Bridget's mama, who'd died when she was four, and he'd been a dear friend of her papa's, who'd promised Thomas that he could spend the rest of his days in the gardener's cottage on the property. Bridget intended to persuade Nate to honor that promise. But that was not yet necessary as Thomas was not ready to put away his shears. Despite approaching sixty years of age, Thomas still had a handsome face, a full head of thick silver hair, and a muscular physique. He worked as he always had—with alacrity and precision—on his beloved garden.

"Thomas, Fred," she said, and it suddenly occurred to her that she had not seen them at all that morning despite the commotion in the garden.

"Are you well, miss?" Thomas asked. "I heard…" He shook his head. "It's unbelievable…there were another body in our garden."

Bridget sighed. By 'another body in our garden,' Thomas was referring to one of the horrific murders which had occurred at Villa De Lacey in the summer. She rubbed the back of her neck, which suddenly ached with tension. "I know. It's rather shocking, isn't it?" she said, for what else could she say?

"I wanted to apologize, miss." Thomas fiddled with his tweed cap, turning it around in his earth-soiled fingers.

"What for? Surely, you don't blame yourself for the body ending up in the garden?"

"No, but I ought to have been the one to find the body, not you, miss. You ought to have been spared that upset. Only I were off the grounds with young Fred here, teaching him about the berries and mushrooms and such. You remember the problems we had in the summer with the mushrooms."

"I do." Bridget nodded. Some guests had arrived with knowledge of the hallucinogenic properties of area fungi, leading to some embarrassing—and dire—consequences.

"So, the lad must be knowledgeable about the plants." He shook his head. "We got an early start this mornin' an' left through the east gates, so we didn't go past the daffodils. I thought I were doing right, but I ought to have done the rounds first, miss."

"Oh no, Thomas! You mustn't blame yourself. How could you have known there'd be a dead man in the daffodils?" Her voice faded with the latter part of the sentence as the horrific image of George's desecrated body reemerged in her mind.

"Have I upset you, Miss Bridget? I shouldn't have mentioned it. I'm sorry."

Bridget tasted blood in her mouth and became aware that she was biting down on her lip. Instinctively, she put her gloved hand to her mouth and pressed it against her wound. When she pulled her hand away, a bright red spot stained her white glove. The sight of it sent her back to the daffodils, where George's blood had stained the lovely golden flowers. Her legs seemed to lose their strength, and she felt unsteady on her feet. Thomas's face became a blur.

"Miss Bridget!" Thomas caught her by the arm. "Are you hurt? Let me take you inside."

Bridget blinked, and Thomas's lined but still handsome features came back into focus. She steadied herself. "No, I'm fine, Thomas. It's only that…well, the way the killer violated Mr. Otis's body after his death was an act of pure evil. It scares me to think someone of that nature lurks among us."

"Aye, but you needn't fret. I have me hunting rifles at the ready, and Mr. Squires has instructed me to start locking the gates after dark. It seems he isn't convinced Mr. Groby is guilty."

"That's a good idea," Bridget said, although the notion saddened her. In all the years she'd lived at Villa De Lacey, there had never been a reason to lock the gates. She'd always suffered from worry when her papa was away, fearing he might not return safely, but she'd never feared for her safety at home. Thomas, who had a stock of hunting rifles, was a constant presence on the grounds, and aside from the previous summer, Villa De Lacey had been the most peaceful place on earth.

Now, many of their guests enjoyed late-night stargazing and moonlit walks by the lake. So, she imagined, they would object to this new situation. Still, it would be for the best, at least for the time being.

"You agree with Mr. Squires, then?" Thomas said. "About Mr. Groby, I mean."

"I've learned the hard way that we never really know anyone. Some people harbor deep, dark secrets, and they hide them well." Bridget swallowed. She hated that she no longer trusted people, and so she fought against this skepticism. *I must remember that most people are good and have honorable intentions.*

She took a deep breath and continued to speak, "That said, we've been purchasing meat from Mr. Groby for years. I've known him since I was a child. Papa always spoke highly of him. And he seems to be a caring husband, father, and neighbor. So, I cannot believe that he would do such a heinous thing—at the very least, I don't think we should be too quick to condemn him. We all need to be certain that an innocent man doesn't hang. That would be another murder, in my opinion."

"Aye. I cannot agree more. I was mighty sorry to hear of Groby's arrest. He's a good man. He said a stupid thing, but he wouldn't do such wickedness to another man. I'm sure of that."

"You were at The Black Horse last night, then? Did you hear what Mr. Groby said?"

"Aye, we both did." Thomas nodded. "Groby were mighty drunk, weren't he lad?" He turned to his apprentice, who nodded in agreement.

"And was that unusual for Mr. Groby?"

"Not for a Sunday evening after a long week. The Black Horse is a place to relax with the lads."

"So, would you say most people were inebriated last night?"

"Everyone was certainly enjoying their ale and cider. They were jolly, to be sure, but none were as bad off as Groby. I've never seen him like that before."

"Was he drinking something stronger than ale and cider, perhaps?" Bridget asked.

"Not that I saw. I can't be certain about what he took in before I got to the tavern. He were already in a bad state when we got there."

Bridget worried her lower lip and then winced, feeling the tender spot she'd bitten earlier. "So, it seems as though he may have been drinking more than usual, which might indicate that something was upsetting him. Still, drunk or not, why should Mr. Groby say such a thing? Do you know if he quarreled with Mr. Otis?"

Thomas squinted reflectively before saying, "Mrs. Groby is a very beautiful woman. And there are many whisperings about her. Why she married a rough country butcher twice her age is a mystery to many. Some say her papa owed Groby money, an' he gave him his daughter instead. Others say her papa were a cruel man, and Groby rescued her from him. I don't know what the truth of the matter is, but I think some of the men are jealous of Groby, and they like to spread stories about him being a cuckold."

"And did someone imply that he was a cuckold last night?"

"Aye. It were that young Rupert. He were intent on getting under Groby's skin, saying things like, 'If I had such a beautiful wife, I wouldn't let her out of me sight, especially not with George Otis. He's a real Don Juan.' Then he hopped onto a table and started spouting some lines about a cuckold and his cheating wife. Had the entire place in stitches, he did."

"Oh my!" Bridget said. "But why should Rupert say those things? It's almost as if he wanted Mr. Groby to hurt George."

"It certainly did seem that way, miss."

"Thank you, Thomas." Bridget frowned. The entire situation seemed very odd. It appeared Rupert wasn't just an innocent bystander. He might have wanted harm to come to his friend. Or was it Groby he hated? If so, why?

Either way, more than ever, Bridget felt convinced that something was amiss and that Groby might be innocent. But mobs of people who'd been whipped into a frenzy didn't have much patience, and spurred on by Rupert, they'd demand swift justice. She'd need to work fast and find something compelling enough to convince the magistrate that further investigation was warranted. She doubted Rupert's little taunt would be enough to sway Magistrate Hunt. If anything, it would only work to convince him that Groby was guilty.

AFTER LEAVING THOMAS, Bridget went straight to the kitchen to collect Bijou. She knew that Nate, her aunt, and Jane would be anxiously awaiting her return, but all she wanted to do was sit quietly in the kitchen with her dog and drink a cup of tea. Yet upon entering, she was met with a blizzard of questions from the servants and frantic barking from Bijou. It seemed that everyone had congregated there, awaiting her return.

"I can hardly believe it. Mr. Groby of all people!" Cook said as

Bridget picked up Bijou and sat down with him on her lap.

"Oh, so you know about Mr. Groby already," Bridget said. "Mr. Squires has been down to talk to all of you, then?"

"No, he hasn't, miss. Not since he came and told us that Mr. Otis were found dead in the daffodils. He's been in with the guests since his return."

"Who then?"

"It were Maria's sister who told us the rest."

"Maria's sister?" Bridget turned to look at Villa De Lacey's newest housekeeper. She was a spinster from Braithwaite who'd lived with her sister and brother-in-law until she'd been hired to work at Villa De Lacey.

"She saw him arrested." Maria straightened her shoulders as if feeling quite important. "And she told us all about how Mr. Groby carved up poor Mr. Otis and fed him to his pigs."

"That's nothing but gossip," Bridget said.

"But he has been arrested." Cook placed a teacup in front of Bridget. "So, who are we to get our meat from now?"

"I hadn't even thought of that," Bridget said. "There are other butchers in nearby villages, but I shouldn't like to take business away from Mrs. Groby now. She'll need the money. Perhaps she'll hire someone to help her."

"Well, I don't want to be cooking her pigs, not if they've been feasting on a man's body parts," Cook said.

"I told you that's only a rumor," Bridget said.

"But it might be true, mightn't it?" Cook said. "And that's enough for me not to serve his swine." The rest of the servants nodded and murmured in agreement.

Bridget sighed. "I realize this situation is disturbing, but please, let's try to be kind. Think of Mrs. Groby and her children. I plan on going to see her again in a day or two. Perhaps you can bake some biscuits for her little ones. They need all the comfort and support they can get."

"I will do so, Miss Bridget. But don't you be bringing any of her pork home for me to cook. I won't do it, I tell you. And if you or Mr. Squires try and make me, I'll—"

"We won't—I mean, I'm sure Mr. Squires will understand. We can adjust the menu accordingly." She broke off a piece of her biscuit and gave it to Bijou, who gobbled it and then turned to look at her with pleading eyes that begged for more.

She gave him the remainder of her biscuit and smiled as he chewed it. But her shoulders felt heavy as the weight of the day's events bore down on her.

$$\mathcal{P}$$

BRIDGET NEEDED TIME to think and breathe before she went in search of Nate or faced her aunt's and any of the guests' questions. Her mind felt overloaded with information. Was Mrs. Groby the faithful, loving wife she professed to be? Who exactly *was* Mr. Collins and what was his relationship with Mrs. Groby? He'd arrived so swiftly, supposedly to render comfort, but why him of all people? And why had Rupert goaded Mr. Groby? Was it to taunt the butcher or to hurt George? Furthermore, why had Groby's friends and neighbors turned against him so quickly?

She exited the villa with Bijou and followed him as he raced across the grass. She thought he might go into the thicket but when he veered right and ran down the main garden, her heart sank. She could not bear the thought of going near the daffodils again.

"No, boy! Come back!" she called, but Bijou paid her no heed and continued toward the bright yellow flowers. He stopped at the edge, just as he'd done earlier that morning. Perhaps he thought George still lay there. She recalled how much Bijou had enjoyed the poet's playful personality. George always had a stick to throw for Bijou and never seemed to tire, no matter how many times her pup wanted him to throw it.

Bridget stood frozen and gazed at the daffodils from afar, recalling the first time she'd met the young man. He'd wandered through the gates of Villa De Lacey, drawn there by the daffodils, which he'd come to admire. She'd spotted him when she'd emerged from the thicket that surrounded the garden—a place Bijou loved. He'd seen a squirrel on the lawn and chased the poor thing back into the thicket where the little creature scrambled up a tree. And there it sat, taunting Bijou from above as he yapped incessantly at it. There'd been no getting Bijou away as long as the creature sat there staring down at him, so Bridget had scooped him up in her arms and taken him out of the thicket. And that's when she'd seen George, admiring the daffodils.

As soon as she'd set Bijou on the ground, he'd raced toward the handsome stranger.

"Hello!" George had knelt to pet Bijou, who'd promptly rolled onto his back so George could scratch his tummy. "Who do you belong to?"

"He's mine," Bridget had said. "And if you keep doing that, you'll have made a friend for life."

George had glanced up at her and smiled. "Good," he said. "I adore dogs as much as I adore Wordsworth and daffodils."

And with those words, he'd won Bridget's friendship.

"Well, you're welcome to come and see them whenever you like. Are you visiting, or have you recently moved to Westmorland? I haven't seen you here before."

"I'm a poet. And I've come on a pilgrimage with my two friends. We're secretly hoping to meet Wordsworth."

"How wonderful. Perhaps your wish will come true. He is sometimes out and about on walks, and he's been known to take a rowboat out on the lake. Where are you staying?"

"In a tiny cottage about half a mile from here. It's the perfect halfway mark between Braithwaite and Lake Windermere. A lovely, secluded spot. Also, we can't afford much else." He'd chuckled. "Nothing like this place," he said, gazing up at Villa De Lacey. "Are you the mistress of this beautiful villa?" he asked.

"I was once, but now I'm just the hostess."

"I don't understand," George had said.

"It's my family home, but it now belongs to Mr. Squires. Together, we decided to turn it into an inn," she'd said, not wanting to explain her entire history.

"Oh yes." George's eyes had grown wide as he reexamined the villa. "I heard about this place. The 'murder inn' they call it."

The memory of those prophetic words made Bridget's blood run cold, slapping her back to the present. She scanned the garden and, not seeing Bijou, walked cautiously forward, her legs shaking and her heart thumping in her chest. "Bijou." She clapped her hands together. She hoped he hadn't gone into the daffodils again. "Bijou!" She ran toward the flowers, her heart racing.

"Bijou!" She stopped by the daffodils and scanned the flower beds. "You know you're not supposed to be in here," she said weakly. "They'll make you sick." Her legs felt shaky, and her body trembled. The image of George's body flashed in her mind.

Just then, Bijou came racing out of the thicket and across the garden toward her, his tail wagging madly. Bridget felt her heart lift. Her dog was safe, and his happiness and joy for life was infectious.

"What were you doing in the thicket again?" She picked up her dog and held him close as she gazed out at the daffodils. Had Papa's death by his own hand left a permanent cloud over Villa De Lacey? Were they indeed now cursed? There was something so sinister and awful about butchering a man in a field of flowers. Especially since the daffodils had been a place that brought George such happiness.

"You shouldn't be here." Nate's voice sounded behind Bridget, and her heart jumped as he came to stand beside her.

"Oh, you frightened me." She pressed Bijou close. "I didn't hear you coming."

"I'm sorry." Nate smiled. "I spotted you from the drawing room, so I came down to meet you. I've been waiting for you to come back. I was worried."

Bridget suppressed a smile. She liked the fact that Nate cared. But his worry had been unnecessary.

"I shouldn't have left you there alone," Nate said.

"Where? In Braithwaite, where I've lived all my life? Or with Mrs. Groby and her children? Do you think little Edmund is the killer?" Bridget immediately felt a stabbing pain in her heart. *How can I joke about George's death? Have I become so callous—so accustomed to murder—that I am able to joke about my friend's brutal killing?* Shame spread from her chest up to her throat and across her cheeks.

"Are you well?" Nate blinked at her. "Did something happen in Braithwaite?"

"No," Bridget said. "I just…it was fine. I did my best to comfort Mrs. Groby, and then Mr. Collins came to check on her, so I left."

"Collins? What did he want?"

"He said he wanted to check up on her. He felt bad for her, I think."

"That's interesting." Nate massaged his jaw. "Because I am certain that I saw Collins in the crowd today. Not in Groby's slaughterhouse, but outside. There was a mob jeering at Groby while he was being led away by Magistrate Hunt."

"Was Collins jeering at him?"

"I don't quite remember." Nate frowned. "No, I don't think so. But he was in the crowd."

"An observer, then." Bridget said, "I don't see anything wrong with that. But there was something odd. I went into the kitchen at the Groby's to make tea and when I returned to the parlor, I walked in on Mrs. Groby and Mr. Collins having a private conversation. It made me feel a bit uncomfortable. It felt as though they were a little too familiar with each other. That's when I decided to leave."

"Odd, indeed," Nate said, with a thoughtful frown. "We shall have to look further into that."

"I heard from the servants that you were busy explaining things to the guests. Are they very confused and upset?" Bridget asked.

"Some are. Others seem a bit excited."

"By that, you mean Colonel Kendall, I presume," Bridget said with a halfhearted smile.

"Yes, and I got a similar impression from Mr. Angert. Strange fellow."

"What about the others?"

"Lady Armstrong hardly seemed to care, except for the effect it had on her companion. Miss Jennings was visibly upset, but I can't say if it was because of Otis or because of Lady Armstrong's bullying. She's quite awful."

"Poor Miss Jennings," Bridget said. "She reminds me a bit of Jane when she first arrived at Villa De Lacey last year—the way Lady Darby constantly beat her down with her bullying. It's just terrible."

"I agree. And then, of course, there's Lady Matheson."

"Yes, all eyes *must* be on Lady Matheson." Bridget giggled. "I expect she was quite dramatic."

"She was, but I also learned something quite interesting. She was the last person to see George alive—aside from the killer, of course. They met for a moonlit walk, and he recited a poem to her. After their walk, he escorted her back to the villa. She swears that's the last time she saw him."

"It might not even be true," Bridget said with a sigh. "Lady Matheson likes to be the center of attention. She might be making the whole thing up."

Nate gave a short laugh. Then he slipped his hands into his trouser pockets and gazed at the horizon, and Bridget could not help but notice how handsome he looked. "There's a lot to consider," he said. "But there is nothing to suggest that Groby is not the killer. All the evidence still points to him. He had a motive, and he had the means to kill George."

Bridget's heart sank. In these past months, her world had been turned upside down. People close to her had betrayed her. Still, she could not dismiss her neighbor and a man she'd known all her life based on another's actions.

"If he is guilty, then he should be punished. I just can't believe he would do such a thing. And there's something else…" Bridget frowned as she thought back to her conversation with Thomas.

"What?" Nate asked.

"I met Thomas in the garden. He was at The Black Horse last night, and he said Groby was highly intoxicated—more so than usual. I just have a bad feeling about it. Thomas said Rupert was goading Groby, calling him a cuckold. He even recited a humorous poem about it. Everyone was laughing at him and I think it embarrassed Groby. That, together with too much drink—or whatever else he'd consumed—made him say something out of character."

"It may have also caused him to act out of character—to do something he'd never have ordinarily done. Even good men do terrible things sometimes, especially when blinded by jealousy. Shakespeare taught us that."

"'It is the green-eyed monster that doth mock the meat it feeds on.'" Bridget recited Shakespeare's famous line from *Othello*.

"Well, *someone* was a good student." Nate grinned. "I'm impressed."

"I had a lot of time to read before Papa…" She bit her lip, not wanting to finish her sentence.

Nate cleared his throat and looked down at the ground before saying, "I think you're right. Mrs. Groby's relationship with her husband, as well as Mr. Collins and George, warrants closer investigation. But you must be prepared for the fact that it may prove rather than disprove Groby's guilt."

"All I want is to catch and punish George's killer. He didn't deserve to die that way—no one deserves something like that…" The swelling in her throat stopped her speech as she thought of her papa.

It always came back to him. She would never find peace with how he was buried.

She swallowed her pain. "Perhaps I'll pay Mrs. Groby another visit tomorrow. But I must say, it feels rather invasive, digging for information about a man's relationship with his wife."

"We have no choice," Nate said solemnly. "The people are going to demand swift justice, and Magistrate Hunt is going to want to give it to them."

CHAPTER SIX

THE NEXT DAY, Nate rode back to the village of Braithwaite and managed to persuade Magistrate Hunt to let him speak with Mr. Groby.

"It won't do you any good to give the man false hope, Mr. Squires." Magistrate Hunt rested his folded arms on his round belly. "I know Miss De Lacey has a soft heart and wants to believe the butcher is innocent, but I've got twenty men who heard Groby swear he'd carve that young poet up and feed him—"

"Yes, I know." Nate held up his hand to stop the magistrate from going on. "All I'm saying is that you've known Groby for years. He is your neighbor and your friend. Are you simply going to condemn a man without an investigation? Surely, there must be an inquest to decide if he should stand trial."

"Why call an inquest when we already know what the outcome will be? Yesterday was proof enough. The people of Westmorland have already decided that Groby is the killer and must stand trial for the slaughter of George Otis. We don't need an inquest for that. But…if the formality is what you want, then I shall do one. Just don't expect a different outcome."

The magistrate had a point. At best, an inquest would yield the same result as yesterday. At worst, it would create more anger and chaos. Nate shuddered at the thought. "I'd like to ask him if there is anything I can do to help his wife and children. They're innocent, aren't they? If you're going to send a man to his death, at least let him go in peace."

Magistrate Hunt shifted his stance, unfolding his crossed arms and reaching into his pocket for the keys to Groby's cell. "I suppose I can't see any harm in that. Follow me."

Nate followed the magistrate across the street to the local jail, which was most often occupied by intoxicated men needing to sober up.

"I'm taking Mr. Squires to Groby's cell," Magistrate Hunt informed the guard, who jerked up from his slouched position as they marched past his desk.

Groby sat in a cell with a wooden bench that acted as his bed and looked as though it were only big enough for a child. The bear of a man looked up in surprise as Nate and the magistrate approached his cell.

"I'm afraid I can't let you inside," Magistrate Hunt said, slipping the keys back into his pocket. "Too much of a risk after the heinous act he committed."

"Well, we don't know that he's guilty. The man hasn't had a trial yet," Nate reminded the magistrate.

"All the same," Magistrate Hunt said, "this is as far as you're going."

"Very well," Nate said. "Thank you, Magistrate."

The magistrate nodded and strode away.

"I hope you don't mind the intrusion," Nate said, and Groby shrugged in response.

"Can't intrude on a dead man, now can you?"

"You will have a trial. There's a chance you might be found innocent."

Groby snorted. "Is that why you came? To try and save my neck?"

"I'd like to try. If you are innocent as you claim, I—Miss De Lacey and I—would like to help prove as much."

A faint smile appeared on Groby's gruff face. "Aye, Miss De Lacey. She's a sweet lass. Known her since she were the age of me daughter."

"She thinks very highly of you, too, and that's why she—

we—want to try and help you."

"That's mighty good of you. But how will you do that?"

"If you can answer a few questions for me, that will be a start."

Groby shrugged again. "What is it that you want to know?"

"Do you recall what you said in The Black Horse last night?"

"I know what people told me I said, but I don't remember saying it."

"Some of the patrons that night remember you as being very intoxicated—more so than usual. Did you start drinking earlier than normal?"

"I don't remember," Groby said. "It's a blank space in me head."

"Do you remember if something happened to upset you that night?"

"It's all dark up here." Groby tapped his finger against his temple. "But it's no mystery. It's happened to me before. Drink a little too much ale, 'an you can't remember a thing of what occurred the next day." He chuckled, but then quickly grew somber.

"Your wife was taking reading lessons from Mr. Otis, and I've been told you ordered her to stop, but she continued against your will. Were you jealous of Mr. Otis?"

"Jealous? Not of that whippersnapper, I weren't."

"So why did you order your wife to stop the lessons? Was it because of money?"

Groby ran a hand through his shaggy black mane. "It weren't Otis who had me raging. It were Collins."

"Collins?" The hairs on the back of Nate's neck stood on end.

"Aye. She'd take her lessons with Otis an' then she'd meet up with Collins after. It weren't too long 'afore she stopped the reading and only went out to meet Collins."

"How do you know that?"

He hung his head. "I had Trent follow her. He owes me some money, so..."

"And did you confront her about Collins?"

"Nay, I did not."

"Why not?" Nate asked, but he already knew the answer. Groby loved his wife and confronting her would mean facing a reality that was easier to ignore. Nate had behaved similarly when he'd been betrothed to Helen. "So, when Rupert taunted you about being a cuckold, you became enraged. And you don't remember what you did after that?"

"It's all dark, like I said."

"So, it's possible that in your intoxicated rage, you attacked and killed Otis."

Groby stood. His bulky frame took up a large portion of the small cell, making him look like a caged bear. He turned to face Nate and gripped the cell bars with his large, meaty hands.

"I know I look like someone who can crush a man with his fists, but it's not me nature to act so. I've been a butcher for well-nigh thirty years 'an I know how to kill. But I'm no black-hearted murderer. I don't take pleasure in death like some do. I take care to cause as little pain as possible to the animals an' treat them well when they're alive. I don't abide by cruelty."

Nate's gaze fell on the butcher's beefy hands that gripped the cell bars and the clumps of dried blood under his fingernails. Then he looked up at the man's face. He was gruff-looking, that was for certain, but his soft brown eyes told a different story. They pleaded with Nate to believe him.

"I'm a God-fearing Christian, Mr. Squires, an' I wouldn't condemn myself to an eternity of torment or curse my children with a murderer for a father. If I hang, my wife's and children's good names hang with me. I love my family. I'd not do anything to hurt them."

Nate believed the man. But that didn't discount the fact that Groby may have acted out of character if he'd been in a blind, intoxicated rage of which he had no memory. "Aside from Collins, do you have any enemies? Any person who might want to frame you for this murder?" Nate asked.

Mr. Groby shrugged. "A few men who owe me money, and they've been a little troublesome."

"Owe you money?"

"Aye, I loaned them some at a modest interest."

"When you say modest…" Nate's heartbeat accelerated. Debt and the threat of debtors' prison were a strong motive for framing a man.

"Two percent. I'm not practicing usury."

"How many people?" Nate asked.

"Five or six," Groby said.

"You mean you don't know exactly?"

"It's six, but Wilson finished repaying his debt just last week. So, only five now."

"Have any of the remaining five had any trouble repaying you?"

"Morris, Hornby, and Trent have given me some trouble for a few months now. Sometimes, I let them pay me in with chickens, pigs, or even labor."

"And did you see all five of those men among your accusers tonight?"

Groby frowned in recollection, and then his face took on a pained expression. "Aye. I did. All six."

"Is Mr. Collins one of those you lent money to?"

"Nay, not Collins. I wouldn't have lent him a farthing."

Nate blew out his breath. That at least explained why Groby's "friends" were so eager to see him hanged. Whether or not they framed him, Nate wasn't so sure. Money was indeed a strong motive for murder, but so was love. It appeared as though several people had reason to want Groby gone.

IT SEEMED IN bad taste to play a game of croquet on the lawn beside the daffodils where a man had lain slaughtered just the day before. But Bridget and Nate had agreed that it was best not to dwell on the murder or turn Villa De Lacey into a house of mourning. Nonetheless, Bridget was disturbed that some of the guests—namely Colonel Kendall and Mr. Angert—seemed intrigued and excited by the prospect of playing croquet just a few feet from where the murder victim had been discovered, while others appeared to be indifferent. So she forced a smile and joined the guests in their game, despite her urgent desire to return to Braithwaite and visit Mrs. Groby again.

Teamed with the Harleys, Bridget played against Miss Jennings, Colonel Kendall, and a reluctant Lady Matheson. Lady Armstrong, who had an aching knee, sat on a lawn chair and observed the players, occasionally using her spyglass to get a closer look and act as a self-appointed referee. Mr. Angert declined to play and instead fetched his easel and proceeded to sketch them competing on the grass. And Aunt Marianne, who hated croquet, stayed inside to ensure all was running smoothly within the walls of the villa. After the disastrous summer when the household staff had run amok and two people ended up dead, Aunt Marianne had reassumed the role of managing the servants. Her aunt secretly enjoyed being in charge, but, as she frequently reminded Nate, she was not and would never be a servant. After all, Villa De Lacey was her ancestral home, and she made certain the guests knew as much too.

The game had been going badly because every time someone hit a ball, Bijou would attempt to chase it, and while that made Bridget and Jane laugh, Colonel Kendall was not impressed. For him, everything was a battle that had to be won at any cost. About halfway through, just as Lady Armstrong was admonishing Miss Jennings yet again for playing as though she were "wearing a blindfold," an elaborate black and gold carriage rolled through the gates of Villa De Lacey, causing everyone to pause their game and watch its ascent up the carriageway.

"Someone is here." Lady Matheson's face grew pale as she followed the carriage with her eyes. "There's a crest on the door.

Can you see what it is?" She discarded her mallet and looked around wildly.

"I say!" Colonel Kendall pointed at Lady Matheson's discarded mallet. "We are only halfway through the game. Do you intend to forfeit?"

"Yes, forfeit. Forfeit for all I care!" she said.

"That's a disgrace, madam! We do not abandon our men on the battlefield."

Lady Matheson ignored him, but Jane giggled.

The lady silenced her with a glare. "Who is that? Are you expecting more guests?" she demanded, turning to Bridget.

"Not that I am aware of." Bridget frowned at the approaching carriage.

"Well, it looks to be someone important," Lady Matheson said, and Bridget thought she heard a tremble in her voice. Of what, or who, was Lady Matheson afraid?

The red and gold family crest on the carriage came into focus—two winged griffons on either side of an elaborate shield sporting a medieval castle. Bridget's heart started to pulse. She'd seen a carriage bearing that crest before.

"I think I recognize that crest," Mr. Harley said, "but I can't quite put my finger on to whom it belongs."

"Yes," Jane said. "I can't quite place it either. Although, I agree, it looks familiar."

"It's her." Bridget's voice came out in a whisper.

"Who?" Lady Matheson sounded hysterical, but Bridget couldn't find her voice to answer. They all watched as the carriage rolled to a stop. Then one of the two coachmen, dressed in smart livery consisting of a black and gold-trimmed tailcoat, red breeches, white stockings, and shiny black shoes, dismounted and opened the carriage door.

"The Countess of Luxton," the coachman announced. And then, Nate's beautiful former betrothed—the mother of his young son—exited the carriage.

"It's Lady Luxton!" Jane said. "And she's brought her darling little boy."

The apples of Jane's cheeks brightened at the sight of the child. Her one wish was to become a mother, but with each passing month, her hope diminished. Jane feared she was barren. Bridget was pleased that the presence of little Henry Luxton would bring some comfort to Jane, but for her, his arrival brought new anxiety and worry.

The last time Nate's former betrothed had been a guest at Villa De Lacey, things had not gone well. Worse, Bridget had been the uncomfortable witness to their quarrels and to Nate's agony at finding out he was the father of a boy who'd been claimed by another man.

As far as the world was concerned, Nate's little boy was the son of the Earl of Luxton, who also happened to be the Laird of Lochmaben, owing to his massive estate in Scotland. Neither Nate nor Lady Luxton would do anything to jeopardize that. But Lord Luxton was seven-and-eighty years old and in ill health, so although Lady Luxton had left Nate for the title and money the earl provided, it seemed she now wanted the best of both worlds. Ultimately, Lady Luxton was a vain and cruel woman who liked to use her child to manipulate Nate. And Bridget did not want to see him hurt.

"What a dear little boy," Lady Matheson said, and then she let out a choked sob.

"Whatever is the matter?" Jane asked the lady.

Lady Matheson shook her head, unable to answer.

"Why don't you go inside and lie down?" Bridget suggested. "I'll have some tea sent up to your room." George's death had been an enormous shock to Lady Matheson, and grief had an odd way of expressing itself. After her papa died, the smallest thing could bring forth a flood of tears.

"Yes, that's a good idea," Lady Matheson sniffed. "But I'll want some brandy with my tea. I need something to settle my nerves."

"Of course, my lady," Bridget said.

Lady Matheson turned and walked toward the villa.

"I say!" Colonel Kendall called after her. "This is outrageous. One cannot simply discard one's post in the middle of a game."

Lady Matheson kept walking and paid no heed to the colonel's rantings, which only infuriated him further. "If you were in the army, you'd be shot!" He shouted.

Jane giggled, and Bridget squared her shoulders and prepared herself to face Lady Luxton.

"What's the matter with you?" Jane asked. "You look a bit green all of a sudden. I hope there isn't some sort of illness going around."

"No, don't worry, I'm fine." Bridget swallowed. She could not reveal all that had transpired between Nate and Lady Luxton during the summer. Nor was she at liberty to tell anyone that Lady Luxton's son belonged to Nate and not Lord Luxton. "I wasn't expecting her, that's all. I'm surprised."

"She's not the most amiable, I agree," Jane murmured. "But it's always good to have more guests, isn't it?"

"You're right." Bridget handed Jane her mallet. "I'd best go and see to her needs."

"You too!" Colonel Kendall said, and then bellowed, "Have you ladies no sense of honor—of *duty*!"

"I'm sorry, Colonel. I'll be back, I promise. But I must see to our new guest," Bridget said.

Colonel Kendall threw down his mallet in a huff, making poor Miss Jennings flinch and gasp out loud.

"Lady Luxton," Bridget said as she approached the lady. "What a lovely surprise. Will Lord Luxton be joining you?"

"No," Lady Luxton said dismissively.

Bridget looked at the little boy and swallowed. Eight months had made an enormous difference in the small child's appearance. The boy, now three years old, had Nate's mop of dark curls and his mother's lovely, chocolate brown eyes and long, thick lashes. Dressed in a linen blue skeleton suit with gold buttons, he held his nanny's hand and looked up at Bridget. His likeness was so close to Nate's that Bridget could not take her eyes off him.

"I'll want the same arrangement I had during the summer," Lady Luxton said coolly. "A room for myself—the best you have, of course, and one for Viscount Brayton and his nanny."

Bridget was momentarily taken aback by Lady Luxton's use of Henry's title. She'd not used it once during the summer, and it struck Bridget as awfully pompous and formal. But, she supposed, it was another opportunity for Lady Luxton to exalt her status over Bridget.

"I believe we can accommodate you, but we weren't expecting you, my lady," Bridget said. "Usually, guests send word to warn us of their coming. Did you send word to Mr. Squires?"

"No, I decided to surprise him. Where is he?"

Surprise him? More like blindside him. Bridget's gaze dropped again to the little boy who was Nate's tiny doppelgänger.

"He went into town to see Mr. Groby," Bridget said, then winced at her choice of words. She was so disrupted by the sight of the boy, she'd spoken without thinking. "He should be back shortly."

"Groby?" Lady Luxton inclined her head. "Who is that?"

"He's our butcher," Bridget said, not wanting to talk about the murder.

"The butcher?" Lady Luxton's dark eyebrows came together in a frown. "Shouldn't *you* be handling such a menial task?"

Bridget's chest burned. Lady Luxton never missed a chance to insult her. But before she could reply, Mr. Angert looked up from his easel and said, "You misunderstand. The butcher is accused of murder. And Mr. Squires wishes to save him and deprive us all of a good hanging."

"Mr. Angert!" Bridget had to restrain herself from diving forward and covering little Henry's ears.

"Murder, did you say?" Lady Luxton raised her lush eyebrows. "*Another* one?"

"Oh, yes." Mr. Angert said, his paintbrush poised in midair. "It's most sensational. The murderer cut out the victim's heart and fed it to his pigs. Come see for yourself." As he spoke, drops of red paint dripped from his paintbrush onto his black boot.

Lady Luxton strode to Mr. Angert and peered at his easel. Bridget followed suit.

"Good heavens!" Lady Luxton said as Bridget stifled her gasp with her hand. Mr. Angert had painted a lovely picture of them playing croquet and, lying in the daffodils a few feet away from the joyous game, was the mutilated, blood-soaked body of George Otis.

CHAPTER SEVEN

THE MEETING WITH Groby had disturbed Nate. There was more that needed investigating. Groby had clearly been jealous of Collins, and it sounded as though he had just cause. If Mrs. Groby and Collins were lovers, they'd have had good reason for wanting Groby out of the way. It was far better to frame him for murder than to kill him themselves, in which case the suspicion would fall directly upon them. If all that were true, then George Otis had been a pawn in their scheme.

Nate decided to stop by the butcher's cottage and speak with Mrs. Groby; he suspected he'd find Collins there as well. As he made his way there, he was delighted to see Bridget riding toward him. He tugged on his horse's reins as she neared, and the animal came to a halt.

"Oh, I'm glad to have caught up with you," Bridget said, bringing her chestnut mare to a halt beside his tan gelding. Her cheeks were flushed, and her riding cape was askew as if she'd thrown it on in a hurry. Nate thought she looked beautiful.

"I'm pleased you did," he said. "I was on my way to speak to Mrs. Groby, but I think it's better if we visit her together. That's why you came to town, isn't it?" Nate frowned, suddenly realizing that Bridget had already passed the cottage.

Bridget, in turn, seemed to hesitate as if thrown off guard. "I—yes. That's right. I mean to check up on her. I wanted to reassure her that she needn't worry about our meat order. The poor woman has enough to do already."

"I don't know. I suspect she has some help from Mr. Collins." Nate related what Groby had told him.

"So, it seems I was right. There *is* something between them," Bridget said.

"Yes, it seems you have good instincts. Mind you, that doesn't make them guilty or Groby innocent. He already had suspicions about his wife, and being ridiculed in front of everyone at The Black Horse must have sent him into a blind rage. He can't remember much about what happened that night, though. What if he went in search of Collins but found the poet instead?"

"You don't believe that do you?" Bridget said.

"I have enough doubt not to let the man hang without asking some questions. As for his pigs, if there's even a slim chance he killed Otis and fed his heart to his pigs, I don't think we can risk serving them to our guests."

"Cook had said she wouldn't allow it anyway," Bridget said. "I shall ask Mrs. Groby to remove them from our usual order. Perhaps we can replace it with extra mutton."

"Agreed," Nate said and spurred his horse forward.

Bridget turned her horse around and followed him. Within a few minutes, they were in front of the butcher's cottage and adjacent slaughterhouse.

"It appears as though they are open for business." Nate dismounted from his horse. "I imagine we'll find Collins inside doing Groby's work."

"So soon," Bridget said, also dismounting. "That seems a bit..."

Bridget didn't need to finish her thought. The fact that the butcher shop was open did seem a bit suspect. That was for certain.

"I agree," Nate said. He watched as Bridget reached for a small bundle tied to her saddle. "What's that?"

"Biscuits for the children. I had Cook make them. I don't want any ill will toward Groby's children. Whatever happened, it's not their fault."

Nate smiled. Bridget had a good heart. After everything she'd been through with her papa and the murders last summer, she never wallowed in self-pity or lost her ability to think of others and their suffering.

"That's a lovely gesture." He nodded at the bundle. "Hopefully it will help."

They entered the slaughterhouse and, as expected, found Collins donning the butcher's apron. Mrs. Groby worked diligently alongside him, wielding her butcher's knife quite expertly.

Mrs. Groby looked up from her work. "Miss De Lacey. Mr. Squires." She put down her knife and wiped her bloodied hands on a cloth hanging from her waistband. "I'm surprised to see you here. If you're worried about your meat order, you needn't be. Mr. Collins kindly offered to help me fulfill our obligations."

"How noble of him," Nate said, unable to keep the sarcasm from his voice. "I've just come from speaking with your husband." Nate let that information hang in the foul air of the slaughterhouse.

"Then, the magistrate allowed you in to see him. I wasn't sure—"

"Did you ask?" Nate said. "I'm certain the magistrate wouldn't begrudge a wife from visiting her husband."

"I was going to…later today. But as you can see, I have my hands full here. Somebody has to do the work. Unless, of course, you wish to withdraw your business and find a new butcher as so many of our 'friends' and neighbors have done." She dropped her gaze.

Nate swallowed. He couldn't fault the woman for wanting to survive and support her family.

"No, of course not."

"We just came to tell you that Mr. Groby is well—" Bridget paused—"at least under the circumstances." She held out the bundle. "And to give you these biscuits for the children. I had Cook bake them fresh this morning."

"That's kind of you." Mrs. Groby took the bundle. "The children are both down for naps, and they'll be wanting a little something when they wake. Why don't you come in for some tea? I think Mr. Collins and I could use a small break, too."

"That would be lovely," Bridget said.

Nate smiled to himself. Bridget had such a way with people. Despite the inward anxieties she suffered from, she was always able to put others at ease.

Once inside the comfortable cottage, Nate and Bridget sat on the settee in the front parlor with Collins while Mrs. Groby prepared tea.

"You've only been here a few months, haven't you, Mr. Collins?" Nate took the opportunity to ask the man a few questions. "What made you decide to come to Westmorland?"

"Indeed, I've only been in Westmorland for a few months, but I'm from York. That's not too far away. One day, I picked up Mr. Wordsworth's guidebook and that lured me here."

"Are you also a poet?" Bridget asked.

"No. I'm only a farmer and a bit of a wanderer."

A farmer? The man doesn't sound like a farmer. He's educated, and he can read. Nate was about to ask Collins more when Mrs. Groby's young son wandered into the room, rubbing the sleep from his eyes.

"Just in time for your tea," Mrs. Groby said as she entered the front parlor and placed the tea tray on the table. The child ran to his mother. She embraced him. "Where's Charlotte? Still asleep?" The child nodded, and his mother guided him to his seat.

But it wasn't the child that interested Nate. It was Collins. He saw a change in the man's face as he looked at Mrs. Groby's little boy. He saw the softening of his eyes and the corners of his mouth turn up slightly as he reached out and ruffled the child's blond hair. He saw exactly what he felt when he looked at his own little boy, Henry. It was the look of unconditional love. It was a look a father would give a son.

BRIDGET COULD SEE something was bothering Nate. He'd grown very quiet once the children had woken up. She'd seen him watching young Edmund closely, and she knew immediately why. He was thinking of Henry.

Guilt gnawed at her stomach. She should have told Nate about Henry's arrival as soon as she met him on the road as planned. That was the reason she'd abandoned the croquet game and rushed out of the villa, only stopping to drop Bijou off in the kitchen where Cook had insisted she take the biscuits "afore they grew hard and brittle." But she'd become sidetracked by the visit to Mrs. Groby. She'd planned to go anyway, and after Nate had told her what he'd learned about Mr. Collins, it seemed better that they went together.

Still, now was as good a time as any to tell him. She had no intention of allowing Lady Luxton to blindside Nate as the manipulative woman had obviously planned. She couldn't imagine the shock he'd experience upon seeing Henry playing on the lawn, particularly after Lady Luxton had sworn never to let him see the child again. He'd mourned for Henry these past eight months, and Bridget had ached for him. She knew the unimaginable agony of loss. Nate would be delighted to see his son again, but he needed to be prepared for it. He needed to be in control of his emotions, or Lady Luxton would rule them.

"I know what you're thinking," Nate said as they mounted their horses.

"Pardon?" Bridget asked, startled.

Nate's gelding trotted forward, and she pressed her calf against her mare's side to make her horse catch up with his.

"The little boy." Nate slowed his horse as she came up beside him. "He's the same age as Henry."

"Edmund? Yes. He's three." Bridget's heartbeat accelerated. Why had she waited? It had been selfish of her. "Can we stop a moment? There's something I need to—"

"It's his child." Nate interrupted. "The boy."

"Sorry?" Bridget said, confused.

"You saw the way Collins looked at the boy, didn't you?"

"I…are you talking about Mrs. Groby's son?"

"Of course? Who else would I be talking about?" He paused. "I thought you noticed it too."

"Noticed what, exactly?"

"The way Collins doted on the boy."

"He seemed very kind to the children, especially Edmund."

"You're not hearing me. What I'm saying is I don't believe Collins and Mrs. Groby to be recent friends. I believe they've known each other for a while—more than three years, I'd say."

"Three years," she repeated, finally realizing what Nate was talking about. "Then…you believe that Collins is Edmund Groby's father?"

"I'm certain of it."

"But how…how can you be certain?"

"I told you. I saw the way he looked at the boy, and…well, a father knows these things. His love for the boy was transparent. I thought you saw it too."

Bridget fell silent as she digested Nate's words. She hadn't noticed anything different about Collins's interaction with Edmund, and she wondered if Nate's theory was prompted by something more personal. He missed Henry; she knew as much. Perhaps his longing for his son had led him to jump to this new conclusion.

"Bridget?' he said. "Do you understand what this means? If we can prove that Collins and Mrs. Groby have a long history together, then there is a very good chance that the two of them conspired to get rid of Groby."

"It would certainly complicate things and raise a lot of questions," Bridget said, her mind still on Henry and Lady Luxton. It was time to break the news to Nate. She opened her mouth to speak, but he was too excited about his new theory to let go of it.

"We shall have to do some digging into their pasts," Nate said. "But where would we start? In Collins's hometown of York, I think," he said, answering his own question. "Someone there must know something. And haven't there been rumors about Mrs. Groby's past—I believe I heard something about Groby rescuing her from a cruel father or some such bad situation?"

"Yes," Bridget said. "People have always gossiped and speculated about why such a pretty young woman would marry a gruff old butcher like Groby."

"Well, it's a good question. Why do you think she married him?"

"I don't know. I stay away from gossip, especially after Papa."

"If this is all getting too much for you, I can—"

"No, it's not that at all." She worried her lower lip.

"Then what is it?" Nate said. "You seem…has something upset you?"

"There's something I need to tell you." She swallowed. "I didn't come to town to visit Mrs. Groby. I came to find you."

"But you had biscuits for the children," he said.

"I know. I intended to visit Mrs. Groby, but I needed to find you first."

"Well, I'm glad you did," Nate said. "It was a most informative visit."

"You don't understand. Something happened before I came to find you," Bridget said, the knot in her stomach growing. "Something you need to know about."

Nate pulled on his gelding's reins, and the horse slowed and then stopped. "I'm not following. What happened?"

Bridget stopped her mare and faced him. "A new guest arrived this morning—two guests, actually."

Nate frowned. "Unexpected guests?"

"That's right." Bridget dropped her gaze to her gloved hands. Suddenly, she felt deeply ashamed that she had not told Nate sooner. She'd made the wrong decision. She had no right to make him wait to see his son. And why had she waited? Was it because she wanted to keep him to herself just a little bit longer?

"Well, we have a few chambers available. You were able to accommodate them, I assume?"

Bridget nodded again, still without looking up.

"I don't see a problem. Who are the guests?"

She lifted her gaze and met Nate's deep blue eyes. "It's Lady Luxton and Henry."

🔎

NATE FELT THE color drain from his face. His former betrothed, Helen Morley, now Lady Luxton, had sworn never to let him see his son again, and it had crushed his heart. That had been eight months ago. Eight long months.

Suddenly, nothing else mattered. Not Groby, Otis, or Collins. None of it mattered. He turned to Bridget. "Why didn't you say so earlier? Why did you make me wait…I don't understand."

"I meant to tell you. That's why I came to find you in the first place." Bridget looked visibly upset. "I just—well, after you told me about Collins, I thought it better to wait until after we visited Mrs. Groby." She paused. "And…I was afraid to upset you."

"Upset me?" Nate said. "How could I be upset?" He laughed. He was going to see his son again. And then a terrifying thought struck him. "What if she leaves before I get home?"

"She won't. I showed them to their chambers. She's staying. You needn't worry about that. I just thought you'd want fair warning before you returned home. I think she hoped to shock you with her sudden arrival—to demonstrate that she can snatch Henry away at will and bring him back whenever she wants."

"That's because she can, and I have to take what I can get."

"I know, but her arriving unannounced like that. It's a reminder that she is in control and that you are at her mercy. It's…cruel."

Nate ran his hand through his hair. Bridget was right. Of

course, Helen wanted to control and manipulate him. She couldn't stand the fact that he no longer cared for her—not because she loved him, but for her own selfish need to be the center of everything. Still, as long as she had Henry, she'd have his attention.

He ached to see the boy. How he must have grown during these months. He wanted to spur his horse on and canter home, fall on his knees, and thank Helen for bringing Henry back. Yet, if he showed Helen anything but remote coolness, she'd use the child to torment him forever. Whatever he did, he had to avoid falling into one of Helen's traps. And Bridget's warning had given him the ability to do just that.

"Thank you," he said, turning to Bridget, and she rewarded him with a smile that warmed his heart.

WHEN THEY RETURNED to Villa De Lacey, Lady Luxton was in the drawing room with Lady Matheson and, to Bridget's surprise, Rupert and Charlie. The four were playing a game of cards, and each sipped a glass of port.

Rupert and Charlie got to their feet as soon as Bridget and Nate entered the room.

"Miss De Lacey, Mr. Squires, I hope you don't mind," Rupert said. "We just thought we'd—"

"Oh, do sit down!" Lady Luxton said with a laugh. "You're with us. We invited you. Mr. Squires doesn't mind, does he?" She turned and gave Nate a dazzling smile.

Bridget could see the tension in Nate's jawline as he steeled himself to deliver a cool response.

"Lady Luxton, how kind of you and Lord Luxton to visit us again."

"Who said Lord Luxton is here? He is in Scotland."

Nate gave her a tight smile and then turned to Rupert and

Charlie. "Please sit down. You are most welcome here any time. I am so sorry for everything that has happened."

Rupert nodded, and Charlie dropped his gaze to his feet. "Thank you," Rupert said, and both young men sat down.

"Oh, don't put on such long faces!" Lady Luxton said. "We were having so much fun. Let's get back to it."

Rupert picked up his hand of cards and gave Lady Luxton a weak smile. He nudged Charlie, who then followed suit. But Lady Matheson seemed to have lost her appetite for playing. She picked up her glass of port and wandered to the window, where she stood staring out at the field of yellow daffodils.

Lady Luxton suddenly put down her hand of cards and turned to Bridget. "I hope you don't mind, Miss De Lacey, but my little Henry has kidnapped your mutt—what's his name?"

"Bijou." Bridget scanned the room, looking for her terrier. "Where are they?"

"Henry insisted the pup take a nap with him in his room. I didn't like the idea at all. Dirty little dog. But Henry kicked up such a fuss that I told Nanny to put the mutt on the floor in the corner of the room. Under no circumstances, I said, must that beast go near Henry's bed. Henry is a viscount, you know. His health is imperative, especially as his father is…" She glanced at Nate. "Well…"

"I'll be more than happy to take Bijou from Henry's room," Bridget said icily.

"Oh no, let the mutt stay. If it pleases Henry…"

"I'm afraid I must insist. Bijou needs his walk. Henry is welcome to join us when he wakes up."

"Oh, never mind us. I think we shall take a walk with Mr. Squires." She turned to Nate. "Henry remembers you. He liked it when you played with his boat by the lake. Shall we take him again? Unless you prefer to go with Miss De Lacey and her mutt."

Bridget's chest boiled. She hated how Lady Luxton always managed to make her feel small, like she was a servant in her own home. And she hated even more how she used Henry to make

Nate do her bidding.

"I should be honored to take the young viscount to the lake," Nate said, and Bridget could not fault him for jumping at the chance to spend time with his son.

"Well, it's settled then. I'm sure when Henry sees you, he'll forget all about that little rat catcher." She gave Bridget a smug smile and turned back to her cards. "It looks like Lady Matheson has forfeited her hand," she said. "I believe it's your turn to play, Rupert."

Lady Matheson had not moved from the window and did not seem to register when her name was mentioned. She stood, squeezing her empty glass, with her eyes still fixed on the daffodils.

CHAPTER EIGHT

DESPITE LADY LUXTON'S rudeness, Bridget was secretly pleased that little Henry had taken a liking to Bijou. The child was stuck in a house with grown-ups, and Bijou would make a delightful playmate for him. She knew that Lady Luxton's comments were only said to injure her.

The truth was, Bridget knew, she resented her relationship with Nate. They had developed a solid friendship built on mutual respect, and perhaps Lady Luxton sensed there was something more between them. There was a strong attraction, at least on Bridget's part, but she'd pushed it aside. Her grief for her papa and the horrors that had taken place over the summer had stretched her emotions to the limit, and now she was just beginning to process George's murder. As for Nate, he'd suffered some enormous changes himself. The most important one was discovering that he was a father.

As if that wasn't enough, he had Lady Luxton to contend with.

Bridget heard Bijou's bark behind her, and then her terrier tore into the drawing room, wagging his tail and jumping excitedly upon seeing Bridget. She picked up her wriggling pup and kissed him.

Henry entered the drawing room accompanied by his nanny. He wore the same blue linen skeleton suit she'd seen him in earlier. His nanny had attempted to tame his black curls by flattening some of the more stubborn ringlets with water, but she'd had little success. Though a disaster, it made him look even more adorable.

"Henry, darling. You remember Mr. Squires, don't you?" Lady Luxton stood up and took hold of her son's hand.

The boy looked up at Nate, who gazed down at him and smiled. They were quite the spitting image of one another.

"How do you do, Henry?" Nate said.

"What do you say?" The child's nanny prompted.

"Well, thank you, sir," the child said in an obviously rehearsed line and gave a little bow. Bridget could not stop herself from smiling. In spite of his mother, the child was precious.

"Do you remember when we sailed a boat on the lake?" Nate asked, and Henry nodded. "Would you like to do that again?"

Once again, he nodded.

Bridget swallowed the rising lump in her throat. When Lady Luxton had last departed Villa De Lacey with Henry, vowing never to return, the little boats Nate had fashioned out of paper for his son were all he had left of their time together. He kept a row of them on the window ledge in the office, where Lake Windermere glistened behind the paper vessels.

"Shall we go and find a new boat?" Nate addressed the question to Henry but looked at Lady Luxton as he spoke. Henry nodded but, following Nate's gaze, glanced up at his mother.

"What a marvelous idea," Lady Luxton said, her voice unnaturally cheerful. "Go with Mr. Squires and find your boat, dear. Then we'll all take a walk to the lake together." She gently directed the child toward Nate and briefly closed her hand around his as he took hold of Henry.

Bridget's stomach tensed as she watched the scene. Lady Luxton was a master manipulator. She wanted to gain Nate's trust again only so that she could hurt him later. The woman was like a vampire, gaining her energy by draining it from others.

Bridget turned her attention away from Lady Luxton and back to Nate and his son. Her heart blossomed as she watched Nate leave the room hand-in-hand with Henry. She felt a tear coming, but immediately stiffened when she saw Lady Luxton watching out of the corner of her eye. Against her better judgment, Bridget turned to face the woman. The corners of Lady Luxton's mouth turned up in a smug smile before she returned to her seat and picked up her hand of cards.

"Shall we continue, gentlemen?"

Rupert and Charlie had been sitting in silence, and Bridget had almost forgotten they were there. Charlie, she noticed, seemed fixated on Lady Matheson, who still stood by the window staring at what Bridget knew were the daffodils, which had become terrible to look at but too difficult to ignore.

"Are we going to continue to play, gentlemen?" Lady Luxton asked.

"Certainly," Rupert said and picked up his cards. Charlie turned his head slowly away from Lady Matheson and followed suit.

"Lady Matheson, will you be rejoining the game?" Lady Luxton said.

Lady Matheson blinked and turned away from the window. "I…" She put her hand to her forehead. "I don't think so. My mind feels quite overcrowded now."

"Perhaps you'd care to take a walk outside, my lady?" Bridget said.

"Yes, I think I would like that," she said.

♀

"WE CAN AVOID the daffodils if you like," Bridget said as they stepped outside. She shielded her forehead with her hand as she tried to keep track of Bijou, who'd scampered ahead.

"Thank you," Lady Matheson said. "I've tried not to act the fool about it all. I mean, I only knew the man for a fortnight. It seems silly that I should mourn a penniless poet far below my station. I know everyone is gossiping about it. They think I am some lonely widow desperate for attention."

That was exactly right, though nothing that Bridget would admit to the lady. She veered toward the outer edges of the garden, where the thicket lay, and Bijou raced toward her. He loved the thicket, which was alive with rabbits, squirrels, and voles.

Thoughts gathered, she said, "I don't believe anyone thinks that. And it doesn't matter how long you knew Mr. Otis. You did know him, as did I, and he was your friend." Bridget paused, glancing at the woman beside her. Lady Matheson's face had a pained look. She truly was suffering. "I feel his loss, too," Bridget said. "Mr. Otis had a way of making people like him. He was such a charming young man—so talented and enigmatic."

"If you cared so much about Mr. Otis, why are you trying so hard to free that butcher who killed him? What he did to George was… barbaric."

"I agree," Bridget said. "And I'm not—would never—defend a person who was guilty of such a heinous act. But the rush to judgment and finger-pointing at Mr. Groby seems all too convenient. I've known the man since I was a little girl, and he has always been a decent member of this community."

"Decent? The man publicly declared that he wanted to butcher George. He was jealous of him because his young wife was enamored with George. And why wouldn't she be? He was, as you said, charming and enigmatic." Lady Matheson wiped away a tear from the corner of her eye.

"His loss is a crushing blow for all of us." Guilt gnawed at Bridget's insides. Perhaps she was doing the wrong thing. What if Mr. Groby was guilty? Then she'd have been defending the indefensible—a man who took another man's heart. She'd be defending the likes of those who desecrated her father's body.

"They should hang him, and they should do it soon!" Lady Matheson said, and her vehemence brought Bridget back to her senses.

Lady Matheson's emotions were running high. She understood the feeling very well. But that was also something of which she was afraid. She'd learned from past mistakes that things aren't always as they seem. And a rush to judgment could lead to the death of an innocent man. She had to stay strong and keep fighting for Mr. Groby. His emotions had been spiked the night of the murder, and while that could make one say things out of turn, it did not necessarily make one a murderer. But she knew it was useless to try and explain as much to Lady Matheson. Neither she nor any of George's friends were able to listen to reason. Bridget could only hope that the magistrate would give them a little more time.

They reached the end of the thicket and exited the gates of Villa De Lacey. Lake Windermere's beauty never failed to take Bridget's breath away. In all her two-and-twenty years, she'd never grown complacent to its splendor, for each day the lake looked different. The seasons and the weather changed its mood. Today, the sky was a bright blue, and the sprawling lake sparkled beneath the spring sunshine. The fells surrounding it were as green as emeralds. Bridget inhaled. Here was a sight to soothe the soul.

She glanced at Lady Matheson, hoping the widow was experiencing the same tranquility she was feeling. But Lady Matheson gazed at the lake with furrowed brows as if she wasn't seeing it at all. She was somewhere else—someplace dark—in her mind. Bridget could tell because she'd been to such a place herself after she'd learned how her papa had died. Even the majestic Lake Windermere could not calm her soul then. She'd needed to purge the rage herself—that terrible black anger she'd never known could exist. It had come from a pain so deep that she'd felt helpless. All she could do at the time was scream and rage at the sky, and so that's what she'd done until she'd exhausted her body. And then, it would start all over again. And so it went, until bit by bit, the pain lessened, but it never disappeared. That type of pain came from a deep loss. That's what she was seeing here, and it told her that there was something more to Lady Matheson and

George Otis's relationship.

"I had a child once," Lady Matheson said quietly, as if sensing that Bridget was ready to hear her story.

"Once?" Bridget echoed just as quietly.

"He was only a babe when he died."

"Oh, my lady. I am so sorry."

She smiled sadly. "He was a lot like George. Their coloring was the same. Moses was born with wisps of yellow hair and wonderful blue eyes. Even as a babe, he was full of life and love. I could tell he had a poetic heart, even at an early age."

Bridget frowned. It sounded as though Lady Matheson was talking about George—as if she'd imagined her infant as a full-grown man in the form of the young poet. "So that's why you gravitated toward George," Bridget said. Finally, Lady Matheson's relationship with him was making sense. She'd lost her son, but if he had lived, he would have been George—at least in her mind.

"Losing George has been like losing my boy all over again. He drowned in a pond behind our estate—stepped on the ice. He wanted to slide across it—adventuresome little one. But it was too thin, and…"

"How awful." Bridget's heart sank. This story kept getting stranger. *How can a babe step on ice? Or decide he wants to slide across it all by himself?* But perhaps he'd been a toddler—just a babe in her memory. "Was he alone?" Bridget asked and then instantly regretted her question.

Lady Matheson pressed her gloved hand to her eyes. "No, I…well… it was many years ago. He was so beautiful—perfect. It was no fault of his, you understand. No fault of his whatsoever."

"Of course not," Bridget said.

"The nanny failed in her duty to protect him. But he was always running away from her. He wanted to be free, and who could blame him?" Lady Matheson was becoming increasingly upset and confused, it seemed.

Bridget silently admonished herself for asking the poor woman to divulge the traumatic details of her child's death and feeling guilty for assuming that Lady Matheson had had a romantic interest in George when she'd viewed him as her lost son.

"The heart never truly heals from such a loss," the lady said. "And now the pain…it's come back. It's quite unbearable."

"I know that all too well." Bridget put a hand on the woman's arm.

They strolled along the shore of Lake Windermere, taking in the sparkling lake and the green fells surrounding it. A sense of calm settled within Bridget as it always did when she was surrounded by the beauty of her home, and she hoped it was doing the same for Lady Matheson.

After a while, they turned and made their way back to Villa De Lacey. It was then that Bridget spotted Nate and Lady Luxton playing with Henry. All three were laughing as they watched the child's paper boat bob along the water. Emotions warred within her. Her heart lifted for Nate. He was, she knew, the happiest he'd been since Lady Luxton had threatened to take Henry away for good. But she could not help feeling somewhat envious and also a little cross. Lady Luxton had owned Nate's love, and she'd thrown it away. It did not seem fair that she continued to have such a strong hold on his life.

"That's his child, isn't it?" Lady Matheson said, and Bridget jumped, startled by the question.

"No, of course not. The child belongs to Lord and Lady Luxton."

"Don't look so frightened. I know how dangerous it is to say such a thing, and I won't repeat it, I promise. I only want you to remember that what you see before you—this happy scene—is simply a father who loves his son, not a man who loves a woman. I've watched the two of you, and I'm certain you have his heart."

Bridget felt her face redden. "That's—no—you've got it all wrong. I'm still mourning my papa. You mustn't—"

"I won't," Lady Luxton said. "Don't worry. I shan't say another word." She took hold of Bridget's arm and gently pulled her away.

Bridget glanced at Lady Matheson, seeing her in a new light for the second time that day. Her words had both pleased and comforted Bridget. It was refreshing to have guests who treated her like the granddaughter of the man who built Villa De Lacey, rather than a burden to the man who now owned her home and her heart.

THE NEXT DAY, as Bridget was returning from her morning walk with Bijou, she made her way to the servants' quarters at the back of the house. Bijou scampered eagerly ahead of her, knowing that a bowl of delicious scraps would be awaiting him in Cook's kitchen. But he stopped abruptly as he neared the rear of the house and cowered back.

Bridget raced forward to see what had alarmed him, but before she reached him, she heard a ruckus that told her all she needed to know.

"Don't you dare set that down, hear me! This be my kitchen an' I don't want it, so get it out!"

"I'm not going anywhere until I have delivered the order Mr. Squires himself requested." Mr. Collin's voice sounded.

Good heavens! Bridget picked up her pace. *The meat order must have arrived!* She rounded the corner toward the back of the villa and saw Mr. Groby's loaded meat wagon parked outside. A few feet away, Cook stood with her hands on her ample hips, glaring at Mr. Collins as she blocked him from entering the kitchen.

"What's the matter?" Bridget asked as she approached them, even though she knew full well what the problem was.

"Our new butcher—or so he calls himself," Cook said, her cheeks as fiery as her red hair. "I told him I don't want none of Groby's pork, and he keeps insisting that Mr. Squires ordered them for us. As if I'd believe that Mr. Squires went to the butcher and put in for a meat order! Gentlemen don't handle their own meat orders, Mr. Collins. If you were a *real* butcher, you would know that!"

"Now, everyone, please calm down," Bridget said. "As it happens, Mr. Squires and I *did* place the order when we visited Mrs. Groby yesterday." She turned to Cook. "I took the biscuits you made for her children, remember?"

Cook nodded begrudgingly. "Aye, I remember. But it was just you who took them, not Mr. Squires."

"We met on...Well, never mind that. The point is that we told Mr. Collins to deliver our meat order as usual. I meant to tell him without the ham, but I believe I forgot."

"Forgot, miss? How? When they've been given a man's heart in their feed? And it's no wonder if Mrs. Groby was carrying on with that poet the way she's carrying on with Mr. Collins now." Cook gave a self-righteous sniff and re-planted her fists on her hips as she glared at the man.

"How dare you!" Mr. Collins said. "Mrs. Groby has done nothing wrong. As for me, I'm only trying to help a family in need."

Cook opened her mouth and leaned forward to argue but Bridget got between them.

"Stop!" she said. "There's no use in us standing here squabbling. Perhaps we can compromise. Mr. Collins, you'll take the ham back with you to Mrs. Groby's butcher shop and tell her we have no need for it this week. And you will leave the rest of the meat here."

Mr. Collins gave Bridget a cold stare, and she almost regretted her offer of compromise. Instead, she straightened her shoulders and said, "It's better than taking back the entire order, is it not, Mr. Collins?"

Collins stiffened his back. "I wish to speak with Mr. Squires."

"Then you're in luck, Mr. Collins," Nate said as he came around the corner. "What seems to be the problem?"

"Your servants are refusing the meat you ordered."

Bridget's chest tightened. She was not a servant.

"I'm only refusing the ham," Cook expostulated. "We don't want to turn our guests into cannibals, that's all."

"Mr. Collins, first let me thank you for delivering our meat order so promptly. Now, why don't you do as Miss De Lacey suggested? Carry the meat inside, but take the pork home, and we'll pay for the full order. Mrs. Groby and her children can enjoy the ham as our gift."

Collins narrowed his eyes. "Very well," he said in a clipped voice, "I shall explain your position to Mrs. Groby."

"You'll send Mrs. Groby our best wishes," Bridget said sternly, still stinging from the way Collins had referred to her as a 'servant'. She was more than that, and he needed to be aware of that fact. "And you will thank her for the timely delivery of our meat order, considering the circumstances."

Mr. Collins blinked and seemed to shrink down a little. "Of course, Miss De Lacey," he said. "I will relay your message as you told it." He doffed his cap. Then he hauled the mutton out of his truck and headed for the pantry.

"I don't trust that one," Cook said after Mr. Collins was out of earshot.

"I thought it was Mr. Groby you didn't trust," Bridget said.

"I don't know no more. All I know is that I don't like how quick Mr. Collins stepped into Groby's butcher's apron. It's like he knew what was coming—like he—they…planned it all."

"They? Do you mean Mrs. Groby and Mr. Collins?"

"Aye." Cook narrowed her brown eyes. "I know you think Mrs. Groby an innocent woman, but people are mighty suspicious of that Collins taking over the butchery the day after her husband were locked away."

"I don't know that he's taken it over. Mrs. Groby seems grateful for his help."

"Seems right convenient." Cook narrowed her eyes. "If you ask me, *he's* the one who took Mr. Otis's heart and fed it to those pigs."

Just then, Mr. Collins came back outside and picked up the remainder of the meat order.

"Well, I'd best go see to my kitchen," Cook said and followed Mr. Collins inside. Bijou chased after her, barking. She stopped and laughed at the terrier. "Don't worry. I 'aven't forgotten your scraps. Come along."

Bijou's tail wagged madly, and Bridget laughed. "I'll be there in a minute," she called after them. Then she turned to Nate and said, "So we're not the only ones who suspect Collins."

"Not anymore," Nate said. "And if people in the town are expressing similar doubts, that might slow the magistrate down a little, but we need to take advantage of the time we have."

"So, what do you suggest we do?" Bridget asked.

"I think it's time we take a trip to York," Nate said.

CHAPTER NINE

B RIDGET NEVER TIRED of York. Despite the long carriage ride from Westmorland, she never refused an opportunity to visit the magnificent medieval city. The first glimpse of the spectacular gothic towers of York Minster always sent a thrill down her spine. The breathtaking cathedral, with its elaborate architecture and stained-glass windows, dominated the area. But there was so much more about the historic town that Bridget loved. York's Roman walls, narrow cobbled streets, overhanging timber houses, and bustling markets never failed to fascinate. She'd spent many happy hours perusing York with her papa, and so it held her heart and some of her most precious memories.

Bridget leaned her head against the carriage window and sighed as the vehicle rambled through York's cobbled streets. In her mind's eye, she saw a young girl walking arm-in-arm with her doting papa, who insisted on purchasing yards of beautiful fabric along with bows, hats, and gloves for his only daughter. Her heart ached for the return of those days. What she would give for just one more day—one more hour—with her papa.

"You're very quiet," Nate said, pulling Bridget back to the present. "I do hope you're not worried about your aunt."

"Aunt Marianne?" she said, turning from the carriage window to face him. "Not at all. She is perfectly at home in York." They'd left Aunt Marianne, who'd accompanied them on the trip, to care for Bijou and peruse the markets while they went about their business—only Bridget wasn't quite sure what that "business" entailed. "Actually, I was wondering where we are going?" she said, glancing again outside as the carriage left the city center and rambled through an open road lined with trees. "We don't know anything about Mr. Collins. Where do we start searching for information?"

"We know more than you think," Nate said just as the driver slowed the horses, and the carriage rolled to a stop.

Bridget peered out the window and saw that they had stopped in front of an ancient-looking stone building attached to a church. In front of the building lay a sprawling green, the type one would find at a prestigious public school. Indeed, affixed to the black iron gates that protected the grounds from outsiders was a red shield with white letters that read *St. Paul's of York.* "We're at a school," she realized aloud.

"That's right. Our man Collins is too well spoken and has far too many airs to be a mere farmer's son—unless farmers are using Latin phrases nowadays."

"What are you talking about?"

"The other day, when we visited Mrs. Groby, and I asked Collins to recount Groby's outburst at The Black Horse, he mumbled the Latin phrase, *'in vino veritas.'* I knew, then, that we were dealing with a man who has two identities."

"In wine, there is truth," Bridget said. "I don't recall him saying that."

"And I don't recall you telling me that you knew Latin."

"I don't—not really." She smiled. "Papa liked to pepper his speech with Latin phrases, so I picked up a few here and there."

"Aah, I see. Well, either Mr. Collins has spent a lot of time with educated men, or—he is one of them."

"And you think this is the school he attended?"

"If he lived in York as he claimed he did, then this is very likely where he would have gone to school."

"But what good will it do us? We can't simply walk inside and ask for information about a former pupil. We're not magistrates."

Nate smiled. "Sometimes there are advantages to being the

second son of an earl." Then he pushed open the carriage door, stepped outside, and extended his hand to Bridget.

She slipped her gloved hand into his and felt a tingle travel up her arm and down her back. She wondered if he felt it, as well.

🔍

IT DIDN'T TAKE long before Nate and Bridget were seated inside the headmaster's office. Headmaster Egan, who'd stood to greet them upon their arrival, was a tall, wiry man, with a neck and legs as long as those of an ostrich. He had a bird-like face, too, with a beakish nose that supported a pair of round spectacles. Nate could imagine the towering stick figure looking down admonishingly upon his pupils, most likely with a cane in his hand. That's how most of the headmasters operated, in his experience. He shivered at the memory. The slice of the cane biting into his flesh had never stopped him from doing as he pleased, and it had pleased him to get into a lot of mischief, much to his father's and his brother's disdain.

"How may I help you?" Headmaster Egan asked as he re-claimed his seat.

Nate scanned the walls behind the headmaster's desk, eyeing the portraits of his predecessors. "How long have you been headmaster here?" he asked.

"Seventeen years." The headmaster straightened his back, indicating his pride in that fact.

"Excellent," Nate said. "The school is preeminent among public schools in England. I'm sure that's largely down to you." *A little flattery never hurt a headmaster.*

"Well, I cannot take too much credit. After all, the school has been open for centuries."

"Of course." Nate smiled.

"Do you have a son you are interested in enrolling, perhaps?" Headmaster Egan glanced at Bridget, and his brow creased slightly as if he were confused by her presence. A boy's education was his father's business, after all.

"No," Nate said and then added, "not yet." He smiled. "We are here to inquire about one of your former pupils."

"Oh?" The headmaster lifted his brows.

"We need some information and hoped you'd be able to enlighten us," Nate said. "It would be several years ago now that he attended."

Headmaster Egan folded his long fingers together. "We do keep records on all our students—not too detailed, but with the dates they attended and other such facts."

"Well, I'm hoping you'll remember a lot more than simple dates. I am sure you pride yourself on knowing every young man who passes through your school."

"Indeed, I do. But what type of information are you after? I shouldn't be comfortable divulging information of a private or sensitive nature to those who are not family." He raised his eyebrows. "Are you family?"

"Not family," Nate said. "But this is a matter of life or death."

Mr. Egan blinked rapidly behind his gold-rimmed spectacles. "Life or death, you say?"

"I do, but I cannot divulge more than that."

The headmaster frowned, drawing his feathery brows together. "I must say this is a little unusual. What is the name of the young man you wish to inquire about?"

"His surname is Collins." Nate paused, uncertain of Collins's first name.

"Mr. Douglas Collins," Bridget added. Nate had to admire her. She *would* know his first name, focused on people as she always was. "He is today approximately seven-and-twenty years of age."

Headmaster Egan narrowed his eyes. "Do you know, that name sounds familiar? But it's not because he was a pupil at our school. No, I don't recall a Collins here."

Nate frowned. "But you must have so many pupils; how can

you know for certain? He would have attended ten years or more ago. Perhaps check your records."

The headmaster gave Nate a tight smile. "I remember all of our boys. Most of them come from aristocratic families, so I am not likely to forget a name."

"But you do remember something, correct? After all, you just said the name sounds familiar to you."

"Indeed, I do. May I suggest you visit a school called St. Joseph's in Harrogate?"

"Why?" Nate asked.

"There was some sort of a scandal a few years ago at St. Joseph's—about four years ago, if my memory serves me correctly, and I believe the name Collins was attached to it."

"What kind of scandal?"

"I'm afraid I can't say. I don't know all the facts, and I have a strict policy against gossip. It would be a waste of your time to learn about half-truths, and as you said, yours was a case of life or death; I'd hate to mislead your inquiry in any way."

"Of course." Nate nodded. He was eager to learn more about this scandal and whether or not it involved Collins, but it would do him and Bridget no good if they were to receive incorrect information. The headmaster was right. It was better to go to the source. Nate got to his feet, and Bridget followed suit. "Thank you, Headmaster, you have been most helpful. If you remember anything at all, I would most appreciate it if you would send word to Villa De Lacey on the shores of Lake Windermere."

"Villa De Lacey?" the headmaster asked, standing up. "Is that the one where—I read about it in the *York Herald*. A poet was murdered and found lying in the daffodils, of all places. How intriguing. Someone must have been trying to make a strong statement."

"Oh, you mean…?" Nate gestured to his heart. "Yes, I suppose they were." He glanced at Bridget, worried the conversation had taken an upsetting turn for her. But she remained admirably poised.

"Not only the taking of that organ but more specifically, leaving the body in the daffodils," the headmaster said.

"Do you mean because he was a poet, and Wordsworth wrote a poem about daffodils?" Nate asked.

"Precisely. Wordsworth is Westmorland's greatest poet, after all. And those young poets make the journey there as some sort of pilgrimage, do they not? They aspire to be like him—perhaps meet him and learn from him. So, when I read in the *York Herald* that a local butcher had committed the crime, I thought they must have the wrong man. It cannot be a coincidence that this young poet ended up dead in the daffodils. Unless, of course, the butcher is a poetry aficionado." The headmaster blinked behind his spectacles.

"Yes, we are questioning the arrest of the butcher too," Nate said, turning to Bridget who nodded her agreement.

"So why do you ask about Collins? Is he involved in this somehow?" Though he'd said he had a policy against gossip, the headmaster was doing a poor job of following it.

"We don't know. We are only trying to make sure an innocent man doesn't hang for the crime—that is not to say the butcher is innocent, only that we wish to make sure he is guilty and not innocent." Nate frowned at how convoluted his own words had sounded.

Beside him, Bridget shifted. Apparently, she was tired of being treated as invisible by Egan. "We want to make sure a potentially innocent man doesn't hang," she clarified for him.

Headmaster Egan seemed a bit affronted to be addressed by a female in such a forthright manner. His eyes narrowed behind his glasses. "Well, if you care to consider my humble opinion, I'd say that while a cuckolded butcher might be the obvious choice, the symbolism of this crime seems too complex for a *simple* butcher." He stressed the word "simple", perhaps for Bridget's benefit.

It didn't sit well with Nate. Still, despite his arrogance the headmaster had a point. Perhaps he hadn't given the connection between Wordsworth's poem and Otis's murder enough thought.

"Of course, I wouldn't expect your local magistrate to understand any of that. You, on the other hand, must have received a gentleman's education." The headmaster cocked his head and raised an eyebrow. "An Eton boy, perhaps?"

"Westminster," Nate said. "And Oxford."

"Well, then, sir, I expect you are the perfect man to solve this crime."

"Not me," Nate said. "Miss De Lacey is the aficionado when it comes to Wordsworth." The headmaster's expression clouded, and Nate suppressed a satisfied smile. Although he'd liked the classics well enough, he hadn't been inclined to read much popular poetry after leaving school. But perhaps it was time to indulge in a little Wordsworth.

🔍

"It doesn't make sense," Nate said once they were back in the carriage. "Four years ago, Collins would have been three-and-twenty and no longer a schoolboy. Are you sure of his age?"

"No, I was only guessing. He looks to be about the same age as you."

"I'm six-and-twenty."

"That's why I said approximately," Bridget answered. "Either way, you are right. Unless he is much younger than we think, he would not have been a schoolboy four years ago."

"Well, the only way we can find out is by taking a trip to Harrogate and visiting St. Joseph's. Unfortunately, we shan't be able to make it to and from Harrogate today. So, I'm afraid we will need to spend an extra night in York and make our trip in the morning."

"That shouldn't be a problem. Mrs. Harley will do perfectly well looking after the inn."

"Yes, I believe you're right. But I was thinking of your aunt. If she wants to return, then I can make the journey to Harrogate by myself."

"Don't you dare!" Bridget laughed. "We can leave early in the morning and return by afternoon. Aunt Marianne will be thrilled to spend another day perusing the markets in York."

Nate smiled to himself. Bridget was a true puzzle solver, and whether she'd admit it or not, investigating this murder had energized her.

"Perhaps we can get ourselves a copy of Wordsworth's poems in the meantime. That headmaster left me wondering if there are any hidden clues in that daffodil poem. I don't believe I can remember much beyond the first line. Let's see. *'I wandered lonely as a cloud, that floats on high o'er vales and hills...'"* He shut his eyes, trying to remember the rest.

"*'When all at once I saw a crowd, a host, of golden daffodils,'"* Bridget finished the stanza for him. "Would you like me to go on?" She cocked her head at him and smiled cheekily, revealing two small dimples at the corners of her mouth. His heart gave a little leap, and he checked himself.

"You know the whole thing, then?" He could not help but smile back at her.

"I do," she said. "But it's only the last stanza I feel we need to focus on."

"It contains some hidden clues, you think?"

"I don't know about clues, but that headmaster was certainly right about the symbolism. Actually, now that I'm thinking about it, I believe I know exactly what he's talking about."

"What do you mean?"

"Take a moment to listen carefully," Bridget said. "*'For oft, when on my couch I lie, in vacant or in pensive mood, they flash upon that inward eye, which is the bliss of solitude; and then my heart with pleasure fills, and dances with the daffodils.'"* Bridget recited the final stanza of the poem. "He's talking about recalling the daffodils he saw and how the memory fills him with joy."

"Yes," Nate said. "That's simple enough."

"Now, focus on those last two lines. *'And then my heart with pleasure fills, and dances with the daffodils.'* It's as though the killer is sending a sinister message by perverting the delight that Wordsworth experiences when he recalls the daffodils. Remembering the daffodils, Wordsworth feels connected to nature, and his heart overflows with joy."

"Unlike Otis," Nate said, "who lies among the daffodils, lifeless and with no heart. The very core of his being was ripped from his body. Not to mention that daffodils are spring flowers. They symbolize renewal and hope. And of course, there is no hope left for Otis. Such an ugly death suggests just the opposite."

"His murder was likely a punishment," Bridget said. "Perhaps he stole someone's heart and broke it, and so the killer condemned him to spend eternity without hope or heart," Bridget said.

"Contrapasso," Nate nodded in understanding. "That's exactly it."

Bridget frowned. "Now you've lost me. What's contrapasso?"

"It's from Dante's *Inferno*. In Dante's version of Hell, the sinners' punishments echo their crimes. In other words, they are punished in a way that befits their crimes—it's called the *law of contrapasso*," Nate explained. "For example, those guilty of gluttony are condemned to wallow in filth like pigs and being bitten by the three-headed dog, Cerberus."

"How awful," Bridget said.

"Yes, but the point is that the punishment fits the crime."

"I tremble to think what happens to murderers."

"Murderers are condemned to wallow in a river of boiling blood. Their punishment resembles their crimes on Earth. They have blood on their hands, and so they are mired in blood for eternity. The punishment fits the crime."

"That makes sense." Bridget shuddered.

"It might sound awful," Nate said. "But Dante wanted to illustrate that the Lord is just. Sinners receive a punishment that befits their sins—nothing more and nothing less."

Bridget went silent for a moment. Then she asked, her voice trembling slightly, "And what of those who self-murder?"

Nate's heart broke for her. She so wanted to believe her papa was at peace. "It's only a story, Bridget. All of it conjured up in Dante's mind. He'd been expelled from Florence, and he was furious. Do you know, he put all his enemies in the lowest levels—"

"I know it's not real," Bridget said. "But I want to know, nonetheless."

"Those who self-murder lose the right to their earthly bodies for eternity, and their souls are instead trapped inside trees…" He stopped, hoping that would be enough to satisfy Bridget.

"Is that all?"

"All that I can remember," he lied.

"There are nine circles of Hell in Dante's *Inferno*, are there not?"

Nate nodded.

"And the self-murderers are in what circle?"

Nate exhaled. "The seventh."

"And they don't suffer any torture?"

"The trees"—Nate hesitated—"are attacked by harpies. They pull at the leaves and claw at the branches. The souls cry out but are unable to speak of their suffering until Dante breaks a branch from one of the trees and makes it bleed."

"I understand. The souls are tormented and in constant pain. They cannot freely express their anguish, and they will never know peace or their human form again."

He glanced at Bridget, whose eyes had welled up, and he silently cursed himself. Why had he brought up the damned *Inferno*? "Bridget," he said, "you mustn't—I mean, your father was—"

"So if we are correct in our thinking"—Bridget forced a smile—"then it's as I said. Whoever killed George must have had their heart broken by him. He ripped out someone's heart—took away their joy, hope, and future, so they did the same to him."

Bridget worried her bottom lip. "Now we just have to find out if that person is Collins."

"Exactly," Nate agreed, still eyeing Bridget worriedly. "Let's hope the headmaster at St. Joseph's is the same one who was there four years ago, and that he's willing to talk to us."

CHAPTER TEN

BRIDGET'S CONVERSATION WITH Nate continued to sting long after she'd returned to The King's Head on Low Petergate, where she was sharing a room with her aunt. She hadn't been able to stop herself from pressing Nate about the self-murderers' fates in the *Inferno*. And now it ate away at her heart. Was her dear papa suffering torments for his final act? She refused to believe it. Dante's *Inferno* was only a story, and the punishments in his hell were all figments of his imagination. But his message was correct. The Lord was just, and He knew that her papa had been decent and kind his entire life. He knew that her papa belonged with her mama, who was with the angels. Still, she would never know for certain—at least, during this lifetime—and that left her stomach in a knot of pain.

"Well, Bridget. What do you think of the gloves?" Aunt Marianne asked as she admired a set of white gloves laid out on the bed.

Bridget petted Bijou absentmindedly and glanced down at them. "Oh, yes. They are lovely, Aunt."

Aunt Marianne was very pleased with herself after purchasing Jane Harley a new pair of gloves to thank her for tending to Villa De Lacey and their guests while she and Bridget traveled to York.

"Perhaps, I should have gotten a pair for you, too, Bridget. I saw a lovely blue pair that would make your eyes sparkle. It's been a year since your papa's death. You no longer need to wear mourning dresses."

"I know, Aunt," Bridget said. She had transitioned to wearing half-mourning colors of lavender, gray, and white, but could not bear to shed her mourning wear so soon. One year had flown by, and it seemed to Bridget that she'd lost her papa only days ago.

"I don't like how glum you look, dear. I believe this murder has upset you greatly."

Bridget forced a smile and placed Bijou in his basket. The terrier was no doubt exhausted from his day out with Aunt Marianne. "I'm just a little tired, that's all."

Aunt Marianne picked up the gloves and placed them back in their ribboned box. "I do wish you'd leave things up to Magistrate Hunt this time," she said. "We don't want a repeat of what happened last summer when you ended up getting hurt."

"How can I do that after everything we have discovered about Mr. Collins and Mrs. Groby's ongoing dalliance?"

"Really, Bridget!" Aunt Marianne's cheeks turned pink. "A young lady should not be so outspoken about such things."

"I'm sorry, Aunt, but we cannot ignore that fact because it may mean they schemed to kill George in order to frame Mr. Groby for the murder. After all, they must have wanted to be rid of Mr. Groby."

"And how will you prove such a thing?"

That is the real dilemma. "Well, for a start, we will need to go to Harrogate tomorrow."

"Harrogate!" Aunt Marianne exclaimed.

"Yes, there's someone we need to interview. You don't mind staying in York an extra night, do you?"

"What about Jane?"

"I think she'll be fine for an extra day."

"Well, I don't like it, Bridget," Aunt Marianne said. "Poking around and asking questions might lead to you being harmed again. And I—well, if anything were to happen to you, I don't know what I would do. Your poor father would never forgive me."

Bridget's heart contracted. She wasn't the only one who'd

suffered after Papa's death. Poor Aunt Marianne had lost her brother and the quiet, peaceful life he'd provided for her since the death of her husband.

"You don't have to worry, Aunt," she said. "I shouldn't be able to forgive myself if anything I did led to you being miserable."

"Then you'll drop this nonsense and leave it to the magistrate?"

Bridget walked to the window of her inn and gazed out at the cobbled streets lined with overhanging timber houses. "No, but I do promise to be careful," she said. That was the best she could do to comfort her aunt, but she had no idea if being careful would be enough. George's killer was a dangerous and vengeful person who would not be afraid to strike again if he felt cornered. She and Nate would need to move carefully but quickly. A crime of this magnitude could not go unpunished for long.

$$\rho$$

AFTER A TWO-AND-A-HALF-HOUR journey to Harrogate, Nate and Bridget were disappointed to find that the black iron gates to St. Joseph's Grammar School for boys were shut. And the school building that stood behind them looked to be in disrepair. The green in front of the building was overgrown and neglected.

"It's no longer in operation," Nate said. "I wonder why?"

"Perhaps it had something to do with the scandal Headmaster Egan was talking about."

"Perhaps." Nate sighed. "The question is, who can tell us?" He scanned the area, and his gaze landed on a church that stood beside the old school building.

It was exactly what he'd been looking for. Most public schools were tied to churches, so the chance of the vicar knowing something about Collins and the scandal at St. Joseph's was high. The chances that the vicar would talk to them, on the other hand, remained to be seen.

He turned back to the school and rattled the locked gates in frustration.

"I'm afraid that won't help. They've moved," someone said behind Nate. He immediately let go of the gates and turned around to see a short, balding man wearing the vicar's cloth standing a few feet away. "I saw you from across the street"—the vicar pointed to his church—"and I was wondering if there was anything I could help you with."

Nate straightened his jacket and cleared his throat. "Yes," he said and proceeded to tell the vicar why they'd come.

The vicar clasped his hands together and nodded. "I knew a Mr. Douglas Collins. But he wasn't a pupil at St. Joseph's. He was one of the masters."

Bridget gasped. "A schoolmaster!" She glanced at Nate, and he knew what she was thinking. The mystery of Mr. Collins's age had been solved. He had been too old to be a pupil at the school, but he was not too young to have been a teacher.

"He was only a young man. In his first or second year of teaching," the vicar said, "but very clever. He'd received an excellent education—although I cannot recall where he'd studied." The vicar scratched his lined forehead. "Anyway, he seemed a respectable sort. And he was popular with the boys, but maybe a little too gentle for the headmaster's liking. He used to complain that Collins wasn't fond of corporal punishment." The vicar stuck out his chin in apparent disapproval. "I must say, the headmaster had a point. Young boys need a firm hand, you know. And there's nothing wrong with a smart cane to keep them in line."

Nate flinched as if a thin wooden cane had come down against his flesh. The sound, the sting…those were memories that could never be erased. He swallowed. "Can you tell us what caused him to leave his post at St. Joseph's?"

"He was terminated." The vicar sighed. "It was an unpleasant business, but it had to be done."

"May I ask why?" Nate tried to keep the eagerness out of his voice.

"I was wanting to ask the same thing of you. Why are you so interested in Mr. Collins? Did something happen to the man? Or are you looking to employ him?"

"Indeed, I am," Nate lied. "As a tutor for my son." He could feel Bridget's eyes on him. *How can you lie to a vicar?* He heard her scold him in his mind.

"Oh, well, in that case, I'd better explain everything and give you fair warning."

Nate glanced again at Bridget, suppressing his smile. He'd told a small lie to the vicar, but it had worked. The man was now eager—if not determined—to tell them everything he knew about Douglas Collins.

"I'm afraid Mr. Collins was involved in a scandal of a somewhat delicate nature."

"Oh dear," Nate said, continuing his charade.

The vicar glanced at Bridget and rocked back and forth on his heels, indicating that he was uncomfortable saying what was necessary in front of a young lady.

Bridget must have understood immediately because she said, "I'm just going to have a look inside your lovely church."

"Excellent idea. Be my guest." The vicar gestured toward the building.

Nate watched her go. He knew it must have irked her to leave, but he admired the grace and understanding with which she had handled the situation. The vicar would likely not have spoken freely in front of her.

Once Bridget was out of earshot, the vicar continued eagerly, "One of the students claimed he caught Mr. Collins in a 'lewd act' with a young woman. He told the other students, and word spread like fire around the school. Disgusting things were said, which I am certain were exaggerated, but that was of no matter. The man's reputation as a respectable teacher and gentleman was tarnished. The headmaster had to act swiftly. Boys at St. Joseph's come from good Christian families, and the school prides itself on producing upstanding, moral young gentlemen. Their reputation depends upon it."

"Understandable, of course," Nate said. "But did Mr. Collins admit to these charges against him?"

"He didn't deny knowing the young lady in question, but he vehemently denied having engaged in any…well…ungentlemanly behavior. Of course, none of that mattered. The scandal was enough to ruin him. So they had to get rid of him."

"Do you happen to recall the name of the young lady in question?"

"I'm afraid not. All I know is that her father had a farm. I believe he'd sell his meat and buy cattle in Harrogate on market days. And that's how Mr. Collins became acquainted with his daughter."

Sell his meat? So, she was a butcher's daughter.

"And what about the student who reported Collins? Do you recall his name?"

"Oh, yes. Mr. Phillips."

"Is he perhaps still a pupil at St. Joseph's? Was he one of the younger lads?"

"Oh no. Phillips was eighteen. He was in his final year."

"Does Mr. Phillips still reside in Harrogate?"

"I have no idea. I typically lose touch with the pupils after they leave St. Joseph's, and now that the school has moved, I don't have contact with any of them."

"Well, do you remember anything about his family? Anything at all that could help us locate him today?"

The vicar scrunched his eyes. "I don't recall much beyond his name. He wasn't one of the charity boys, that I *do* know. The charity boys tended to get bullied by the others, and they would often seek comfort in my church, so I knew most of them well."

"Would the current headmaster of St. Joseph's know more about the student in question?" Nate asked.

"I doubt it. The current headmaster has only been serving for two years. The headmaster at the time of the incident has since passed away." The vicar eyed Nate. "But why should you want to locate Mr. Phillips? I think you have sufficient information regarding Mr. Collins. Even if Phillips was lying, you wouldn't consider hiring a man with a tarnished reputation to be your son's tutor, would you?"

"Of course not," Nate said and looked toward the church. He was anxious to tell Bridget what he'd learned. "You have been most helpful, Vicar. I thank you for your time."

"Yes, I'm sorry I couldn't give you better news. Mr. Collins would have been an excellent tutor for your son. He taught the classics at St. Joseph's, and I remember him being well-versed in them. He was a bright young man."

Nate blinked. *A classics master.* So, Collins would have been familiar with Dante's theory of contrapasso. And what classics master didn't love poetry, both classical and contemporary? Collins would most certainly have read Wordsworth's most popular poem. It was all starting to make sense.

CHAPTER ELEVEN

As Nate's carriage rolled through the gates of Villa De Lacey, Bridget gazed up at her beloved home. She was pleased to see that the blue shutters and curtains in all the rooms were open, allowing daylight to infiltrate. So many of the rooms had been shuttered for years, when it had just been Papa, Aunt Marianne, and she, occupying the villa. Papa had closed eleven rooms to save money, and she'd never realized how silent and isolating it had been. Her grandfather's home was meant to be seen, appreciated, and enjoyed. And for a time, it had been. Until once again, it was marred, by murder.

She sighed and stroked Bijou, who lay curled in a ball on her lap. He opened his eyes and looked at her. Upon seeing her smile, he sat up and tried to lick her face. Then, noticing his cherished garden out the carriage window, he started yapping madly.

"Bridget, make him stop!" Aunt Marianne put her hands over her ears. They had started their journey in the wee hours of the morning, and Aunt Marianne was tired and irritable.

"He's excited to be home, that's all." Bridget stroked the terrier, who now stood on his hind legs with his paws resting against the carriage window and his tail wagging.

The carriage rolled to a stop outside the stables, and Aunt Marianne was the first one out the door when the driver opened it for her. She nodded at Jane, who'd come outside to greet them, bustling past her and disappearing into the villa, no doubt heading straight to her chamber for a well-earned rest.

Bridget exited behind her aunt, letting an excited Bijou scamper forward to greet the footman James, who bent to pet the dog as it spun in a circle driven by his excitement.

"Downstairs, Bijou. Go and see Cook. I'm sure she has some nice scraps of meat for you."

Nate came up behind Bridget and together they watched the terrier race down the stairs to the servants' quarters.

When Bridget took her eyes off her dog and faced Jane, she saw that the woman's expression looked grim.

"I do hope everything went smoothly whilst we were away," Bridget said, feeling apprehensive. "We cannot thank you enough for your help."

"Indeed, it did. Aunt Marianne has trained the servants so well that this place practically runs itself." A nervous laugh escaped her throat, and Bridget noticed that she clasped the fingers on her right hand as if uneasy.

"Is everyone well?" Nate asked. "There hasn't been another…"

"Heaven's no! Nothing like that," Jane said.

"Then what is it? I can tell there's something."

"I'm afraid Mr. Angert and Colonel Kendall have stirred up a bit of trouble."

"Good Lord!" Nate groaned. "What have they done now?"

"Well, Mr. Angert has started selling miniatures of the murder scene, and it has brought an influx of villagers to see the site. And Colonel Kendall has taken it upon himself to give the 'visitors' a tour and a detailed explanation of what occurred that day."

"Good grief!" Nate said. "They are turning Villa De Lacey into a circus."

"Indeed. And their actions have greatly upset Lady Matheson, who has taken to locking herself in her room."

"This will not do," Nate said. "I shall have to put an end to it immediately."

"I should say so," Bridget said.

"It has also upset Rupert and Charlie a great deal."

"Rupert and Charlie are not our guests, so why is that a concern?" Nate asked.

"But they are our guests. They've moved in."

"Moved in?" Bridget said with a gasp. "Do you mean to say they've abandoned their cottage?"

"Oh, yes. They cannot afford to stay there anymore, what with the loss of Mr. Otis and his share of the rent."

"If that's the case, then they definitely can't afford our rates," Nate said.

"Oh, but we can't throw them out onto the streets," Bridget said. "After all, their friend was murdered on our property."

"Payment is not a concern," Jane said. "Lady Luxton is paying for their keep."

"Lady Luxton?" Nate exclaimed, his voice sounding both surprised and relieved. "So, she is still here?" Bridget saw some of the tension leave Nate's body. He likely knew the day would come when Lady Luxton would take Henry away again, and his chances of seeing the child after that would be filled with uncertainty.

"Oh, very much so," Jane said. "You might say she was running the villa in your absence, the way she took to ordering the servants."

Bridget's chest tightened. Lady Luxton was obviously quite bored at home with her husband and so had decided to become mistress of Villa De Lacey. "Well," she said frostily, "We'd best get inside and put an end to these shenanigans, which seem to be disturbing the peace of our guests."

NATE'S PRIORITY UPON his return was to see his son. But he was sorely disappointed when he approached Helen and asked if he could spend a little time with Henry.

"Rupert and I are taking Henry to the lake," she said.

"Rupert?" Nate asked, unable to keep the irritation from his voice.

"Yes. Henry adores him."

"Well, I can see why. That poet is but a mere child himself."

"He is no child"—she gave him a coy smile—"that much I can assure you."

Nate felt the tension in his jaw as he bit back his retort. "What about tomorrow?" he said as amiably as he could manage.

"Why is it you want to see him now? You have shown no interest in days."

"I've been in York. I thought you knew."

"Yes, of course," she drawled, and Nate saw a flash of malice in her eyes. "Am I expected to arrange my time around your little excursions with your blond orphan? If Henry were your priority, you would remain here for the short time he is present. It won't be long before I take him back to Lochmaben. His papa misses him terribly, you know."

Nate swallowed the sorrow that rose in his throat. Perhaps Helen was right. He knew Henry would only be at Villa De Lacey for a short time, yet he'd spent three days in York investigating a murder that, as far as the magistrate was concerned, was already solved. Still, he could not allow Helen's manipulation and attempt to control him to continue. She was still trying to punish him for rejecting her the previous year. Rejection was not something Helen could accept. She wanted every man in her path—even those she'd discarded—to worship her.

"It's just as well," Nate said, suppressing the ache in his chest, "I have busy days ahead. Good day to you, Lady Luxton." Then he turned on his heels before she could say more and walked in the opposite direction.

Thrown off course by his encounter with Helen, Nate strode aimlessly forward and almost collided with Mr. Angert's valet, who was carrying his master's easel and painting utensils out to the garden.

"Excuse me, sir," the man said in a thick German accent.

Nate stopped. He'd almost forgotten about Angert and his blasted paintings. "Where is your master?" he inquired.

"I'm here," Angert said, coming toward Nate. The man was impeccably dressed as always in a dark suit, gray waistcoat, white shirt, and black cravat. He also wore expensive leather boots and gold-rimmed spectacles perched on his beak-like nose. It suddenly struck Nate that the man reminded him of a crow as much as the headmaster had reminded him of an ostrich. He chuckled to himself.

"What is so funny?" Angert demanded.

"I was just thinking what a fine suit that is for a day of painting."

Angert lifted his pointy chin. "I am a gentleman as well as an artist. One does not cancel out the other."

"Of course," Nate said. "I hear you've been keeping quite busy."

"Ja. It's wonderful. This murder. The interest in my paintings is enormous. I cannot thank you enough."

"I find it both strange and unsettling that you think murder wonderful, Mr. Angert. And thanking me—well, I'd prefer you didn't. In fact, I must ask you to stop selling paintings of Mr. Otis's murder. I hardly think it appropriate for you to exploit a man's gruesome and tragic death."

Angert's long, thin face became even more drawn as he looked sourly at Nate. "I am an artist, Mr. Squires. I do not exploit. I make art. Death is part of life, and it can be beautiful. People find my paintings majestic. Come"—he gestured for Nate to follow him—"see for yourself."

Nate followed the man to his chamber. Upon entering the room, he was aghast to see the walls lined with paintings of the most gruesome nature. There were several portrayals of Mr. Otis's murder. At the start of the row, the paintings depicted the sea of daffodils in Villa De Lacey's Garden against the idyllic backdrop of Lake Windermere, surrounded by greenery and a brilliant blue sky. Then, upon closer inspection, one could see drops of blood seeping from the daffodils. The first picture showed only one or two drops, which were hard to detect upon first glance. In the next, the blood trickled between the flowers, and in the third, it stained some red. The fourth picture grew more macabre. It showed George Otis's stiff hand, in a frozen, petrified death grasp, emerging from a bloodied patch in the flower bed.

As the row of paintings went on, they became even more graphic, showing details of the murder and Otis's mutilated body. Nausea rose in Nate's throat. There was something very wrong with Herbert Angert.

"Well, what do you think?" Angert beamed at his work. "I imagine you are wondering how I painted so many in such a short time. It's because I am what they call *beidhändig* in German. It means 'two-handed.' I use both my hands to paint two pictures at a time—one with the left hand and one with the right hand. It's a talent I was born with." He turned to his paintings and grinned. "Masterpieces, are they not?"

"I won't deny your talent, Mr. Angert," Nate said, trying to be diplomatic. "But I must say, these are in bad taste. In that respect, I must ask you to stop."

"Stop!" Angert spat out the word as if it were an obscene object stuck in his throat. "You ask an artist to stop painting? That is like asking him to chop off his hands."

"I'm not asking you to stop painting. Westmorland has some of the most exquisite scenery in the world. You can paint endless landscapes. I thought that was why you came here."

"It is. And I have captured Lake Windermere on my canvas." He reached down and extracted a painting from a pile leaning against his wall. "See."

Nate nodded at the landscape, which depicted a rather dark and gothic-looking Lake Windermere with stormy skies above. It was a somewhat exaggerated portrayal of how ominous the lake could look during a storm. "I see you have a penchant for the gothic," Nate said wryly. "All I'm asking is that you stick to painting scenes like this one. There are even lovelier views from Orrest Head, and Buttermere is quite breathtaking. Why don't you venture out there with your easel?"

"Demand for depictions of Mr. Otis's murder is high, Mr. Squires."

"You cannot possibly need the money. Isn't your father a baron?"

"Wasn't yours an earl?" Angert said, coolly.

"He was. But that title now belongs to my brother, who inherited all my father's wealth, along with the title."

"Leaving you at your brother's mercy." Angert's fists curled into a tight ball. "I know something of that injustice myself. Nothing irks my brother more than me selling my paintings. He says it besmirches the family name. And that is exactly why I continue to do it." The corners of his mouth curved into a sinister smile. "You and I are alike in that respect, are we not?"

Nate swallowed. Was Angert correct? After all, he'd been profiting heavily since the first murders at Villa De Lacey. The notion made him sick.

"I see that made you uncomfortable," Angert said. "But the truth is that people love the macabre. Public executions in Germany delight the masses as they do in England. Have you ever seen a man drawn and quartered, Mr. Squires? It's a most gruesome spectacle, yet Englishmen flock to see it. They bring their wives and children. That's why these murders have been good for you. Why should they not be good for me too? The colonel is also profiting in a different way, no?"

"Don't tell me he is charging villagers too," Nate said.

"No, but he delights in the attention. What is the harm?"

Nate squeezed the bridge of his nose. It was obvious that he was not going to be able to convince Angert to stop the sickening paintings or Colonel Kendall from being a self-appointed authority on the murder. And that left him with only one solution.

CHAPTER TWELVE

T HE NEXT MORNING, Nate opened his eyes as his valet entered
his room, carrying his tea. Bennett set the cup down next to
his bed with a "Morning, sir," and then drew back the curtains,
allowing the sun to stream into the room.

Nate stretched, sat up in bed, and reached for his cup. "Is it
done, Bennett?" he asked before taking a sip.

"It's done, sir," Bennett replied.

Nate took another satisfying sip of tea before putting it down.
Then he threw off his covers and waited for Bennett to help him
into his robe before he went to the window. When he'd first
come to live at Villa De Lacey, he'd only had one goal in mind,
and that was to return to London. He thought he'd never be
happy living anywhere else.

But Westmorland, with its pristine lakes, lush green landscape, and high fells, had won him over. Moreover, country life
had turned him from a late riser into an early lark. Now, the idea
of not seeing the magnificent Lake Windermere upon waking
every morning was unthinkable. But this morning, his gaze fell
directly to the garden and the place where the daffodils had been.
The beautiful sea of yellow flowers had been pulled out of the
ground from their roots, and the soil smoothed over like a mass
grave. He sighed. The sight hurt him, but it was for the best.

"Thomas and Fred must have started before dawn to get
everything finished this early," Nate spoke his thoughts out loud.
"It's a shame, but it's what had to be done."

"You did right, sir," Bennett said. "All kinds were trespassing on your land to come and gawk."

With Bennett's assistance, Nate washed and dressed for the day. As the valet buttoned his waistcoat, a great hue and cry sounded in the distance.

"Good Lord, has it started already? I thought we could at least wait until after breakfast."

"Shall I see what it's all about, sir?"

"I think I know what it's about. It's Colonel Kendall, no doubt. Discipline from his army days made him an early riser. I don't believe he has a view of the garden from his room, so he must have only just ventured outside and seen the daffodils."

"Shall I go and speak with him, sir?"

Nate sighed. "It's best I do it. Fetch my jacket."

When Nate stepped out of his room, he almost ran into Bridget, whose face looked creased with worry. "It's Mr. Angert," she said. "It sounds like he has taken the loss of the daffodils very badly."

"Indeed," Nate said. He could hear the artist shouting expletives in his heavy German accent coming from downstairs.

Just then Colonel Kendall came out of his room, fully dressed and ready for the day. "I say, what's going on? I was enjoying my morning tea and newspaper when someone started screaming like a lunatic." He glanced toward the stairs. "Good heavens! It's coming from down there."

"Not to worry, Mr. Angert is simply a bit upset. I shall see to it."

Lady Armstrong peeked out from behind her chamber door. "What's all that racket?" she asked. Then, before Nate had a chance to answer, she opened the door and shoved Miss Jennings out, saying, "Go and tell whoever's making that noise to be quiet!"

Miss Jennings stood by the door, looking bewildered.

Then, Angert, himself, came rushing up the stairs in his robe. His face was purple with rage. "Monsters! Savages!" he cried.

"Who would do such a thing? I ask you! Who?"

"Calm down, Mr. Angert. It's only a few daffodils."

"Only a few daffodils?" the man thundered. "What are you talking about? It's my work. My art. Someone has murdered my art!"

Doors opened, and the guests, most still in their robes, peeked out of their rooms. "Did someone say *murder?*" Mr. Harley asked, and the rest of the guests gasped.

"No one has been murdered." Nate held up his hands in a calming gesture. "There's nothing to worry about. Just a minor mishap. You can go back to bed." Then he turned to Angert and said, "I told you yesterday, Mr. Angert, you can make more art. There's plenty of…"

"*More* art!" Angert leapt forward like a crazed animal and grabbed Nate by his jacket. "You dare to destroy my art and tell me to make *more?*" His pale blue eyes bulged in their sockets as if his head were about to explode.

"Mr. Angert"—Nate removed the man's hands from his lapels—"calm down!" He smoothed his jacket. "I had my gardener take out the daffodils on the lawn because it is the site of a murder—a gruesome, tragic murder—and you and Colonel Kendall were making a spectacle of it."

"I say"—Colonel Kendall stepped forward—"have you removed the daffodils? That was uncalled for. One doesn't remove a battlefield because soldiers died on it. No! One goes there and relives the great moments of history."

"The daffodils?" Angert blinked. "You think I'm speaking of daffodils?" He spat out the words. "Those daffodils are imprinted in my brain. I can paint them from memory. But to destroy my art—my paintings—was unforgivable!"

Nate heard Bridget gasp beside him.

"Destroy your paintings? Whatever are you talking about?" Nate asked.

"My paintings! Someone slashed them with a knife. They're ruined, I tell you. Ruined!"

"Good grief!" Bridget cried.

"Come see for yourself." Angert raced back down the stairs, crying, "Savages, murderers," as he went. Nate, Bridget, and a host of others followed him to his chamber.

"Do you see!" The man fell to his knees on the floor of his chamber and howled like a mother grieving for her babe. "All my beauties, ruined. The entire collection—gone!"

Nate entered the suite and froze. It was exactly as Angert had said. Someone had taken a knife to his daffodil paintings, slicing through each canvas multiple times and destroying them beyond repair.

Several guests crowded into Angert's room, their faces aghast. Suddenly, Miss Jennings let out a single high-pitched squeal. Everyone turned to look at her. Another shrill sound escaped her throat. She put her hand over her mouth but could not stifle the growing feeling—be it excitement or nerves—that was building inside her, and she broke out into hysterical laughter.

"How dare you?" Angert sputtered with rage.

It was obvious that the poor woman could not stop herself from laughing.

"Stop it!" Angert shouted. "Stop it, at once!" He advanced on the woman, and Nate quickly stepped in front of him.

"Now, Angert, control yourself."

"Control? Me? Are you mad?" He blustered. "It is she who—"

A sharp slap sounded, and the laughing ended abruptly. Nate turned to see Lady Matheson glaring down at Miss Jennings, who held her hand to her bright red cheek. She stared at Lady Matheson with a look of utter horror.

"She was hysterical," Lady Matheson said. "Her shrieking was rattling my nerves. Someone had to do something."

"What sort of a place is this?" Angert said, eyeing the guests. "Which one of you destroyed my paintings?"

"Perhaps none of us did it, Mr. Angert," Lady Matheson said, her voice sounding savage. "Mayhap it was George."

"George? He is dead."

"Have you ever heard of a vengeful spirit?" she asked. "I'd destroy what's left of those if I were you," she said, and then she turned and walked out of the room, leaving Angert staring after her.

Miss Jennings, apparently emerging from her state of shock, suddenly dashed from the room.

Bridget ran out after her. Lady Matheson had had no right to hit her, no matter how upset she'd been.

"Miss Jennings," Bridget called as she followed the woman outside and into the garden with Bijou at her heels. "Wait, please!"

The woman kept running but then came to an abrupt stop in front of the uprooted daffodils. Bridget slowed her gait and approached Miss Jennings cautiously. "I'm so sorry for what Lady Matheson did to you," she said. "It was uncalled for. She had no right."

Miss Jennings put a hand to her cheek. "Well, it's not the first time a lady has slapped me. I seem to try the patience of my betters."

"Don't say that. They are not your betters. You have just as much right to be treated with dignity as they do."

"That's what Geor—Mr. Otis used to say whenever Lady Armstrong mistreated me." She gave her a half smile.

"Were you very fond of Mr. Otis?" Bridget asked.

"He was kind to me. Few people have been in my life. I seem to be one of those people who are always in the way of others, so I try to stay quiet and go unnoticed, but Mr. Otis—well, he noticed me. He talked to me and asked my opinion—no one ever does—did—that." She blinked furiously and Bridget knew she was trying to stop tears from falling.

"I liked him too. He was a dear friend." Bridget paused. "And I do hope you and I can be friends."

"I should like that. I miss my walks with Mr. Otis." She stifled her laugh with her hand. "Do you know, I'd give Lady Armstrong a pinch of laudanum, a few minutes before I was due to meet Mr. Otis. She would have never allowed me out of her sight otherwise."

Bridget felt a niggling in her stomach. It came as a warning. Then she pushed it aside. Would she have acted any differently were she under the thumb of a woman like Lady Armstrong? Probably not. Miss Jennings had limited choices, and if someone was keeping one as a caged pet and curtailing one's freedom, then one had no choice but to steal it back.

🔍

"IT HAD TO be Rupert and Charlie," Nate said, once he and Bridget were alone in the garden.

"That's rather unfair," Bridget said.

"It's the only logical explanation. Those pictures were painful to look at—even for me—can you imagine how horrible they must have been for Rupert and Charlie? And to think, Angert was *selling* them. People in town have miniatures in their pockets and on their walls. I hardly blame them for doing it, but I cannot condone such behavior at my inn."

"But you have no proof," Bridget said.

"I don't think it will be difficult to get them to confess. I believe they are, in all probability, proud of what they've done. It's a statement, you see. They've taken action on behalf of their friend. Just as they did in getting Groby arrested and locked away. It's the only way they can help him and preserve his dignity now."

Bridget sighed. "Death has a way of making the living feel helpless," she said. "Poor Rupert and Charlie. What will you do?"

"The only thing that can be done," Nate said. *And I won't be sorry to see the back of them.*

"Then, you'll throw them out?" Bridget said, and Nate could hear the distress in her voice.

"I have no choice," he said, and he meant it. Despite being

happy to have Rupert gone, he really did not have a choice.

"I think you might have a difficult time of it. They seem to have made some friends here." Bridget looked toward the Villa as she spoke, and Nate followed her gaze. Then his heart sank. Rupert had exited the villa in the company of Helen and Henry. Nate's son stood between the pair, each of whom held one of his dear little hands. Nate watched as they lifted the child off the ground and swung him in the air between the two of them. The child laughed hysterically.

"She'll accuse you of being jealous," Bridget said.

"I know," Nate said, his chest tightening with every breath.

"Then it's best you leave well enough alone. We can't prove that Rupert did anything to those paintings. And if I'm not mistaken, I saw an empty bottle of brandy next to Mr. Angert's bed. For all we know, he could have done that damage himself when inebriated. His behavior is a little strange at times."

"Strange is an understatement," Nate said, his eyes still fixed on Helen, Henry, and Rupert. He could not believe Helen was making such a spectacle of herself. How long would she punish him for disappearing for three days with Bridget and her aunt? Helen had taken it as a personal insult, which was ludicrous. She thought the entire world revolved around her. Whatever happened, he could not let her think she had any control over his life or his emotions.

"It certainly looks like Rupert's mood has improved," Bridget said. "It's almost as though he's taken George's place as the popular young poet among the ladies."

"I don't know. I think he's just Helen's pet project at the moment. She must have the attention of every man in her vicinity. What I don't like is her palming off my son to every man who takes her fancy," Nate said, lowering his voice as the trio approached them.

"Oh," Helen said, clearly pretending to be startled at seeing Nate. "You're here."

"Yes." Nate smiled at Henry and crouched to the child's

height. "Hello, Henry. Have you been having fun?"

The child nodded.

"I was wondering, do you like horses?"

Henry nodded again. "I like Prince."

"Prince? Is he your pony?"

Another nod and a grin.

"How would you like to come riding with me someday? My horse is very tall, probably not like your Prince, but you can sit in the saddle with me. Would you like that?"

"Yes!" The child's round face beamed.

Nate stood and faced Helen. "How about tomorrow?"

"Not tomorrow. Rupert and I are taking Henry on a picnic. Perhaps another day. It all depends."

"On what?" Nate asked, his chest tight with both disappointment and anger.

Helen merely shrugged and gave Bridget another cold stare before sauntering away, taking Henry and Rupert with her.

NATE SIGHED AS he watched his son leave. "I suppose it's for the best," he said. "I do need to go and have that talk with Collins."

"You don't expect him to admit anything, do you?"

"He might if he is innocent. If he and Mrs. Groby do have a history together, it doesn't mean he killed George, but it is something we need to know. I got the distinct feeling that the vicar in Harrogate wasn't telling me the entire truth."

"Perhaps I should have another chat with Mrs. Groby," Bridget said. "She might be more willing to—"

"Not yet. We don't know enough about these people. If, indeed, they worked together to kill George and frame Groby, then they are dangerous individuals. I can't risk you going into that house alone and confronting her."

"You'll want to be careful too," Bridget warned.

"Are you afraid he will chop me up right there in the slaughterhouse?" He grinned.

"Don't make light of it," Bridget said, remembering George's hacked chest with a shudder. "Although it is strange. He doesn't strike me as being dangerous. He seems to be quite the gentleman. The vicar in Harrogate even said that Collins was reluctant to use the cane on his pupils, which would indicate that he's not inclined to violence. If I didn't know Mr. Groby, I'd certainly think he was more inclined to be a killer than Mr. Collins."

"Agreed. Collins seems quite amiable and genteel to me too. But haven't we learned that killers don't always look and act the part?"

A pain shot through Bridget's heart. The events of the last summer were still raw. "Perhaps you should ask him to come to Villa De Lacey, then?"

"No, I don't want him lurking around Villa De Lacey. I prefer to keep the investigation as far from us as possible. I think it will be best to invite him for a drink at The Black Horse. He will be on his best behavior there, wanting to keep himself in check in public."

"That seems like a good idea." The tension in Bridget's body eased somewhat.

"Well, I suppose I'd best get that message written and sent, then." Nate glanced in the direction of Henry again, and Bridget followed his gaze. The party of three had reached the end of the garden. Lady Luxton and Rupert were still periodically swinging Henry between them. Nate slipped his hands into his pockets and watched until they exited the gates. Then he sighed and excused himself, saying, "I'll be off now."

Bridget silently cursed Lady Luxton as she watched Nate go. Not only was she using Rupert, but she was toying with the bond Nate was forming with Henry. But there was little Bridget could do. Perhaps if she kept her distance from Nate, it would help the situation.

She called for Bijou, who was rolling on his back in the grass.

He jumped up upon hearing his name and raced toward her. She crouched to receive him with open arms. The terrier sprang up to lick her face while letting out a series of excited yips.

Once inside, she headed upstairs with Bijou in tow, intent on finding Charlie. She guessed he would be in the library, working on his poetry, and she was correct.

Charlie sat on the window seat with some papers on his lap. He appeared to be in deep thought. Bridget loathed to disrupt him and considered leaving when Bijou trotted into the room and curled up in his little basket that sat permanently next to the fireplace. Charlie turned and smiled at the dog. Then he saw Bridget.

"Miss De Lacey." He scrambled to his feet. "I hope I have not taken your seat. I'll just gather my things and—"

"Oh, no, please, sit down. How are you enjoying your stay at Villa De Lacey?"

"It's a lovely house." Charlie remained standing despite Bridget's invitation for him to sit. "This library suits my needs very well."

"It's my favorite room," Bridget said. "And I don't mind sharing it." She smiled. "George loved it in here too."

Charlie pressed his lips together, and Bridget could not tell if he was suppressing a grimace or a smile.

"I'm going to ask you a question that might seem a bit unfair, but I'd like you to be honest with me." Bridget waited for his reaction.

"You want to know if I slashed Mr. Angert's paintings," Charlie said.

"Actually, yes." Bridget felt somewhat relieved that Charlie had been expecting her question. "I couldn't blame you if you did. They were tasteless."

"Well, you can put your mind at ease. I didn't. Although I'm not sorry someone did it. He's an awful man."

"What about Rupert?"

"He didn't do it. He's been spending all his time with Lady

Luxton." There was a hint of bitterness to his tone.

"Does that upset you?"

Charlie shrugged. "He's forgotten, that's all."

"Forgotten?" Bridget said. "What do you mean? What has he forgotten?"

"What some rich people are like. She'll discard him when she no longer has a use for him."

Bridget couldn't argue with that. She paused. The young man had had some kind of experience in his past, and she wanted to find out what it was.

"When did you meet George?" she asked.

Charlie gazed out the window as if recalling a memory. Bridget noticed that his body stiffened. "I'm sorry if this is too difficult for you," she said. "We don't have to continue this conversation."

He seemed to slump and turned to look at her. "We only met about six months ago," Charlie said, "through some friends. We were all aspiring poets and such. At first, I wasn't sure about George. He was different. Posh. But he claimed to be an orphan. He didn't like to talk about his past. It seemed to make him cross."

"Six months ago? I thought you'd been friends for years."

"We bonded over our mutual love for poetry. George was…well, it felt like we'd known him all our lives even if we hadn't."

"Yes, he did have that effect on people." Bridget felt a tinge of sadness. "What about you and Rupert? Where are you from?"

Charlie gave her a faint smile. "Dorset. Our father was a groundskeeper for a wealthy gentleman, Mr. Wareham. He was part of the landed gentry. He had no children of his own, so we had access to a great deal of books from the family's library. He even paid for us to have a private tutor. I daresay, we had as good an education as George. We were lucky in that respect."

"And is your father still in Dorset?"

Charlie shook his head. "No, he passed away last year, right after Mr. Wareham died. Wareham's estate went to his next of kin. But the kind old gentleman left Rupert and me a little money. We took it and traveled up north to York. That was our first stop before Westmorland."

"York? And that's where you met George?"

"Yes. He was heading to Westmorland too. He had one of Wordsworth's guidebooks, just like us. So we came together."

Bridget frowned. "I don't remember George saying he was from York."

"He wasn't. I believe he was from Harrogate—or at least, he went to school there."

"Harrogate," Bridget said with a sinking feeling in her stomach. Did George and Mr. Collins have a history together? Or was it simply a coincidence that they both had been at schools in Harrogate?

❧ ❧

CHAPTER THIRTEEN

COLLINS ENTERED THE Black Horse, looking every bit a gentleman and very little like a butcher. He wore a pair of beige trousers with a white shirt and cravat, a navy-blue waistcoat and matching tailcoat. He removed his top hat when he greeted Nate and sat beside him.

"I took the liberty of ordering you an ale," Nate said.

Collins glanced down at the glass of ale and thanked Nate before taking a thirsty sip.

"Long day?" Nate asked.

"Butchering is hard work," Collins said. "It requires a lot of physical strength. And a strong stomach as well."

"More difficult than teaching, I imagine." Nate picked up his ale and eyed Collins as he sipped it.

Collins kept a straight face, revealing nothing.

"I just returned from a trip to Harrogate," Nate said casually.

Collins's cheeks paled. He picked up his ale, took another sip, and said, "What is it you wanted to see me about, Mr. Squires?"

"About a school called St. Joseph's, where you were once a teacher."

"So you've been investigating me, have you?" He lowered his mug. "On what grounds, may I ask?"

"Because you and Mrs. Groby have a history together—a *long* history."

Collins shifted in his seat. "You have no proof of that."

"The young woman involved in the scandal that got you

dismissed from your position at St. Joseph's was Mrs. Groby, wasn't it?" Nate saw Collins's jaw tighten, and he knew he'd stumbled upon the truth. "You met her in town where her father would come to sell his meat and buy cattle on market days, and the two of you fell in love. But her father disapproved of you. Although I can't think why. You are a gentleman and well-educated. Why would a butcher not think you good enough for his daughter?"

Collins made a face and when he answered, his voice was bitter. "For those exact reasons, you stated. I was educated, and he was not. He didn't want anyone better than himself for his daughter. He treated her like she was one of his cows. I wanted to take her away from all that."

"But then one of your students caught you together in a compromising situation and reported you to the headmaster. You lost your job." Nate paused. "So how is it that both of you ended up in Westmorland with her married to Groby?"

Collins ruffled his blond hair and sighed. "I didn't abandon her if that's what you think. We were going to run away together, but her father discovered our secret and kept her under lock and key. He watched her every move. I had the idea of paying him off. But of course, there was the problem of money. I didn't have enough, so I was forced to return home to Kent to borrow some from my father."

"Kent? You said you were from York."

Collins shrugged. "As you can see, I had things in my past that I wished to stay hidden."

"Fair enough. And did your father give you the money?"

He chuckled sadly. "Of course not. I don't know why I thought he would. He's always been a bastard. But I was desperate."

Nate nodded. He could relate. He knew what it was like to have a father who was constantly disappointed and refused to trust you. It was hurtful, and he'd made the same mistake Collins had made countless times—thinking things would change. They never did.

"He'd received a letter from the headmaster, detailing my dismissal—as though I was a rusticated schoolboy and not a grown adult and schoolmaster. It was humiliating. He was furious to learn that I had been dismissed, especially under the circumstances. As far as my father was concerned, I'd disgraced the family name and dragged everyone down into the lowest gutter, and he wanted nothing more to do with me. He threw me out and cut me off without a penny."

Nate could not help but feel some sympathy for the man. He knew all too well his pain. But he reminded himself, Collins could be a killer, and if so, he was likely a liar as well.

"Did the headmaster tell your father about the child?" Nate asked.

Collins paled.

"Mrs. Groby's boy is your son, isn't he?"

"How did you find out?" Collins said in a whisper.

"I guessed. It wasn't difficult. I saw the way you looked at him."

Collins ran a hand over his face. "None of this means that I killed Groby."

"Agreed, but you have to admit it doesn't look good. So why don't you tell me how she ended up married to Groby instead of you?"

"Her father found out that she was with child, and near beat the babe out of her." He swallowed as if the thought choked him. "Then he forced her to marry Groby. Sold her to him like one of his cattle."

"All of this happened while you were in Kent, I presume," Nate said, and Collins nodded.

"By the time I returned to Yorkshire, she was gone. He refused to tell me where she was. I inquired—begged—the surrounding farmers to tell me what they knew, but they all refused. I was an outsider—an interloper—and moreover, they were afraid of Lockwood."

"So what did you do?" Nate asked. "How did you find her?"

"You wouldn't believe it if I told you."

Nate remained silent, watching the man. Whatever had happened had obviously taken an enormous toll on him. He'd paid a heavy price to find the woman he loved and his child, and it had been humiliating. That much, Nate could tell from the pained look on the man's face. Nate felt a lump in his stomach. He, too, was having to pay a price and act the fool to stay in his son's life. And that would continue for as long as Helen desired. He was at her mercy.

"Lockwood said if I worked on his farm for a year, he'd tell me where she'd gone. He said he'd turn me from 'a posh know-it-all' into a real man—a farmer who worked the land and a butcher who brought home his own supper. So that's what I did." He hung his head. "But one year turned into two and then three. He kept saying I wasn't ready."

"Good God!" Nate said.

"Then one day, his heart gave out, and he keeled right over in the field. I thought I would never find Alice, then, but a few days later, she arrived at the farm with Groby and my son, and another babe in her arms. I could hardly believe it when I saw her. All that time, Lockwood had been lying to me. Alice was already married."

"But you weren't prepared to lose her again, were you?"

He shook his head. "I'd follow her to the ends of the earth if I had to. Even if she didn't love me anymore. I wanted to be close to her and to my son. But as it turns out, she did still care for me. Groby was good to her, but she didn't love him."

"Is that what she told you?"

"Not in so many words, but I knew. I could see it in her eyes when she looked at me."

"Still, she was married to him, so that should have been the end of it."

"It should have, but it wasn't. I let about a week go by after she departed the farm before I followed her to Westmorland.

Once I got there, we started meeting in secret. She was already taking reading lessons with Otis, so we'd meet briefly after her lessons. She was earnest about her reading. She said she didn't want to be like her father. She wanted to learn how to read so she could teach our son. I think she wanted to be on more of an equal footing with me. I told her I'd teach her, but she refused. She said it would make people even more suspicious if she suddenly came to me for reading lessons. Otis was a poet. People respected that, so it made sense for him to teach her. No one knew I was a former schoolmaster. To them, I was just a farmer."

"And you never became jealous of Otis? He was a charming young man, and he was spending far more time with her than you were."

"I had no reason to be jealous of Otis. Alice and I had a strong bond. We shared a child. And Otis was doing me a favor. If not for him, we would not have had the opportunity to see each other at all. His lessons gave us a chance to meet thrice weekly."

Nate got the distinct feeling that Collins wasn't being entirely truthful. "I can't understand why Groby would let his wife go off with a handsome young Don Juan like Otis. Surely, people talked," he baited Collins.

Collins shrugged. "They did. But Alice is a strong woman. She was raised by a tyrant and survived. Town gossips weren't going to bother her. But the gossip *did* bother Groby. He ordered her to end her reading lessons, but she refused. The gossip grew worse. And then came the night at The Black Horse when Rupert taunted Groby about being a cuckold. His patience must have reached its limit, and so he killed Otis."

"You really believe that?"

"I do," Collins said.

Nate recalled his conversation with Groby when he'd visited him in jail. The man had told him that he'd been suspicious of Collins, not Otis. He'd had his wife followed and discovered she'd been meeting Collins in secret, which Collins had just confirmed. Why, then, would Groby kill Otis? It made no sense at all. It was far more likely that Collins had grown jealous of Otis and killed *him.*

A man who spent three years laboring—for a butcher!—so he could find out where the love of his life had disappeared to would not take kindly to losing her heart a second time. And if anyone could steal a woman's heart, it was that charming charlatan, George Otis.

Bridget attempted to read while she waited impatiently for Nate to return. She sat with Bijou by the drawing-room fire, foregoing the library where Rupert and Charlie worked late into the night. Most of the other guests had retired to bed, but Bridget suspected that Lady Luxton was waiting for Rupert to make a late-night visit to her room. She was doing everything in her power to make Nate jealous, but the only real power she had over him now was her son.

Bridget lowered her book and sighed. Why was Nate taking so long to return? She hated that he'd gone out in the dark after dinner. He should have met Collins during the day. If there was a connection between George and Mr. Collins, then the latter was certainly the killer. A vision of Nate's mutilated body lying in the daffodils flashed in her mind, and she shuddered.

Bijou, who sat in his basket next to the fireplace, lifted his head. A low growl emanated from his throat. Then he stood up and let out a flurry of high-pitched barks.

"Quiet, boy." Bridget held a finger to her lips. But Bijou could not be mollified. Something had gotten his attention. He shot out of the library, barking. Bridget grabbed her lantern and followed her wayward dog, only to almost collide with Nate, who'd caught Bijou and secured him under his arm. Her heart almost exploded with relief and happiness upon seeing him in the dim passageway.

"You're awake," Nate said. "Sorry, I didn't mean to frighten

Bijou."

"He's excited, not frightened," she said, taking the terrier from him. "And it wasn't Bijou you frightened; it was me. I've been worried sick about you."

They moved back into the drawing room, where Nate put down his lantern and picked up the crystal brandy decanter. Then he paused and put it down again as if having second thoughts. "Why were you worried?" He asked. "You knew I'd gone to meet Collins at The Black Horse."

"Exactly. You went to meet a potential killer late at night." She put Bijou on the ground, and he trotted back to his basket. Then she placed her lantern back in its place on the table.

"Bennett drove me there in my carriage, so I wasn't alone. Furthermore, I'm not about to let Collins or anyone else, for that matter, kill me." He gave her a teasing smile, but Bridget could not find the humor in his comments. What she'd learned from Charlie had truly frightened her and set her imagination running.

"What's the matter?" Nate asked, glancing at Bridget's hands tightly clasped together.

Aware of his gaze, she released her hands and went to sit on the settee. "I spoke with Charlie today, and I asked him about George. He doesn't know much about his background—he said George was always evasive about that—but he did mention something that I found quite alarming."

"What is it?" Nate came to sit beside her on the settee.

"He said George had gone to school in Harrogate. And I think that cannot be a coincidence."

Bridget could see Nate's body momentarily freeze. "Good God," he finally said. "It's all coming together."

"My sentiments exactly," Bridget said. "Did Collins confirm his past relationship with Mrs. Groby?"

Nate hesitated.

"If you withhold information from me like you did in the summer, Nate Squires, I shall never forgive you!"

Running a hand through his dark, wavy hair, Nate sighed.

"Very well," he said. "But you must promise not to do anything rash. Promise you won't attempt to talk to Mrs. Groby or Collins without me."

"Believe me, I shan't go anywhere near Collins on my own."

Bridget listened as Nate told her about his meeting with Collins. "So, after being dismissed and disowned by his father, Collins worked for Alice's father for three years in the hope of discovering what had happened to her?"

"That's right," Nate said.

"Astonishing! Just like Jacob worked for Laban in the Bible. Only he worked for seven years, not three."

"Collins might have labored for longer except that Lockwood died unexpectedly after three years, and he was able to reconnect with Mrs. Groby. So, I suppose he got what he wanted in the end—until George Otis took it all away from him—at least that's my hypothesis. We still have no proof that it happened. But now that you've told me George went to school in Harrogate—assuming that's correct and the school he attended was St. Joseph's—I have to wonder why Collins didn't tell me that he knew George."

"I agree. If George was one of Collins's pupils at St. Joseph's, he would have known about the scandal," Bridget said, putting it all together in her mind. She paused. "Do you suppose he was the one who reported Collins to the headmaster?"

"The vicar said the boy's name was Phillips. I think it's more likely he came to some arrangement with Collins—possibly for money—where he agreed to help facilitate meetings between Collins and Mrs. Groby under the guise of giving her reading lessons. But then the unthinkable happened. Otis and Alice Groby fell in love, and she lost interest in Collins."

"It's a strong motive for murder," Bridget said.

"Exactly my thinking," Nate agreed. "Collins slaved for three years for Alice's father in the hope of winning her hand, not knowing she was already married. But since that was a forced marriage, and they shared a child, he still had hope. They resumed their relationship. And then George stole Alice from under him. That would be intolerable to bear."

"Yes, it fits perfectly. George took Alice's heart away from Collins, so Collins, quite literally, took George's heart," Bridget said. "Unfortunately, it is all based on a lot of guesswork. We have no proof that any of this is true."

"Not yet," Nate said. "But I have a feeling we are on the right path. All we need to do is a little more digging."

CHAPTER FOURTEEN

THE NEXT MORNING at breakfast, Nate became increasingly irritated by Helen and Rupert. Unable to consume his attention, she'd taken her "act" with Rupert a step further, and it was becoming embarrassing. The two of them shared glaringly obvious smiles and flirtatious glances. It did not bode well for a countess to behave in such a manner, especially when the countess was the mother of his son. Henry would one day replace his father as the Earl of Luxton, and his mother was doing all she could to tarnish that title.

Just when he thought he could take no more, Angert, who'd been glaring at everyone seated around him, suddenly slammed the butt of his knife into the table, rattling the dishes, cups, and utensils.

"My word!" Lady Armstrong said, as her tea sloshed down the sides of its cup. "What are you about?"

"I demand to know which one of you butchered my paintings. Was it you?" He suddenly turned to Rupert, swinging his butter knife in the poet's direction.

Both Rupert and Helen burst out laughing.

"You find it funny to destroy my work? You demon!"

"Mr. Angert"—Nate squared his shoulders—"put that knife down at once."

But Angert sprang from his seat and swung the knife in Charlie's direction. "*You* did it, you worthless little—"

In a flash, Colonel Kendall shot out of his seat, grabbed Angert's wrist and, with a sharp twist, forced the butter knife from his hand. Angert squealed as the knife fell onto the floor.

Nate felt his mouth physically drop open. The retired colonel took on a new level of admiration in his eyes.

"You barbarian!" Angert cried. "You've broken my wrist." The artist held up his limp wrist.

"Don't be absurd," Colonel Kendall said. "It's merely bruised. Good heavens, man, straighten up and stop whimpering like a little boy."

Angert took a few steps backward and scanned the room. "You will not get away with this," he shouted. "Mark my words, all of you! The culprit will pay."

"Oh, do be quiet," Lady Matheson said. "You nasty little man!"

Everyone fell silent. Lady Matheson's mood had darkened considerably since Otis's murder.

"You!" Angert pointed a finger at Lady Matheson. "How dare you? I demand that you return my portrait."

"Portrait? What portrait are you talking about?" Lady Matheson said.

"You know which one. The one you begged me to paint of the dead poet."

"I know of no portrait. You're deranged!"

Suddenly, a strange sound emanated from Miss Jennings, who'd been quietly observing the madness. Nate wasn't sure if it was laughter or tears. She covered her mouth, and her body trembled.

"What on earth are you doing?" Lady Armstrong hissed. "Get a hold of yourself."

The young lady apparently could not do as she was bid because she rose from her chair and hurried out of the room, still shaking, either with laughter or tears.

Angert stormed out of the breakfast room.

Nate had had enough. He pushed his plate of eggs and kippers away and stood up just as Bennett entered and handed him an envelope on a silver tray. He took the envelope and, seeing it was from his brother, thanked Bennett and exited the breakfast room. Wanting some fresh air, he went downstairs and headed for the garden, where he opened the letter, which bore the seal of the Earl of Westerly. What could Edward have to say to him now? No doubt, it was yet another threat to cut him off. He'd already informed Edward that he no longer needed his money, but his brother had kept it coming anyway, along with the threats. And Nate knew why—the earl couldn't bear to give up control of anyone or anything. Nate sighed as he unfolded the letter, and as he did so, several banknotes fell into his hands. He pocketed them and turned back to the letter.

Brother,

I hear you are stubbornly and shamefully continuing to make a mockery of our family name and me by running an inn. Villa De Lacey—an estate I gracefully bestowed upon you out of the goodness of my heart—has now become known in London as the 'murder inn.' And while you might think yourself clever, and while people might find your little scheme amusing, may I remind you that in the long run, they will shun you and make you a persona non grata *in society. Because, brother, as you well know, gentlemen don't run inns.*

Now to my main point, it is with great pleasure that I inform you that the Countess of Westerly is with child. As such, it is even more imperative that you drop your shenanigans immediately. Should the child be a boy, you will no longer be my heir, but you will continue to receive your thrice-yearly allowance if you behave accordingly. Bear in mind that if you do not, I shall do more than cut off your funds. Trust me when I say, I will not have my son growing up under your disgraceful shadow.

Your ever gracious and benevolent brother,
Edward Squires, Earl of Westerly

Nate felt his entire jawline tighten. He crumpled the letter and mumbled, "Just you try, brother." Then he laughed out loud.

Thank heavens for Lady Westerly! If Edward were blessed with a son, he would no longer have to endure the burden of being his brother's heir. It was what he'd been hoping for, but now it seemed that a son would only make Edward more determined to control him than before. Nate looked at the crumpled paper in his hand. He needn't worry about it now. Edward was being premature. Whether or not Lady Westerly gave birth to a boy remained to be seen.

He turned back to the spectacular view of Lake Windermere and saw Bridget and Jane Harley coming up the garden toward him. They must have breakfasted early and gone out for a walk—no doubt to escape Helen and Rupert. It's what he should have done, too.

Both women were smiling and looked delighted to be in one another's company as they came toward him. But it was more than the smile that made Bridget lovely, something…he suddenly realized she'd come out of mourning. Instead of the severe black she'd worn, or the somber grays and lavenders, this morning she wore a pink dress. She was transformed. Nate blinked, overwhelmed by how the color complemented her soft, sweet features. She looked as feminine and delicate as a pink rose, and her face was joyful as she chatted and laughed with Jane. It filled his heart with pleasure that Bridget had a true friend in Mrs. Harley, who was a changed woman since coming to Villa De Lacey.

"Good morning," he said as the women approached him. "Out for an early walk, I see."

"Oh, yes," Mrs. Harley said. "It's the most glorious day." Her blue eyes, which had been droopy and always sad when she and her husband had first arrived at the villa eight months ago under the large thumb of Mr. Harley's draconian aunt, now sparkled with enthusiasm. What a difference a few months can make away from those who seek to oppress you, he thought.

"It certainly is a day for celebrations," Nate said, hiding the crumpled letter from Edward behind his back. "I've just had some excellent news from my brother. Lady Westerly is with child."

"How wonderful!" Bridget cried. "She has been waiting for so long." Then she turned to Mrs. Harley and squeezed her arm. "Isn't it wonderful, Jane?"

Mrs. Harley put her hand on her stomach, and her cheeks flushed pink. "Well, it seems there must be something in the air this spring."

Nate hesitated, momentarily taken aback. "What are you saying?" he asked. As far as he knew, Mrs. Harley was barren. This sounded like a miracle.

"I am with child," Mrs. Harley confirmed. "Mr. Harley and I are delighted. We can't thank you enough for allowing us to stay at Villa De Lacey. Even with all the…well, it's been a breath of fresh air for us."

"I must say, I am stunned. I should go and find Harley and congratulate him. He didn't say a word about it at breakfast." Nate frowned. He couldn't remember if he'd seen Harley at breakfast that morning because he'd been too distracted by Helen, Rupert, and the madness that had ensued with Angert.

"Yes, he is thrilled. After all our troubles…" She bit her lip. "I only hope Lady Darby won't force us to return to London."

"Don't worry about that now." Bridget patted her friend's arm. "All you need to concentrate on now is resting and securing the health of yourself and your child."

Mrs. Harley's cheeks flushed as she inadvertently touched her belly again. Nate felt a lump form in his throat, and he shifted his gaze to Bridget. He adored Henry, but what would it be like to share a child with a woman he loved? The thought caught him by surprise. Did he love Bridget? She caught his gaze and her sweet lips curved into a shy smile, revealing the two minute dimples at the corners of her mouth. And Nate knew the answer to his question.

🔍

"DID YOU HEAR what I said, Nate?" Bridget's words cut into Nate's thoughts. He'd been lost in a blissful moment where it was Bridget rather than Mrs. Harley who stood before him with sparkling eyes and bright cheeks, holding her belly with one hand and clasping Henry's small hand in her other.

Nate sighed inwardly. "Forgive me. What was that?"

"I said that I've invited Mrs. Groby and her children for a picnic by the lake. I sent out a note by messenger, requesting her to come at noon."

"You've *what*?" Nate said, completely snapping out of his reverie. "Do you think that wise?"

"It's the perfect environment for a casual conversation, and with the right prompting, who knows what she might reveal about her relationship with Mr. Otis? Jane will be with me, of course. So it will just be a few ladies and children enjoying a day at the lake," Bridget said.

Nate nodded. "I suppose that sounds harmless enough. Still, do be careful."

"Oh," Bridget said, peering behind Nate, "here comes—"

"Excellent morning, isn't it?" Nate groaned inwardly as he heard Colonel Kendall's voice behind him. He forced a smile as the colonel joined their party and greeted the ladies.

"Good morning, Colonel," Bridget said. "What do you have planned for this fine day?"

"Well, I've already prevented another murder, so I think it's time now for a brisk walk along the lake." He chuckled.

"Prevented another murder?" Bridget said. "Whatever do you mean?"

"It was nothing. Only a small skirmish involving a butter knife at breakfast." The colonel puffed out his chest.

"A skirmish?" Bridget's eyes widened.

"Mr. Angert is still furious about his paintings," Nate said, and then proceeded to tell Bridget and Mrs. Harley what had happened at breakfast. "I had hoped to smooth things over by replacing his damaged easels, but I imagine that after today, he'll be returning to Germany. After all, he won't be able to paint with an injured wrist."

"But he *can't* go," Bridget said. "He has proven to be violent and bloodthirsty. He could be the killer."

"Nonsense," the colonel said. "He's no killer. Only a temperamental artist. And you don't need to worry about him leaving. He won't want to miss the gibbeting."

"The gibbeting?" Nate's stomach plummeted. "What are you talking about?"

"The butcher. After his trial in York. He will be hanged and gibbeted. It's the law. The Murder Act, don't you know?"

Bridget's hand flew to her mouth as she stifled her gasp.

Nate's gut twisted. Gibbeting would be torturous for Mrs. Groby and her children. It meant that Groby would be hanged and then his corpse would be encased in a cage that fitted his body and held it in place, so he could then be displayed to rot away in public. It was a cruel punishment meant for murderous, evil criminals. But if John Groby was found guilty of George Otis's murder, he would indeed be considered the worst of the worst.

"The magistrate is going to request that Groby be brought back to Westmorland to be hanged and gibbeted. It's only fitting that those of us who witnessed this heinous crime should see justice meted out."

"Who told you this?" Nate said.

"I heard men talk of it when I went into town yesterday. After a spot of shopping, I stopped at The Black Horse for some refreshment. And I overheard some men talking about it. I must say, I think it's a fine idea. I like a good hanging. And I expect Angert's mood will be restored as soon as he has the opportunity to watch a man hang and then rot away in a cage. It will make for a fine painting—a rotting corpse against Westmorland's pristine landscape. Oh, the contrast is delicious." Colonel Kendall chuckled.

"That's quite enough," Nate snapped.

"Oh, heavens!" Mrs. Harley clutched Bridget's arm. "How awful."

"Awful? I hardly think so. That butcher deserves the very worst of punishments. His corpse should rot as an example to others who plan to commit such wicked crimes. In the army, we have no tolerance for criminals of any kind. When deserters are caught, they are—"

"I said, that's enough," Nate barked. Any earlier admiration he'd felt for the colonel in handling Angert quickly dissipated.

"Well, I daresay, there's no need to be rude!" Colonel Kendall said. "I think I'll take my leave of you. Good day, sir." He bowed stiffly. "And to you ladies." He marched away in a huff.

Good Lord, what kind of guests is Villa De Lacey attracting now that it's become known as 'the murder inn'? I meant for this to be a respectable establishment. A place of relaxation and beauty. Perhaps Edward is right. Perhaps it is time to shut Villa De Lacey's doors.

"I must go and see Magistrate Hunt at once," Bridget said, breaking into Nate's thoughts. "I must talk him out of this madness. To subject Mrs. Groby's children to this horror—why, it's too much!"

"No, I'll do it," Nate said. "You have your plans already set for this afternoon with Mrs. Groby, and I think you can do better here with her."

"Oh heavens, what am I to say to her?" Bridget cried.

"You'll need to break the news to her gently if she hasn't heard already. And if she cares for children at all, she will do all she can to be honest with you and prevent this atrocity from taking place."

"You're right." Mrs. Harley said. "Few women would put their love for a man over their love for their children." She caressed her belly and smiled lovingly down at it.

Nate nodded. He only hoped that was true for Mrs. Groby.

CHAPTER FIFTEEN

EAGER TO GET to Braithwaite and talk sense into the magistrate, Nate wasted no time in summoning his valet and ordering his horse to be readied. But before he could escape out the back door, Lady Matheson approached him.

"May I have a word, Mr. Squires?" she asked.

Nate hesitated, surprised to see that she had changed into black mourning clothes. *Is that for George?* The question almost slipped from his tongue, but he held it back. Lady Matheson looked exceedingly pale and unwell, and he didn't want to upset her further. She had taken George Otis's death to heart, and her grief and attachment to the poet seemed to be growing every day. It was odd, indeed, and he was certain that the unpleasantness at breakfast hadn't helped her nerves either.

"I'm on my way to Braithwaite," he said. "I only have a minute."

"Braithwaite. That's what I wanted to talk to you about. Are you going to see the magistrate?"

"Yes," Nate said cautiously. He wondered if Lady Matheson had heard about the prospect of Groby's hanging taking place in Westmorland. If she thought he was going to advocate that the magistrate go forward with it, she was quite mistaken.

"I want to know what he has done with George's body," she said. "I think George deserves a poet's burial—someplace marvelous with a monument honoring his memory—and I want to pay for it."

"That's very generous of you. I believe he was an orphan, but I'm afraid you're too late."

"Too late? What do you mean?"

"Magistrate Hunt took the body for further investigation, but I can't imagine he'll still have it. I am certain he disposed of the body already. One cannot keep a corpse—forgive me my bluntness, my lady—in such warm weather, you understand."

"Disposed of the body? How? Do you mean he just threw George away like a dog?"

"I don't know...No." Nate frowned. He didn't know what had happened to Otis's body. The man had been an orphan, but he wasn't a pauper. He was well educated and had worn decent clothing. He wondered if Bridget knew. It wasn't customary for women to attend funerals, so perhaps it had all been up to Charlie and Rupert. "I am certain his friends arranged for his burial. Have you spoken to them?"

"His *friends?*" Lady Matheson scoffed. "Why should they bury him? How long have those two known George? A few months? How dare they?"

Nate blinked, taken aback by Lady Matheson's vehemence. "I really don't know. But at least here in Westmorland they were his closest friends. You only knew him for a matter of weeks yourself, did you not?"

"How could you allow something like this to happen?" She bared her teeth at Nate, and he backed away, thinking she was suffering from a bout of hysteria.

"I'm sorry, Lady Matheson, but why didn't you talk about this before? It's been a little over a week. That's far too long to keep a body unburied in the spring. I imagine you know that."

She blinked, and her anger dissipated. She seemed confused. "Over a week, you say? Has it been that long? Impossible. Why, I saw him just the other day." An eerie smile played on her lips. "Some days, I quite forget he is...gone."

Nate swallowed. He'd always thought of Lady Matheson as a sophisticated and beautiful woman, but now, he could see that she was quite unstable. If he didn't know better, he'd think she was mad.

"No matter. I want you to tell the magistrate to exhume his body, so I can give him a proper burial—one fit for a poet of his talent. Perhaps on the shores of his beloved Lake Windermere."

"I don't think that will be possible. If he's already buried—"

"I insist. I don't care what it costs. A poet like George needs a shrine. He deserves to be remembered. He shall have a resting spot where those who admire him centuries from now will be able to visit his grave. He does not want to rot in a common grave and be forgotten. His friends, indeed!"

"I'll speak to the magistrate. I promise," Nate said, backing further away and reaching behind him for the door handle. He would promise anything to keep Lady Matheson calm at this point. Had the lady and George Otis been lovers after all? It certainly seemed that way. She was behaving more like a grieving widow than a woman who'd been slightly charmed and mildly entertained by a young poet she'd just met.

MAGISTRATE HUNT STOOD to greet Nate as he entered the gentleman's study in his home, located across the street from Braithwaite's small jail where Mr. Groby was being held.

"Mr. Squires," the magistrate said. "Please, sit down. What can I do for you today?"

"I'm here about Groby." Nate took a seat across from the magistrate's desk. "I was told you are getting ready to send him to York for his trial." Nate wanted to ease into the conversation before bringing up what he'd heard regarding Groby's possible gibbeting.

"Indeed, so if you've uncovered any new evidence, it's best you let me know now."

"I think there is a possibility Collins is involved—and perhaps

Mrs. Groby herself."

Magistrate Hunt tapped his fingers together. "I've given that some thought too. Collins has practically taken over Groby's farm and slaughterhouse. It looks suspicious."

"There's even more to it than that," Nate said.

"Oh?" Magistrate Hunt leaned forward. "I'm listening."

Nate told the magistrate all he'd learned about Collins and Alice Groby's past together.

"Interesting." The magistrate folded his arms and leaned back in his chair. "Very interesting. Do you think Groby knows the boy belongs to Collins?"

"I don't know. But if he does, why not kill Collins? Why kill Otis?"

"Yes. I see the possibility that Collins could be the guilty party, but we have no proof, and without proof, all I have is a man who threatened to kill Mr. Otis the night the murder took place." He blew out his breath. "Although there is the matter of Otis's head wound."

"What about it?" Nate leaned forward.

"I had Dr. Elias examine the wound, and he concluded that Otis was hit several times in the back of the head with the rock found next to his body."

"We knew that already, did we not?"

"We knew he'd been struck with the rock, but we didn't know he'd been hit several times. It made me wonder why a man with Groby's strength would need to strike so many blows. Someone of Groby's size and brawn would likely have used a much heavier object and struck one fatal blow." Magistrate Hunt shrugged. "On the other hand, he was inebriated, so it's possible he was clumsy."

"Or it was someone else," Nate said, not wanting to lose the magistrate. "Collins is a much smaller man than Groby."

"True," Magistrate Hunt said. "Still, it is all speculation. And even if I have an inkling of doubt in my mind, I cannot turn a man loose who promised to butcher the victim and had cause to do so. Jealousy is a powerful motive. The people are convinced Groby is guilty, and they want him to hang."

"Not just hang," Nate said. "He'll be gibbeted."

"Nothing I can do about that—it's the law. That's the appropriate punishment for this crime."

"But I hear you are going to request that his punishment be carried out in Westmorland, rather than York, where he will stand trial."

"That's right. It's what the people want."

"Which people? Who is advocating for this?"

"Hornby, Morris, and Trent were in my office just yesterday, demanding that he be hanged and left to rot in Braithwaite."

"Hornby, Morris, and Trent?" Nate thought back to his conversation with Groby. "Three of the five men who owe Groby money. Substantial amounts. Do you think that's a coincidence? These men resent Groby for his success, even though he was good enough to loan them money. I am certain they played as large a part as Rupert did to whip up hatred against the butcher. It's no wonder his so-called friends turned on him so quickly."

"That may be so, but this is 'a murder most foul,' to use Shakespeare's expression, and such a crime warrants a harsh punishment."

"Think of his children!" Nate said.

"His children are too young to be affected. If their mother keeps them away from the gallows, they won't have to witness their father's decomposition."

Nate massaged his temples as a growing headache began to spike. "At least wait until we clear up this business with Collins. If Groby is guilty, then I agree he should hang. But how will you live with yourself if the man is innocent? He has been your friend and neighbor for years. At least give him a few extra days."

"I'm afraid I don't control when the assize court meets. They will arrive in York next week, and I intend to transport Groby there three days from now."

Nate's chest tightened. The assize court traveled around the country and tried the most serious of offenders—murderers and traitors. Their guilty verdicts were frequent. Mr. Groby's statement of intent to harm Otis was all the jury would need to convict him. That, coupled with Mr. Groby's brawn, gruffness, and especially his successful skills at his trade, would almost certainly seal his terrible fate. "But the assize court comes to York twice a year, does it not? If you just wait—"

"The people want justice. This crime was simply too vicious. It must come to a just end. That gives you three days. Use it wisely. But do consider the fact that Groby may be guilty after all."

Nate nodded. Perhaps Groby *was* guilty. If he could not prove otherwise in three days, then he would have to accept the fact that he and Bridget had tried their best to ensure that an innocent man did not hang. After all, it was Bridget's determination not to see another innocent man die like a criminal, the way her poor papa had. That was truly what all this was about. His motivation was to alleviate further pain and suffering for Bridget, not necessarily to save a man of whose innocence even he was uncertain.

"Thank you for your time, Magistrate." He stood to leave when he remembered Lady Matheson's request. "There's one more thing," he said, sitting down again. "Otis's body. Where is it? Lady Matheson is insistent on exhuming the body, so she can bury the poet herself—or at least give him the burial she thinks he deserves. I told her that it would be difficult, but she is adamant. She said she didn't care what it cost. But I can't imagine anyone will want that job."

"Oh, someone would, mark my words. If you pay enough, you can always find people to do your bidding. But I didn't bury the body," Magistrate Hunt said. "Mr. Otis's family came up from Knaresborough a few days after the murder."

"His family? I thought Otis was an orphan."

"Yes, so did I. I'm uncertain why he made that claim. But I take it there was some type of family rift between the parents and their son. Nonetheless, when they read about Otis's death in the newspaper, they wanted to bury him at home. So, after they identified their son's remains, I released the body for transport." Magistrate Hunt leaned back in his chair and rested his hands on his rotund belly. "You can tell Lady Matheson that her wish has been granted. The poet has received a proper, Christian burial at no expense to herself."

"Knaresborough?" Nate said, thinking out loud. "That's near Harrogate."

"Yes, just outside."

"But when did Mr. and Mrs. Otis come and collect George's body?"

"About four days after his murder. When you were in York, I believe. But his parents aren't called Mr. and Mrs. Otis. That wasn't Otis's name—or at least not his complete name. His full name was George Otis Phillips."

"Phillips!" Nate almost jumped out of his chair.

"Yes. He must have dropped the Phillips part after his rift with his parents—the Reverend and Mrs. Phillips from Knaresborough."

"Phillips is the name of the student who reported Collins to the headmaster of St. Joseph's. Don't you see! George Otis was responsible for Collins being dismissed from St. Joseph's and losing Alice. Then, over three years later, Collins arrives in Westmorland only to find Otis is there giving Alice reading lessons!" Nate shook his head and laughed. "It all makes sense now. Otis must have tracked Alice to Westmorland, and Collins would have been enraged to find that Otis had wormed his way into Alice's life after all the damage he had done. He must have wanted to get rid of him once and for all. Collins has to be the killer!"

"That doesn't prove anything. It's all hearsay," Magistrate Hunt said after Nate explained the full extent of Otis's relationship to Collins.

"Of course, it does," Nate said. "Otis ruined Collins's life. It is entirely his fault that Collins lost his position as a master at St. Joseph's and, if that wasn't bad enough, he ended up losing the love of his life as well. Then, when Collins finally reconnects with Alice, Otis arrives and ruins everything yet again."

Magistrate Hunt shifted in his seat. "But we have a near confession from Groby. He is the one who declared he'd butcher Otis, not Collins. The people have decided he is guilty."

"The people?" Nate said. "They are in no position to judge. They've been whipped into a frenzy by the horrific details of the murder. Their judgment is clouded."

"It's not their fault—they are good people—they want justice. Groby needs to hang, and his body needs to remain rotting in public for all to see—not because we are bloodthirsty, but because—"

"What if we can get a confession from Collins?" Nate interjected.

"How? Do you intend to beat it out of him?"

"Of course not. But let's pay him a visit and see what happens when he realizes we know that George Otis is George Otis Phillips."

Magistrate Hunt sighed. "I don't know—"

"How long have you known John Groby?" Nate asked. "Thirty years or more? And in all that time has he ever acted aggressively or caused any trouble?"

"No," Magistrate Hunt said. "He's been quite an upstanding citizen."

"Exactly. Yet you choose to ignore the possibility that a stranger, newly arrived in Braithwaite, who has a strong connection to the victim, might be the killer? Don't you owe Groby—an 'upstanding citizen' in your own words—better than that?"

The magistrate nodded. "You're right. Let's go and pay Collins a visit."

ALICE GROBY ARRIVED at Villa De Lacey with her two children in a horse-drawn cart. She wore a pale-green dress that showed off her slim figure and complemented her lovely green eyes. Her light-brown curls were set in a loose bun and ringlets around her face. She had a creamy complexion that showed no trace of the hardships she'd suffered through in her life.

As she climbed down from the cart with the footman's help, Bridget approached her.

"Welcome," Bridget said. "I'm so glad you could come. This is my friend Mrs. Jane Harley. I hope you don't mind if she joins us today."

"Nice to meet you, Mrs. Harley." She smiled at Jane. And then, turning back to Bridget, said, "Thank you for inviting us. It's good for the children to have an outing."

Bijou, who'd been off in the garden, came racing toward them, wagging his tail. Edmund clung to his mother's leg as the dog approached.

"Don't be afraid, Edmund. Bijou wants to be your friend." Bridget petted Bijou. "He likes to be petted. Do you want to try?"

Edmund nodded and came forward to pet the dog. Bijou jumped up and put his paws on the boy's chest, making him giggle.

Little Charlotte kicked her legs and squealed in her mother's arms.

"Shall we go down to the lake? Cook has prepared a delicious picnic for us to enjoy." She held up the basket containing the feast.

"Oh, yes," Alice said, and Bridget was pleased that the woman appeared relaxed, but she dreaded the conversation they'd need to have later in the day.

Once they were settled on a blanket on the shores of Lake Windermere, Bridget laid out the bread, cheese, cake, biscuits, and tea that Cook had prepared for them. After a few minutes of munching heartily, the women sat back and watched Edmund as he played with Bijou.

"Oh no," Alice said as Edmund wandered too close to the water. "He can't swim." She started to get up.

"Sit," Jane said. "I'll go. I should like to stretch my legs a bit after all those lovely biscuits and cakes."

"Thank you," Alice said as she watched Jane race toward Edmund.

Bridget smiled to herself. Jane was going to make a wonderful mother.

"It's good to see him so happy." Alice pulled Charlotte onto her lap and handed the child a biscuit. "They need more days like this. But with Mr. Groby gone…"

"How are you coping—especially with little Edmund?" Bridget asked.

"It's difficult. He wants to know when his papa is coming home. Charlotte is young yet, but it's been hard for Edmund. I don't know how I'm going to explain things to him if his papa is…" She shook her head.

Bridget bit her lip. Was all this an act to appear innocent on Alice Groby's part? Or was she indeed ignorant of what had happened to George? *Dare I mention the prospect of Groby being gibbeted in Braithwaite?*

"If not for Mr. Collins, I don't know where we would be. He's been a great help with the farm and slaughterhouse."

Bridget opened her mouth to comment, but the words wouldn't come out. She needed to take this opportunity to question Alice about her relationship with Collins, but it went against her very nature to do so. It felt horribly impolite.

"I know what people are saying about us," Alice said as if reading Bridget's thoughts. "But they're wrong. Douglas—Mr. Collins is—well, he's a dear friend, and I couldn't manage without him."

"It does seem rather convenient that he was ready to take

over from Mr. Groby the day he was arrested," Bridget said, hating herself.

"I know it looks that way, but me and Mr. Collins have a history. We was friends before I were married. He used to work for my father, you see. That is why he were so quick to help me."

"Yes," Bridget looked down at her lap. "I know about that."

"Oh?" Alice said.

Bridget inhaled and looked Alice in the eyes. "The fact is, you weren't merely friends, were you? Mr. Collins followed you to Westmorland. And the two of you started a romance again in secret. Mr. Collins has already confessed as much to Mr. Squires."

Alice lowered her gaze and smoothed her daughter's frock. "I did love Mr. Collins once. He were the first man who were kind to me. My papa was…well, he treated me cruelly. I were grateful for Mr. Collins's love. So grateful that I gave myself to him before marriage. And he would have married me too. I know that. He loved me then, and he still does. But my father had other plans for me. I thought I'd die when he forced me to marry Mr. Groby, a man I thought would be a monster like my father. But he weren't. He were good to me, and he gave me a good life—a better life than I'd ever known. We had a family and were happy. I grew to care deeply for John."

"That's what I'd always thought. Despite the gossip in the village, you seemed very happy with Mr. Groby. He is a good man. So, what happened?"

"After my father died, Mr. Collins reappeared in my life. I were shocked to learn that he'd been working for my father for three years—shocked he'd done it in the hope of finding me. It were a grand gesture. I can't say I felt nothing for him because that wouldn't be true. Maybe I encouraged him—I don't know. I felt responsible for his troubles—he'd lost his job as a teacher and bound himself to my father because of me. So after he came to Westmorland, I started meeting with him in secret because…." She dropped her gaze.

"Because Edmund is his son," Bridget said.

Alice looked up, her eyes troubled. "How did you know? Did Mr. Collins say something?"

"No. He kept your secret. But Mr. Squires guessed, and Mr. Collins didn't deny it." Bridget paused. "That's the reason your papa forced you to marry Mr. Groby, isn't it? Because he knew you were with child."

Alice gazed at her son, who was clapping his hands as Jane threw a stick for Bijou to fetch. "I felt beholden to try and find a way for Mr. Collins to be in Edmund's life. I hoped he could be a family friend—a sort of uncle to Edmund. But John didn't like Collins. I think he felt there was summat more between us. He questioned me about why Collins had come to Westmorland after leaving my father's farm. He knew something weren't right."

"And what about George? Was Mr. Collins jealous of him at all?"

"He were leery of him. He said he couldn't be trusted, and like John, he wanted me to stop my reading lessons. He said he would teach me himself. But I was quite happy with George's lessons, and I didn't like being told what to do by Douglas or my husband." Her face reddened. "I have a stubbornness about me. It's in my nature. But as it happens, I should have listened to them because they were right. George wasn't a good man."

"What do you mean?" Bridget said as a prickle of apprehension swept over her.

"He did just what my husband said he would do—he demanded another form of payment for his lessons. And when I refused, he became nasty. I believe if he weren't afraid of my John, he'd have forced himself upon me."

Bridget stifled her gasp with her hand. *George?* It couldn't be true. He'd always been a perfect gentleman when in her company. She couldn't even imagine…

Alice seemed to understand her inability to comprehend her revelation. "I don't expect you knew that side of him. He wouldn't have taken such liberties with you. He enjoyed the advantages of being your friend too much. He wouldn't have wanted to spoil that."

"I can hardly believe it," Bridget said.

Alice smoothed her daughter's curls. "That's because George hid his darkness well."

Bridget swallowed. Yet another person in her life who'd deceived her. How many more would there be? "Did you tell Mr. Groby about this?"

"Of course not," Alice said. "I knew it would send him into a rage. I haven't told anyone, and you mustn't either." She reached out and grabbed Bridget's wrist. "Please! It won't help John if you tell him. He will only say he wishes he *had* killed George." Alice's daughter began to squirm on her lap, and she set the child down next to her.

"So you didn't mention this to Mr. Collins either?"

"There was no need. I could manage George Otis on my own. I did warn George that if he ever bothered me again, I'd let the whole town know what a scoundrel he was—including my husband. He apologized and begged me not to say anything. He said he couldn't help himself—that he'd fallen in love with me. I didn't believe him, but I wanted no trouble, so I promised not to say anything, as long as he kept away."

"Then you stopped the lessons? And Mr. Groby thought you were finally complying with his request?"

She shook her head. "I pretended to keep on with my reading lessons, so John wouldn't think anything was amiss. Also, I wanted to keep meeting Mr. Collins as usual. That was stupid of me. But I didn't have the heart to stop. He'd done so much for me. And he is Edmund's father, after all. In the end, I didn't have to keep it up for long because a few days after the problem with George, he were dead."

Bridget sighed and glanced down at Alice's daughter. The little girl gave her a toothy grin. "And you have no idea who could have killed him?"

Alice pressed her lips together. "I..." she began. Then she

shook her head.

"Alice," Bridget said gently, "if you know something, you'd best say it. I hear Mr. Groby will be sent to York soon for his trial, and the magistrate is likely to find him guilty."

A tear rolled down Alice's cheek. "I know."

"But it's even worse than that," Bridget said, hating herself for having to tell Alice what would happen to her husband. "There's talk that he'll be hanged and gibbeted in Westmorland."

The woman sucked in her breath so forcefully that Charlotte began to cry. Alice pulled the child onto her lap and sobbed, covering her mouth with her hand.

Bridget felt a lump rise in her throat and tears sting her eyes. What was happening to Westmorland? Once again, darkness had descended on her tranquil and idyllic home.

"There is one thing." Alice sniffed and wiped her eyes. "Whenever I met with George near his cottage, I felt as if someone were watching us."

Bridget went cold. Hadn't Nate said that Mr. Groby had had his wife followed? And didn't that mean that he would have known everything? Perhaps she'd been incorrect from the beginning.

Mayhap Mr. Groby *did* kill George.

CHAPTER SIXTEEN

NATE NOTICED THAT something was amiss the minute he and Magistrate Hunt dismounted their horses outside the Groby's cottage. Several sets of departing bloody footprints dotted the dirt path in front of the butcher's slaughterhouse. And while the blood could have come from an animal, the multiple sets of footprints struck Nate as unusual. He glanced at the magistrate, and they both quickened their pace.

Upon entering the slaughterhouse, Nate recoiled as the smell of blood, flesh, and death assailed his nostrils. He'd never been able to abide the stench of animal slaughter and had always taken care to avoid Smithfield's and other like areas in London.

"Good Lord!" Magistrate Hunt cried and raced forward.

"What is it?" Nate asked, following the magistrate, but then slowed when he almost slipped on a wet pool on the floor. "What the devil…" And then he saw Collins. The man lay there, covered in blood. "Is he dead?" Nate asked as he came closer to inspect Collins's battered and swollen body. His entire face was a purple and bloodied mess.

"Not yet." Magistrate Hunt knelt, not appearing to care about what he was kneeling in, and put an ear to Collins's heart before he lifted his head and looked at Nate. "Help me carry him inside. Then run and get Dr. Elias."

As they picked up Collins by his arms and legs, the man groaned.

"Careful," Magistrate Hunt said as they shuffled Collins outside.

They moved slowly so as not to slip or further injure Collins. Then, just as they reached the cottage, they saw Alice Groby's wagon roll to a stop outside her gate.

"Let's get him inside before the children see him." Nate tried the cottage door, and it swung open. They carried Collins inside and laid him gently down on the kitchen table. Then Nate went back to intercept Mrs. Groby and the children before they entered the dwelling.

"What has happened?" Alice Groby asked as Nate met her by the front door. "What are you doing in my house? And why is there blood outside?" She glanced down at Nate's bloodied hands and gasped. "Why…what? Are you hurt?"

"There's been an accident," Nate lied. "It's Mr. Collins. We've put him on the kitchen table. You will want to steer the children away from him. They might be frightened."

Alice nodded, and Nate stepped aside to let her in. Holding her babe in her arms, she ushered her on through the parlor and into the rooms beyond. She returned several minutes later and said, "I've put them down to sleep. They had a long day at the lake."

"That's good," Nate said, stepping aside so she could get a good look at Collins.

Her hand flew to her mouth as she gasped at the sight of him. "How did this happen?"

"We don't know," Magistrate Hunt said. "We found him like this a few minutes ago. But judging from the bloody footsteps outside, he had more than one hostile visitor this afternoon."

Mrs. Groby fetched a bowl of water and a cloth and began tending to the battered Collins, who could barely open his swollen eyes to look at her.

Nate left the cottage and ran to fetch Dr. Elias. Upon his return, he and Magistrate Hunt waited for the doctor to finish tending to Collins before meeting with him in the front parlor.

"It was a vicious attack," Dr. Elias said, "but I don't believe the intent was to kill him. Although his attacker, or attackers, could have done."

"I agree," Magistrate Hunt said. "There were plenty of knives in the slaughterhouse. If the attackers wanted to kill Collins, they would have used one of those. This was a beating intended to punish."

"Do you have any idea who could have done this to him?" Dr. Elias asked the magistrate.

"Well, I would say Groby, but he's in jail," Magistrate Hunt said.

"I think I may have an idea," Nate said, turning to Mrs. Groby. "Do you know what Mr. Collins planned to do today?"

"He were going to collect some of the payments owed to my husband."

"From Morris and Trent, correct?"

She nodded. "Mr. Hornby, too. Mr. Brown and Mr. Whittle paid my husband what they owed for the month before he…" She squeezed her hands together. "I told Mr. Collins it weren't a good idea. They wouldn't pay me on account of my being a woman, and I didn't think they would take kindly to paying him either."

Nate glanced at Collins's motionless body on the settee. "It certainly looks that way," he said.

"Are you going to arrest them?" Mrs. Groby asked.

"Not without proof, and that would mean waiting for Collins here to wake up and tell us who did this to him." Magistrate Hunt leaned over Collins and shook his head. "Might be a while before he can talk again."

"You can't let them get away with this!" Mrs. Groby said. "You arrested my husband without nowt evidence!"

"Your husband declared his intention to kill a man who was found dead the very next day. I think that's proof enough."

One of Mrs. Groby's children began crying, and she excused herself, only to return seconds later holding her small daughter in her arms. Mrs. Groby soothed the child as tears fell from her own eyes. "What shall I do now?" she said. "Without that money and Mr. Collins's help, we are doomed."

Nate glanced at the magistrate, who looked uncomfortable. *This isn't right. Something must be done to protect this woman and her children. What if the attackers return?*

THE BLACK HORSE—A whitewashed building with black beams, a heavy, black wooden door, and a thatched roof—stood at the corner of an otherwise quiet cobblestone street in Braithwaite. Inside, the low-beamed tavern smelled like sweat and ale. It was a small establishment, and Nate and Magistrate Hunt immediately spotted the three culprits sitting at a table drinking pints of ale.

"Gentlemen," Magistrate Hunt said as he stopped by their table. "May I have a word?"

"Aye, Magistrate," Morris said. He was the oldest of the four men, aged about five-and-fifty, with a slim build and a sharp, sour face. "What can we do for ye?"

"According to Mrs. Groby, Mr. Collins came to collect Groby's money from you today. Did you pay up?"

"Why should we pay Collins? We don't owe him the money," Trent said. He was a short but powerful man who enjoyed pugilism as a sport. Nate noted a cut on his hand as well as his bruised knuckles.

"He was collecting it on behalf of Mrs. Groby, as you well know," Magistrate Hunt said. "But you lot didn't want to pay your debts, so you beat the man half to death."

"Says who?" Trent said. "We've been here all day. Just ask Peterson. He'll vouch for us."

Nate and the magistrate turned to the publican, who glanced at the table of men before giving a slight nod.

"There you are," Trent said, turning back to his ale. The other two men at the table grinned.

"Very well," Magistrate Hunt said. "Mind you keep out of trouble now." Then, much to Nate's astonishment, he turned and strode out of the tavern.

"We cannot leave Mrs. Groby and her children in the house with Collins while those men are on the loose," Nate said as he followed the magistrate outside. "They are dangerous."

"I don't think so," Magistrate Hunt said. "They have made their point. But I will ask Dr. Elias to take Collins home and care for him. His injuries are severe, and Mrs. Groby has her hands full with her children."

"Perhaps, I should ask her to come and stay at Villa De Lacey. I hate to think of her alone with her children in that cottage. Those men might—"

"You needn't worry. They won't do any more damage. A woman is no threat to them. They owe Groby the money, not his wife. And Groby is…well."

"As good as dead," Nate said.

The magistrate shifted his stance but said nothing.

"You have to consider the notion that those three men could have framed Groby. When I went to see him in jail, Groby told me that he'd hired Trent to follow his wife because he was suspicious of Collins. Trent may have convinced Groby that she was cuckolding him, either with Otis, Collins, or both men. That would have enraged Groby and led him to make the 'threat' he made at The Black Horse, which was likely more of a way to save face than an actual threat. But once he made that threat, he opened the door to being blamed for Otis's death, no matter who murdered the man."

"So you think they could have murdered Otis, knowing Groby would be blamed, to alleviate themselves of their debt?"

Nate shrugged. "It's a strong possibility. Money is always a powerful motive—not to mention jealousy."

"Jealousy?"

"Yes. Groby is successful. He has a decent business and a beautiful wife. He loans them money, and they are indebted to him. When they can't pay with coins, they are forced to give him their chickens or cattle, and sometimes, they must do his bidding. I'm certain that injured their pride."

Magistrate Hunt furrowed his bushy gray brows. "Earlier, you said Collins was the killer, now it's Trent, Morris, and Hornby. Why can't you accept that the killer could just as well be Groby?"

"I can and do accept that. All I am trying to express is that there are many other suspects, and that you should not be so quick to try and execute a man who might be innocent."

"But they are not killers. They proved that today when they spared Collins's life. Furthermore, it doesn't fit."

"What doesn't fit?" Nate asked.

"If those three were responsible for murdering Otis, they would likely have picked Trent to do the deed. After all, he is the strongest of the three. And he would most certainly not have bashed Otis over the head several times with a rock and then cut his heart out. Trent is a pugilist. He would have beaten the man to death with his fists. Furthermore, why would he or any of the others want Otis's heart? I'm afraid you are grasping at straws, Mr. Squires, and I am not sure why. Groby is the only one who made a threat against Otis's life, so he is the guilty party in my mind and the minds of the good people of Westmorland." Magistrate Hunt mounted his horse. Then, looking down at Nate, he said, "I must ask that you not disturb me with this business again. If anything, tonight's events have convinced me that what this town needs is to put this murder behind them. And the only way to do that is to try the culprit in court, and if he is found guilty, hang him as soon as possible. And now, sir, I must bid you goodnight." He tipped his hat at Nate and spurred his horse forward.

Nate sighed as he watched Magistrate Hunt ride away. He had tried his best to convince the magistrate to see reason and consider that many other suspects could have committed this murder. But perhaps he'd gone too far today by trying to put suspicion on Trent, Morris, and Hornby. They didn't strike him as clever enough to frame Groby, and today's event likely had nothing to do with the murder. Collins had stepped out of bounds, and he'd been put back in his place by the locals.

Moreover, Nate still believed Collins to be the most plausible suspect for the murder. All this trouble had started when Collins had come to town in a bid to reclaim Alice. Now Otis was dead, and Groby was in prison facing hanging. That certainly took care of both his rivals. Although battered and bruised, Collins was still looking victorious.

WHEN NATE ARRIVED at the Villa, dinner had already been served.

"Shall I bring you a plate to your room, sir?" Bennett asked.

"That would be nice, Bennett. But I require a bath first." Nate could still smell the stench of blood and death on his body, not to mention the sweat and ale smells that clung to him after his visit to The Black Horse.

"Very good, sir. I will tell the scullery maid to start boiling the water for you immediately."

"Thank you, Bennett. I'll be upstairs shortly."

He mounted the stairs and went to the library, where he knew Bridget would likely be sitting by the fire, reading one of those Austen novels of which she was so fond. Just the thought of seeing her put a smile on his lips, but that was nothing in comparison to what he felt when he walked into the library and saw her sitting with her nose in a book, just as he'd expected. His heart lifted, and the day's troubles floated away as he was transported to another time and place in his mind—a time and place where Villa De Lacey was no longer an inn but his home, and Bridget was no longer the hostess but his wife.

In this place, she put down her book and stood up to greet him, holding out both hands to him. Nate walked to her and clasped her hands in his. Then he pulled her close and pressed his lips to hers. He felt giddy with happiness. When they parted, she said, "My darling, we've been waiting for you all evening."

We? He glanced down and saw Henry smiling up at him, his small hand clasped in Bridget's. And his heart almost burst with happiness.

"Nate," Bridget said. Nate blinked. He was still standing in the doorway of the library, and she was walking toward him. "Did something happen? Where were you? You missed dinner. I can ask Cook to…"

"Bennett is bringing a plate to my room. But I wanted to let you know that I was home."

"Is that…blood?" She pointed to his beige waistcoat.

He glanced down and saw that there was indeed a large blood stain on his waistcoat. "It's not mine," he said. "It's Collins's blood."

"Mr. Collins's blood?" She gaped at him. "Why on earth would his blood be on your waistcoat?"

Nate was about to explain when he caught a glimpse of Rupert and Charlie sitting at a writing desk in the corner of the library. Each held a quill pen, and papers littered the desk. They were both staring at him, presumably having overhead Bridget's exclamation. Nate felt as though a private moment had been invaded. Why was Rupert everywhere all of a sudden? And how had he not noticed the poets before? He stiffened, and Bridget must have sensed why because she turned and looked at them. The two quickly returned to their work.

"It's nothing," Nate said. "You're not to worry. No one else is dead." Then he turned stiffly and walked out of the room.

A little later, when he'd sunk into his steaming tub and was soaking his aching muscles, Nate felt some of the day's tension ease out of him. Still, he could not quite put his mind at rest.

He tried to work out what was troubling him the most. Was it the unsolved murder? Groby's impending trial and inevitable guilty verdict? The prospect of his horrendous gibbeting?

Or was it Rupert, who'd been enjoying long days with his son, stealing that time from Nate? And then there were his growing feelings for Bridget. Did she feel the same toward him? How could she? She'd only just come out of official mourning for her papa, and her heart was still broken over that loss. He'd be a cad to try and take advantage of her vulnerability. Moreover, she depended on him for her security, safety, and livelihood. It wouldn't be fair for him to put her in a position of having to reject him. If he acted on his feelings, everything they'd built together could be ruined.

CHAPTER SEVENTEEN

BRIDGET ROSE EARLY, as she did every morning, and slipped out of bed carefully so as not to disturb Bijou, who was stretched out on her bed snoring softly. She walked to her washbasin and emptied the pitcher of warm water left for her by Harriet, the lady's maid she shared with Aunt Marianne. Then she used a clean washcloth and the rose-scented soap bar she'd purchased on her recent trip to York to wash her face, neck, chest, and arms thoroughly. After cleaning her teeth with tooth powder, she went to sit at her dresser, where she picked up her brush and ran it through her hair.

Minutes later, her chamber door opened, and Harriet stepped inside with her morning tea. "Good morning, miss. Sorry for my lateness, but Cook is in a bit of a fuss. She were out early at the fishmongers, getting what she needs for the fish soup that'll be making up part of tonight's meal, and she said everyone at the fishmonger's were talking about Mr. Collins." She set the tea down next to Bridget and then took the hairbrush from her.

"What about Mr. Collins?"

"He was beaten, miss. Yesterday. Within an inch of his life, they say."

Bridget's heart began to race. The blood she'd seen on Nate's shirt. *It belongs to Collins*, he'd said.

"Whoever did it, left him for dead." Harriet started to brush Bridget's blond locks. "Mrs. Groby came home to find him lying in a bed of his own blood. Can you imagine? An' now Cook says there will likely be no more meat coming from Groby's slaugh-terhouse. An' she'll have to find a new butcher, which she says, we should've done in the first place when Groby were arrested. There's something evil afoot in that…"

Blood rushed to Bridget's ears, and she stopped listening as Harriet rambled on. Had Nate lost his temper and hurt Collins? And what would Alice Groby think? That she'd invited her to spend the day at Villa De Lacey while Nate went to her farm and attacked Collins? Impossible! Nate would never hurt anyone. She was certain of that. But why hadn't he told her what had happened to Collins last night? Why had he hesitated? She chewed the inside of her lip, unable to rid herself of the unsettling feeling in her stomach. Hadn't the last year taught her that everyone had dark secrets—even those closest to her?

Bridget had no appetite for breakfast that morning. Instead, she sat in the breakfast room beside Aunt Marianne and sipped tea while Bijou ate a breakfast of scrambled eggs under the table. It was still too early for the guests, who preferred to eat between nine and ten o'clock.

"I do wish you wouldn't feed Bijou under the table," Aunt Marianne said. "What if one of the guests were to come in?"

"They won't. It's far too early even for the colonel. You know as much, or you wouldn't be here." After last summer, Aunt Marianne had taken to eating separately when some of the guests took to insulting her and treating her like one of the staff. They'd done the same to Bridget, and it had injured her pride at first, but she no longer cared. The murders last summer had put things in perspective.

"I take it you heard about Mr. Collins," Aunt Marianne said.

Bridget nodded. "I shall have to go and see how Mrs. Groby is faring today."

"No, you shall not!" Aunt Marianne said sharply. "I forbid it."

"Aunt Marianne. She was here yesterday, and I owe it to her to…"

"Listen, Bridget. I have no idea what is going on in our once peaceful home, but Westmorland is changing. Ever since Wordsworth wrote that guidebook to the lakes, murder and mayhem have been raining down upon us. I have already lost my brother, and you are my last remaining relative. Should something happen to you, I don't know what I shall do."

"Oh, Aunt." Bridget reached for her aunt's hand.

"Promise me you won't go to Braithwaite unaccompanied," Aunt Marianne said. "I don't want you going to that woman's house. Not now—not until we find out who is responsible for all this violence and that horrible murder. I just cannot believe it is Mr. Groby. He has always been such a lovely man. Your father had great respect for him. The real killer is still walking among us, Bridget."

"I think so too, Aunt."

"It's a terrible thing that has happened to Mr. Groby, but it's not your job to save him. You couldn't save your papa and now you—"

"Don't." Bridget withdrew her hand from her aunt's grasp.

"No, listen to me. You're all I have left, so you'll keep yourself safe. Lest you want to send me to my grave too."

"Oh, Aunt! Don't say such things." Bridget leaned forward and embraced her aunt.

"Promise me, Bridget."

"I promise," Bridget said, crossing her fingers. Aunt Marianne simply didn't understand. She could not let another innocent man be condemned as a murderer for all eternity. Her papa's friend would not suffer the same fate he had. She could not let it happen.

Bridget finished her tea and took Bijou outside. He immediately shot across the lawn, raced around like a demon, and then flopped onto his back and rolled happily in the grass. She strolled after him, unconcerned about Bijou's safety now that the daffodils were gone.

It was still early. She needed to talk to Nate, but she supposed he wouldn't be awake yet. She simply couldn't understand why he hadn't told her about Collins yesterday. Why not, unless he had something to hide? The thought that he was hiding something from her—that he was responsible for what happened to Collins—made her stomach clench. She didn't think that she could withstand another betrayal. She pressed a hand against her abdomen, closed her eyes, and took a deep, calming breath. Her body relaxed.

When she opened her eyes, she saw three figures toward the edge of the garden. She blinked. One of them was Nate. He was crouched down talking to his son, who stood next to his nanny. Bridget watched as Nate picked up the child and gave him a warm hug before setting him down again. The nanny took Henry by the hand and led him back to the villa. Nate slipped his hands into his trouser pockets and watched them go. Bridget could see the heartbreak on his face. *So this is the only way for him to spend time with his son now. How cruel of Lady Luxton. How selfish and vain of her to use her child against his father.*

Nate walked toward her, a smile playing on his lips, and her heart melted. *How could I have doubted him? What is wrong with me? Will I ever be able to trust anyone again?*

"You're up early," Bridget said as Nate came toward her.

"Henry is an early riser. He eats in his nursery, and then his nanny takes him for a long walk. That seems to be his routine. Crossing paths with them allows me to spend a few moments in his company." Nate looked down at his black boots. "It's better than nothing."

"I'm sorry," Bridget said. This time, her heart clenched instead of her stomach.

Nate looked up and smiled, though the smile didn't quite reach his eyes. "What about you? Why are you up so early?"

"I prefer to breakfast with Aunt Marianne. Also, I wanted to talk to you. We didn't get to speak last night after I saw...well. The blood. And then this morning, I heard about Mr. Collins from Harriet. She said someone beat him within an inch of his life." She searched his face for a reaction.

Nate ran a hand through his dark curls. "Yes, it was awful."

"Why didn't you tell me about it yesterday when I saw the blood on your waistcoat?"

Nate sighed. "I was exhausted, and I wasn't ready to talk about it."

"You didn't"—she hesitated—"get into a fight with him, did you?"

Nate took a step back. "You think *I* beat him?"

"No! I—I mean, of course not. But why did you have blood on your shirt?"

"Because the magistrate and I found him lying in a pool of his own blood, and we carried him inside his cottage to tend to his wounds. I got some blood on my waistcoat in the process of helping him."

"Oh." Relief coursed through Bridget's veins.

"You can check with Magistrate Hunt if you don't believe me," Nate said, coldly.

"Of course, I believe you," Bridget said.

"But you doubted me. You *still* don't trust me. After all this time!"

"You have every right to be cross," Bridget said. "After everything you have done for me, yes, I still have mistrust and skepticism in my heart." She shook her head. "My old, trusting self has gone. And sometimes I think I shall never get her back."

Nate's expression softened. "You've been through a terrible ordeal with your papa and the murders last summer. It's no wonder you've lost faith in people." He reached for her hands and clasped them in his, sending a swarm of butterflies swirling in her stomach. "Bridget," he said, "I don't care how long it takes, I'm here to help you regain that trust. Whatever happens, know that I would never do anything to betray or hurt you."

Bridget's throat went dry, and her legs felt somewhat weak as she looked into Nate's deep blue eyes.

"Bridget," he whispered, leaning toward her.

Kiss me. Bridget closed her eyes and waited for the feel of

Nate's lips on hers. She'd never wanted anything so badly in her life.

$$\mathcal{Q}$$

NATE CLOSED HIS eyes and brushed his lips against Bridget's soft mouth. Their lips barely touched, yet he felt his body come alive.

"Mr. Squires!" someone cried. "Miss De Lacey!"

Nate jerked back in surprise and opened his eyes to see Bridget looked up at him wide-eyed. Then they dropped their joined hands and turned to see what the commotion was all about.

Harriet was running toward them. When she reached them, she was so out of breath that she could hardly talk.

"Take a few deep breaths." Bridget put a hand on the woman's shoulder. "What's the urgency? You shouldn't tire yourself so."

Harriet was a woman in her sixties who was more accustomed to doing hair and darning dresses than performing any physical labor. Now she breathed through her pinched nose, and Nate wondered if she was getting any air into her lungs. Her small nostrils flared, and her brown eyes watered as she tried to catch her breath. Eventually, the woman's breathing returned to normal, and she was able to speak.

"Your aunt sent me to fetch you. She says you must come with me immediately. Don't ask the reason, just follow me as though it were a normal day. We don't want to alarm the guests, should any be about yet."

"It *is* a normal day," Nate said with a sinking feeling in his stomach. "Why should we alarm the guests?"

"It's best I don't say anything now—Mrs. Marianne's orders. She is waiting for you. That is all I am at liberty to say."

Nate shared a concerned glance with Bridget. "Very well," he said. "Take us to her."

○

BRIDGET CALLED FOR Bijou, who raced after her as she and Nate followed Harriet inside the villa and up the stairs to the first floor. Most of the guests were still in their rooms, but their lady's maids and valets could be seen entering and or exiting their masters' and mistresses' rooms. Harriet stopped in front of Lady Matheson's room.

"In here," Harriet said and wrenched open the door. "Quick."

Nate shared another puzzled look with Bridget before she stepped inside with Bijou at her heels. Still, he hesitated before following Bridget. It wasn't every day that he entered a lady's chamber without being invited inside by the lady herself. But when Harriet gave him a panicked look, he quickly stepped into the room.

He heard Harriet shut the door behind him as he looked around the bedchamber. It was in disarray. Drawers stood open, and articles of clothing lay on the floor. It looked as though someone had been searching for something. Bijou navigated the items on the floor, sniffing them with great interest. Aunt Marianne stood with a comforting arm around Lady Matheson's crying lady's maid, Louisa. And Bridget hovered near Lady Matheson's canopy bed, her face as white as a winter lily.

"Bridget," he said, not wanting to approach Lady Matheson's bed, partly out of fear of what he'd see behind the canopy and partly out of an absurd sense of modesty. "What is it?"

Bridget turned to him. "She's dead. Lady Matheson is dead."

"What?" Nate rushed to Bridget's side and looked at Lady Matheson, who lay stiff in her bed. Her lovely chestnut curls were fanned out across her pillow, and her amber eyes stared lifelessly at the paneled ceiling. But more noticeable were her lips, which had a blueish tinge to them. Nate scanned the surrounding area, and his eyes fell on a teacup next to her bed. He picked up the cup, which still contained some of the now-cold liquid. It looked considerably darker and thicker than normal tea.

"Did she take anything in her tea?" he turned and asked the distraught maid.

"Lots of sugar but no cream. And oftentimes at night, she mixed in a little laudanum to help her sleep. That's why she liked a lot of sugar, to mask the bitterness."

Just then, the chamber door opened, and Harriet ushered Dr. Elias and Magistrate Hunt inside. They went directly over to Lady Matheson's bed, and Dr. Elias inspected the body, listening to her heart and feeling for any breath or sign of life. Nate thought that somewhat unnecessary, as the woman was already stiff.

"She's been dead for several hours," the doctor said. "I'd say she died last night."

Lady Matheson's maid gasped and began to sob anew.

"Calm yourself, dear," Aunt Marianne said.

"There's a cup of cold tea on the dresser," Nate said. "Her maid says she may have mixed in a little laudanum to help her sleep."

"Well, that's common enough. A little laudanum powder wouldn't harm her." The doctor picked up the cup of tea and inspected the contents, shrugged and put the cup down again.

Magistrate Hunt turned to the sobbing maid and said, "Where does she keep it—her laudanum powder?"

Louisa pointed to the small pedestal table beside Lady Matheson's bed. "In that snuff box. She doesn't take snuff, but she thought the box pretty, she said. That's why she used it for her laudanum powder," the maid said, then buried her face in her hands.

Nate looked at the rectangular porcelain box, decorated with tiny painted bluebells and sparrows. It looked innocent enough.

Dr. Elias picked up the snuff box and opened it. He shook the box, studied its contents, and even gave it a sniff. "It's laudanum powder, as you said. Nothing suspicious here."

Magistrate Hunt glanced around the room.

"Was someone in here? Is the lady's room always such a mess?"

"I'm sorry," Louisa said. "I were so afraid when I saw my lady that I didn't straighten her things…I…"

"Don't worry about that now," Aunt Marianne soothed the maid.

"Yes, but what I'm asking is, how did it get to be such a mess? It's as if someone were in here searching for something. Was it like this when you brought in her tea last night?"

"No, it were tidy. I promise." Tears pooled in Lousia's red-rimmed eyes, and she pressed a handkerchief to each of them as she sniffed, "I wouldn't leave my lady's room a mess."

"So, it's possible someone was in here after you left?" Magistrate Hunt asked.

"I don't see how. My lady keeps her door locked. She always said a lady sleeping alone should never leave herself vulnerable, but I didn't know exactly what she meant by that. I had to get Mrs. Marianne to open her door with the master key this morning when I got no response from my knocking."

Magistrate Hunt frowned. "Could she have been looking for something, perhaps? Something, she misplaced?"

"Oh, yes. She often misplaces things. She can be forgetful at times, and she'd been acting worse of late—since Mr. Otis's murder."

"What do you mean by 'acting worse,' exactly?" Magistrate Hunt asked.

"I…only mean that she's been strange—sad and cross at times, and giddy at other times. Sometimes, she'd rage over nothing. And then a few hours later, she'd be her charming self again. It frightened me. I didn't know what to expect from her."

"Well, if her door was locked from the inside, then she could not have been murdered. What do you suspect killed her then, Doctor?" Magistrate Hunt asked.

"It's difficult to know unless I open the body and examine it. But I couldn't do that without her family's permission or unless you suspect foul play, which you do not. In that case, I'd say it was likely her heart."

"She died of a broken heart?" Louisa said, and then began sobbing into her handkerchief again.

"I suppose you could say that. The heart can be a mystery. One thing we do know is that it can sometimes stop beating, quite suddenly, and for unknown reasons. And that appears to be the case here today."

Nate frowned. Dr. Elias seemed to be making up a reason for Lady Matheson's death. He couldn't know for certain it was her heart unless he examined the body, and he would not do that, so the heart seemed as good a reason as any.

Magistrate Hunt stroked his bushy gray beard. "What do we know of her family? Anything?"

"She was a widow," Bridget said. "And I never heard her mention any children."

"Is that correct, Louisa?" Nate turned to the lady's maid.

She nodded.

"Where was her main residence?" Magistrate Hunt asked.

Louisa attempted to answer but was unable to get the words out. Her chest heaved, trying to catch her breath between sobs. Her hand trembled as she lifted the handkerchief to her nose, which was now running in a most undignified way. Finding her mistress dead had shocked her to the core.

"Why don't I get all the necessary information from the poor girl in a little while?" Aunt Marianne said. "She's too distressed to talk now."

"Give her a pinch of laudanum." Dr. Elias handed the snuff box to Aunt Marianne. "It will help calm her nerves. Perhaps, give her enough to allow her to sleep. When she wakes, she'll feel a lot calmer."

"Thank you, Doctor," Aunt Marianne said, taking the box and pressing the cover into place. Then she led her trembling charge out of the room, the box clenched in one hand, maid's arm gently clasped with the other.

"Well, I suppose my job is complete here," Magistrate Hunt said. "The lady, bless her, died of natural causes."

"Will your men be taking the body with you now?" Nate asked.

"Taking the body? Where shall I take it? The lady wasn't murdered, so it's not evidence, and it's hardly proper to leave her with the carpenter. He has been known to keep a body or two while he prepares the coffin, but someone of this stature—a lady—ought to be prepared and dressed by her maid before burial. You will need to store the body in one of your spare rooms. Once you find out where the body needs to be transported, you can arrange as much with the carpenter. He has a wagon for that purpose."

"Store the body here?" Bridget said. "Impossible! That will be very disturbing to the other guests."

"Bridget is right. We cannot keep her here!" Nate said. "We need to lay her to rest in the churchyard immediately. If her family is in London, it won't do us any good to wait for them. Two weeks in this weather isn't feasible. Tell the carpenter to come immediately with his finest coffin. I'll pay double his asking price."

Magistrate Hunt nodded. "Very well. I'll let it be your decision. She's your guest, after all."

Nate looked at Bridget. "I suppose it's time we go and announce her death to the others."

Bridget squeezed her hands together. "This does not bode well for the inn. I imagine it will unsettle them a great deal. But at least it isn't another murder."

NOT A TEAR was shed on behalf of Lady Matheson. The only guest who seemed perturbed was Colonel Kendall, who thought it was a shame that such a handsome woman should die a widow.

"I wonder what she was searching for," Bridget said later, when she and Nate were seated in the library. Bijou had settled on her lap, and she stroked his white fur. "It must have been something important to leave her room in such disarray. From the state of the room, it looked like she was quite desperate to find something."

"Perhaps it was the portrait," Nate said.

"The portrait?" Bridget asked.

"The other day at breakfast, Angert demanded she return the miniature portrait he'd made of Otis for her. But she denied that she had any such portrait. Anyway, I suspect Angert snuck into her chamber at some point and took the portrait back, just to spite her."

"Why would she have a portrait of Otis?" Bridget asked. "That seems a bit odd, doesn't it?"

Nate sighed. "I suspect she was in love with him."

Bridget kept the lady's disclosure of her drowned son to herself. There was no point in repeating it. "How sad. Perhaps she *did* die of a broken heart."

"Although I can't think why," Nate continued. "A woman of her stature and—may I say—beauty; it seems unbelievable that she would even keep company with the likes of Otis."

"Mr. Otis could be very charming," Bridget said.

Nate shook his head. "I don't see it. I feel as though there was more to their relationship—something we don't know about yet. I simply cannot believe that a mature widow who has both wealth and beauty would fall madly in love with a young man she barely knew. It doesn't make sense. A woman like that doesn't die of a broken heart. That's the stuff of romantic novels, not of real life."

"Oh really?" Bridget could not stop herself from smiling. "And just how many romantic novels have you read?"

Nate frowned. "That's not the point. The point is—"

Just then, Aunt Marianne burst into the library, her face ashen. "I gave her a pinch—just a pinch like the doctor said."

"Aunt!" Bridget jumped out of her seat and went to her aunt. "Whatever is the matter? You look like you've had a terrible shock."

"Only a pinch, Bridget. You heard the doctor, did you not? He said to give her a pinch and it will calm her down." Tears rolled down Aunt Marianne's cheeks.

Nate, who was already on his feet, raced to Aunt Marianne's side. Then with his help, Bridget led Aunt Marianne to the settee.

"I'm going to pour her a brandy," Nate said.

Bridget sat beside her aunt, holding her hand while Nate went to pour the brandy.

"I…I only gave…" Aunt Marianne's words were lost in a sob.

"Shh, Aunt. Don't try to speak now. Try to calm down first."

Nate returned with his cognac and handed it to Bridget. "Here, Aunt. Take a sip of this. It will help your nerves."

Aunt Marianne took the glass, but her hand shook so badly that Bridget had to hold the glass for her. She put it to her aunt's lips. After a few small sips, Aunt Marianne seemed to steady.

"Now, Aunt, tell us what has made you so upset."

"It's Louisa," she said. "I gave her the laudanum from Lady Matheson's snuff box, just as the doctor told me to do. Remember?" She looked at each of them in turn. "It was to help her sleep."

"Yes, that's right. And is she sleeping soundly now, Aunt?"

Aunt Marianne looked at Bridget and blinked. "She's dead."

CHAPTER EIGHTEEN

"SHE SUFFERED A seizure and lost consciousness, but I believe she will survive." Dr. Elias addressed Bridget, Nate, Aunt Marianne, and Magistrate Hunt in the study after he'd concluded his examination of Louisa.

"Oh, thank goodness!" Bridget felt the weight lift off her body.

"But I saw her!" Aunt Marianne said. "She…she was as cold as marble and as pale as snow. Her mouth—there was—"

"It was a reaction to the poison," Dr. Elias said. "You've never seen the body react in such a violent manner, I'm sure. It's completely understandable that you thought she was dead."

"The poison?" Nate asked.

"Yes, someone tampered with the laudanum." Dr. Elis opened the snuff box and handed it to Nate. "I'd say they mixed it with arsenic, which is both colorless and tasteless. It would not have changed the look or the taste of the laudanum. It's a good thing she only took a pinch of the powder. Lady Matheson on the other hand…"

"Good heavens!" Bridget pressed Bijou close. Her heart was beating wildly. "Are you saying that Lady Matheson was murdered after all?"

"It wasn't necessarily murder," Dr. Elias said. "Earlier, the maid had spoken about her mistress's erratic moods. It sounds to me as if her ladyship may have been suffering from an extreme case of nerves or hysteria, perhaps brought on by Mr. Otis's death. Either way, sometimes, serious bouts of hysteria can result in self-murder." He glanced apologetically at Bridget as he spoke.

"That complicates matters," Magistrate Hunt said. "Self-murder will change how the law allows the lady to be buried."

"Good grief," Nate said, sweeping his hand through his hair. "What are we to do then?"

Magistrate Hunt sighed. "Considering the circumstances, I'll keep the lady's body as evidence, while we conduct a short investigation. But, if no evidence of murder can be found after three or four days, I'm going to declare it death by self-murder and dispose of the body accordingly. I don't think it's feasible to keep the body longer in this weather."

A familiar pain shot through Bridget's heart. She reached for her aunt's hand and squeezed it. Only Aunt Marianne understood what she was feeling at this precise moment.

"Thank heavens it was only the maid who took the laudanum to calm her nerves. It could have been Miss De Lacey or her aunt," Magistrate Hunt said.

Bridget wondered if he thought the comment would some-how cheer her. It was a callous thing to say—"only the maid" as if poor Louisa's health was worth less than anyone else's. Still, Bridget shuddered. She felt awful about Louisa, but the idea that her aunt could just as easily have taken a pinch of laudanum to settle her nerves made her turn cold with fear.

Then a thought struck her. Hogarth's *Marriage à la Mode*! When she'd turned seventeen, Papa had brought home from London a miniature set of the six frames by Hogarth that told the tragic story of a wealthy merchant's daughter forced to marry a bankrupted, philandering earl. Papa had given the set to Bridget and promised never to force her into such an unhappy arrange-ment. The calamitous saga ended with the young lady's self-murder by poisoning—and her poison of choice was a bottle of laudanum.

"If Lady Matheson was intent on self-murder, why the need for arsenic?" Bridget looked to Dr. Elias for an answer. "Isn't laudanum fatal in large doses?"

"Yes," Dr. Elias said slowly, "but it would take a large amount to kill an adult, especially one who takes laudanum often. It's generally quite safe. That said, ingesting too much accidentally could, and does, happen."

"So, if Lady Matheson was intent on self-murder, all she needed to do was take a larger than usual dose of laudanum. She would not have needed arsenic at all. On the other hand, if someone else wanted to ensure that Lady Matheson ended up dead, they'd need to add another poison to her laudanum powder—one that required a smaller dose to kill."

"I see what you mean," Dr. Elias said, reluctance in his tone.

"Do you think the person who tampered with Lady Matheson's snuff box is the same one who killed George?" Bridget directed her question at Nate, but the magistrate replied instead.

"No. We have Otis's killer. It's John Groby, and the day after tomorrow I'm going to be transporting him to York for his trial next week."

Bridget's stomach clenched. *Next week!*

"Surely you realize this changes everything," Nate said. "There's been another murder. Do you suppose we have two separate killers?"

"I don't know if we have one or two murderers, or even if Lady Matheson was murdered at all. But I do know that Groby will stand trial for the murder of George Otis Phillips next week. And if he is innocent, the court will find him not guilty, so you needn't worry. If you find out any new information before the trial, you can request to be called as a witness and testify in front of the jury. They will hear you and decide Groby's fate."

"Would you at least consider postponing Mr. Groby's transport to York?" Bridget asked. "If only to give us a chance to discover what happened to Lady Matheson."

"I already told Mr. Squires that that it is out of the question. The assize court arrives in York next week. I have no choice but to transport him there before they arrive. He leaves the day after tomorrow, but you'll have a few days before the trial."

Bridget inhaled deeply and then exhaled slowly. "Then, we shall have to find out who killed Lady Matheson and George Otis within the next few days. For I believe their killer is one and the same."

"One caveat," Nate said. "Perhaps we can all agree not to tell the guests that Lady Matheson was murdered. After all, we don't know it to be a fact just yet, and we don't want to create panic. Secondly, we won't want to alert the killer, should there be one residing among us, of course."

A chill ran down Bridget's spine at hearing Nate's words.

"Agreed?" Nate said.

Aunt Marianne whimpered and nodded, along with the magistrate and Dr. Elias.

"Agreed," Bridget said.

🔎

AUNT MARIANNE CALMED down considerably after she and Bridget checked on Louisa, who was being carefully nursed by Harriet.

"She had a terrible time of it—retching violently—but now she's sleeping soundly," Harriet spoke in a whisper so as not to disturb her patient. "I think she'll be feeling much better tomorrow."

"Thank heavens!" Aunt Marianne dabbed her red-rimmed eyes, which had begun to water again. "I was so frightfully worried for the poor dear. I thought she was…" Aunt Marianne's chest heaved, and Bridget was worried that her flood of tears would begin anew.

"No need to worry anymore, Aunt. Louisa is sleeping like a babe, as you can see." Bridget peered at the sleeping maid. "And now it's time for you to get some rest too." She turned to Harriet. "Some warm milk for my aunt, please, Harriet. That should help her sleep."

"Very good, miss," Harriet said. All three tiptoed out of Louisa's room, and Bridget closed the door gently behind her.

"Will you take Bijou to the kitchen while I see to my aunt?" Bridget kissed Bijou's head and handed him to Harriet. Then she turned to her aunt and put a gentle hand on her back. "Come along, Aunt. You've had quite a shock."

She accompanied Aunt Marianne up to her room and drew the heavy drapes to block out the afternoon sunshine. Harriet delivered the warm milk, which seemed to satisfy her aunt, who settled back on her pillows after draining her cup.

"Rest now, Aunt. You've suffered a terrible ordeal." Bridget clasped her aunt's hand and held it until the woman fell into a deep slumber. Even then, she hesitated to leave her aunt. She thought again about how close she'd come to losing her only living relative. It would not have been out of character for Aunt Marianne to have taken a few pinches of laudanum to ease her nerves along with the maid, but by some miracle, she'd chosen not to and been spared poisoning.

"I am not so grown up, Aunt, that I can do without you," Bridget whispered to the sleeping woman. Then she leaned forward and kissed her aunt's forehead before exiting her chamber.

Bridget went directly to the study, where she knew Nate would be waiting for her. He sat, reclining in one of the leather armchairs with a brandy in hand and smiled as she entered. But Bridget noted the look of worry in his midnight blue eyes. He had removed his cravat and tailcoat jacket and wore his waistcoat open, exposing his white shirt, unbuttoned at the neck and rolled up at the sleeves. Bridget thought about how his lips had brushed against hers in the garden and felt a flutter of excitement in her stomach. She went behind her father's desk and sat in his old chair, immediately embracing the comfort and warmth it always provided her. Though both she and Nate had sat in it countless times since her papa's death, Bridget always felt his presence in that chair.

"I've been thinking about Angert," Nate said.

"Yes, he came to my mind too. If anyone is capable of murder, it's him. I've never met anyone who is so enthralled by the macabre."

"It's not only that." Nate leaned forward and placed his glass on the desk. "A few days ago, before his paintings were slashed, he showed me his collection, and I marveled at the vibrant colors. The emerald green he used to paint Westmorland's fells was incredibly realistic, so like the ones we see outside, and the yellow on his daffodils was truly breathtaking. I complimented him on his colors, and he responded by saying, 'That is due to arsenic.' He always has it on hand to mix those bright pigments."

"Yes, but many people have it on hand. It's commonly used for multiple purposes."

"I know, but Angert was so furious the other day at breakfast. He seemed personally affronted by Lady Matheson's outburst, most likely because he'd thought he'd done her a great favor by painting her a miniature of George. He demanded she return it to him. You weren't there, but the man was frothing at the mouth like a rabid dog."

"I think the thing to do is check Lady Matheson's bedroom for the portrait. I must pack her things anyway. And if we find it is missing, then we will have to find a way to check Angert's room. If he has it in his possession, then we likely have our answer."

"That will be difficult. Since the destruction of his paintings, his valet has been manning his door every time he leaves his room."

"We'll find a way," Bridget said. "In the meantime, is there anyone else we should be considering?"

"That depends on whether or not these murders are linked. I still believe Collins has the best motive for killing George. But he obviously could not have killed Lady Matheson." He sighed. "Either these murders were unrelated, or we have to rule Collins out. If they *are* related, then I'd say jealousy was the motive. Lady Matheson and George appeared to have been more than friends, so someone might have been jealous."

"That opens many possibilities. It could have been anyone in the village or, heavens forbid, one of our servants."

"True, but I was thinking more along the lines of someone who may have been jealous of George himself. He was popular and garnered a lot of attention from the ladies."

"Do you have someone in mind?" Bridget asked.

"Rupert," Nate said without hesitation. "I don't trust him."

Bridget pressed her lips together and dropped her gaze to her lap. That was the answer she'd expected. She understood why Nate disliked Rupert, but the vehemence in his voice puzzled her. Was it just his lack of access to Henry that irked him, or was it Lady Luxton's open dalliance with Rupert that upset him so?

"We can't rule out the possibility that he was jealous of George," Nate reiterated. "Just think about how he taunted Groby on the night of the murder. What did he do that for if not to put George in danger?"

"But then why kill Lady Matheson?"

"I don't know yet," Nate said. "I only know that there is something rotten about that man."

"But Charlie would have to be involved then, too, and I don't see that happening. He's a sweetheart."

"Not necessarily," Nate said.

"Well, I'd say Angert is the one we should be focusing on," Bridget said.

"I agree. But we shall also need to keep a close eye on Rupert."

Bridget nodded. She disagreed with Nate about Rupert, but she didn't say as much. On the other hand, Angert frightened her. And she could very well see him as the killer.

"I think the best thing to do now is check Lady Matheson's room and wait for Louisa to wake up, so we can question her," Nate said.

"I'll take care of searching Lady Matheson's room. Her belongings need to be packed so they can be transported home, and it wouldn't be right for a man to rifle through a lady's things—even if she is deceased."

"You're right." Nate had gone to the window and turned to look outside. "That will suit me well. There's something I need to take care of before we interview Louisa." Nate looked perturbed as he turned away from the window and strode out of the study.

Curiosity took hold, and Bridget walked to the window and looked out. Lady Luxton stood in the garden, staring back up at her.

✦ ════════ ✦

CHAPTER NINETEEN

L ADY MATHESON'S BELONGINGS were decidedly slim for a woman of her stature. She didn't have nearly as many dresses as Bridget had, and barely any jewelry. Perhaps she'd decided against the risk of taking her jewels and expensive gowns on a trip. That seemed sensible to Bridget, but most of the titled ladies she'd come across were far from sensible.

Bridget removed Lady Matheson's neatly folded dresses from her drawer and carefully checked between them for the portrait. When she found nothing, she tucked the dresses into the lady's traveling trunk and moved on to packing her corsets, petticoats, bonnets, and gloves. The final drawer in Lady Matheson's dresser housed a row of shawls. Just as Bridget crouched to open the last drawer, a light knock sounded on the chamber door, and before she could respond, the door opened, and Miss Jennings stepped inside.

Bridget stood and blinked back her shock. "Miss Jennings! Is something the matter?"

"I wanted to offer my help. I heard Louisa is feeling unwell, and you've been so kind to me. I want to repay you in some small way."

"Oh, you needn't worry," Bridget said, "I'm almost fin…" Bridget saw Miss Jennings's cheeks color. The humiliation of rejection was written on her face. Bridget swallowed. How could she be so callous? Miss Jennings was not the type who found extending herself easy.

Bridget smiled. "That would be wonderful. I can use some help."

Miss Jennings entered the room and closed the door behind her.

"I'm just emptying this last drawer where she kept her shawls, and then we can go through her shoes." Bridget lifted a pile of shawls out of the drawer, laid them on the bed, and then carefully refolded each one as she looked for the portrait.

Miss Jennings ran her hand over the night table. "Did you pack all her trinkets away already?"

"She didn't have that many." Bridget pressed another shawl into the traveling trunk. "She didn't bring much with her, from the looks of it."

"Perhaps I can find the carrier for these." Miss Jennings bent to pick up Lady Matheson's soft black leather lace-up boots. "Lady Armstrong likes to keep her shoe cases under the bed." And before Bridget could say anything, Miss Jennings was on her knees, peering under the bed.

Bridget laughed softly and compressed the clothing in the trunk with her hands. It warmed her heart to see Miss Jennings assert herself a little. But her smile faded as Miss Jennings emerged from under the bed, holding an exceedingly sharp knife in her hand.

Bridget's heart leapt into her throat as she backed away from Miss Jennings, despite there being a bed between them. "What are you doing?" she managed to gasp.

"It was under the bed." Miss Jennings dropped the knife onto the bed as if it were a snake.

Bridget then took a cautious step forward and peered at the knife. It was a pocketknife with a sharp blade and an ivory handle. "Was it open with the blade exposed when you picked it up?" she asked.

"Yes, it was lying under the bed, blade out. I don't know what a lady would be doing with a knife," Miss Jennings spoke in a faint whisper as if she were afraid to say the words out loud.

Bridget walked around the bed to where Miss Jennings stood and picked up the knife. She inspected it closely, turning it around and looking at both sides of the blade and handle, but what she was looking for, she did not know. And then she saw something—two tiny flecks of bright green on the tip of the blade—only visible when she squinted and held the blade close to her face.

"Do be careful," she heard Miss Jennings's faint voice behind her. "You might poke yourself in the eye."

"Can you see this?" She pointed to the green flecks on the tip of the blade.

Miss Jennings squinted at the blade but declined to get too close. "I don't see anything."

"There's a little bit of green on the tip of the blade. I do believe it's spots of paint."

"Paint?" Miss Jennings blinked in surprise.

"Yes. I think that this knife was used to slash Mr. Angert's paintings. Perhaps, he'd done a bit of touch-up on one of them and it wasn't completely dry, so a spot of paint got onto the knife."

"You…you think Lady Matheson destroyed Mr. Angert's paintings?"

"I do," Bridget said. "It all makes perfect sense. Those paintings were horrible. They exploited George's death. Anyone who cared about George would have been highly offended by them. I know I was. The pain of losing a loved one, be it a friend or family member, is brutal. It can make you want to destroy things."

The agony Bridget had felt upon learning that her papa had died by his own hand and that his body had been desecrated and buried at a crossroads came flooding back to her. She would have destroyed everything in her path had she not taken herself out of the house and screamed her throat raw in the open air.

"Miss De Lacey?" Miss Jennings backed away from Bridget, her eyes fixed on the knife.

Bridget looked down at her hand and realized that she was squeezing the knife so hard her knuckles had turned white.

$$\wp$$

"YOU NEED TO trust me," Nate pleaded with Helen. "I cannot give you any details, but I'm telling you that it might not be safe here, and I think it's best you take Henry back to Scotland."

"Are you really that threatened by my having a little fun with Rupert?" The corners of Helen's pink lips curved into a smile.

Nate squeezed the back of his neck, which felt as though it might snap from tension. Helen truly would not give up the fantasy that he might still have an interest in her. He cared about his son, and that was all. "I told you that Rupert may not be trustworthy. We don't know anything about him, and there may be a killer on the loose."

"You said Lady Matheson died from a bad heart, and that poet's killer is in jail, so what's to fear?"

Nate massaged his jaw. Every part of his body ached with tension. He would have to tell Helen that Lady Matheson was poisoned, but could she be trusted? He didn't think so. Still, he had no choice. Henry's safety was at stake. "We're not a hundred percent certain that Lady Matheson died from a bad heart. There may have been arsenic involved," he said. "Please don't say anything to Rupert—for your own safety."

"So you think Rupert gave her arsenic?" Helen laughed.

"No…what I mean is…I don't know yet. It could have been anyone. We don't know the level of danger, so it's better to be safe." Feeling his frustration build in his chest, he paused and turned to look at the green fells. Then he inhaled and turned back to Helen. "I need Henry to be safe," he said.

"Henry is perfectly safe. And he is having fun. He's become quite attached to Rupert. He spends more time with Henry than you do."

"That's because you won't let me spend time with him," Nate said through gritted teeth. "I will gladly—"

"Well, which is it? Would you like to spend time with your son, or would you like to send him away?"

Nate closed his eyes and inhaled. Why had he thought trying to reason with Helen a good idea?

"Scotland is a terrible bore. My husband—a man I married to secure your child's future as the next Earl of Luxton—is old enough to be my grandfather. Yet, you have chosen to resent me for it. I offered you a chance to be Henry's father when the earl dies, but your pride won't allow it. And now, you still think you can dictate how I live my life."

Nate felt his nostrils flare as he worked to keep his anger in check. How was it that she had abandoned him at the altar, yet had somehow turned it around to make him the one who'd rejected her? He swallowed his frustration. "I'm not trying to dictate you. I only want to ensure your and Henry's safety."

"Indeed," she said spitefully. "Well, I shan't go back. I'm having too much fun with Rupert, and if you could stand to give up your little blond orphan, then the fun could have been all yours. But then you've always been a hopeless romantic, haven't you?" she said mockingly.

Beautiful as she was, Nate suddenly wondered how he'd ever been attracted to her. She'd lied, cheated, and behaved selfishly at every turn, yet she was Henry's mother, so he was stuck with her. He only hoped she'd do nothing to hurt their son in the future.

Nate placed the magnifying glass in his eye and peered at the blade. "Yes," he said, "I see it. That lovely emerald green Angert uses in his paintings." He lowered the knife and looked at Bridget. "I think you're right. There's a good chance that Lady Matheson used this knife to slash Angert's paintings."

"So it follows that Angert took his revenge by poisoning her."

"It sounds plausible to me. I certainly think him capable of murder."

Bridget sighed. "Now all we have to do is find a way to get inside his room and search for the portrait. If he has that in his possession, we'll know for certain he is guilty."

Just then, a knock sounded on the study door. "That'll be Louisa." Bridget rose and went to open the door. Louisa stood in the doorway with Harriet, who held a tea tray.

"Thank you, Harriet," Bridget said, taking Louisa by the arm and leading her to one of the soft leather armchairs across from the desk. Harriet followed, carrying the tea tray, which she set down on the sturdy mahogany desk. Then she departed.

Bridget poured three cups of tea. "How do you prefer your tea, Louisa?" she asked kindly.

Louisa seemed taken aback. "I…"

"Cream and sugar?" Bridget suggested.

The maid nodded. Bridget added the cream and sugar and placed the cup in front of Louisa. Then she put a few biscuits onto a plate and set them down beside the cup. After pouring tea for herself and Nate, she settled in the chair next to Louisa and waited for the woman to take a few sips of tea before she asked her first question.

"As I'm sure you understand, Louisa, it's important that we inform Lady Matheson's family about her death. What can you tell us about her?"

"I was only with her six months…I don't know much."

"Well, tell us what you do know," Bridget said kindly.

"Her husband, Sir Roald"—Louisa looked from Nate to Bridget—"died these three months past. They had no children."

"Three months?" Bridget said. "But she couldn't have been in mourning. She wasn't in mourning when she came to the villa. And…well…then, there's George."

Bridget's words echoed Nate's thoughts. A lady in deep mourning, who'd recently lost her husband, did not behave the way Lady Matheson had behaved—stepping out late with another man and commissioning a miniature portrait of him to keep in his memory. She'd mourned Otis more than she'd mourned her husband, whom she'd barely mentioned. "Do you know why your lady chose not to wear mourning clothing until a few days ago? Three months is still a deep mourning period for a wife," he said.

Louisa shrugged helplessly, and Nate got the distinct feeling that she wasn't being entirely forthcoming.

"Was Sir Roald a knight or a baronet?" he asked.

"A baronet," Louisa said.

"And where was his estate?"

"Cornwall—St. Agnus."

Nate frowned. "That's a long way from Westmorland. I fail to see why Lady Matheson would leave her home to travel to the other end of the country directly after her husband's death. Unless—" He paused. "Was the estate entailed?"

Louisa looked blankly at Nate. "I don't understand," she said.

"Was Lady Matheson perhaps forced out of her home by her husband's heir?" Bridget said kindly.

Louisa's face cleared, and she nodded. "She said we were to leave directly or the new baronet would have her locked away—" Louisa bit her lip, and Nate knew she'd revealed something she ought not to have.

He glanced at Bridget, whose creased forehead told him she'd also found the remark strange.

"Why would the new baronet have her locked away?" Nate asked.

"No. I don't mean 'locked away'. I meant…'turned away'." Louisa's brown eyes widened.

"Turned away?" Nate felt his irritation rising. The maid was withholding information, and he intended to find out why. "How is that different from leaving on her own accord? If anything, the new baronet would likely have given her more time to prepare—a few months, even. So, please tell us the truth. Why did she run? Is it because she did something to Sir Roald? Was she responsible for his death?"

"No!" Louisa squeaked. "I mean...I don't know...oh, dear!" Her bottom lip trembled.

"How did Sir Roald die?" Nate demanded.

"He fell from his horse and was in a bad way. But the doctor said he would heal and be well again. Then the next day, his valet found him dead in his bed. That is all I know." Louisa started to wheeze as her panic increased.

"Hush now," Bridget said gently as the maid struggled to calm her breathing. "You are not in any trouble and may speak freely. We are here to help you."

Louisa turned to Bridget and blinked back her emerging tears.

"You were following your lady's orders, weren't you?" Bridget continued in a soothing voice. "Whatever decisions she made, they were not yours. The blame will not rest on you. So, tell us. Why did Lady Matheson run away after her husband died?"

Louisa inhaled and let out a shaky breath before saying, "Her name weren't Lady Matheson. It were Lady Patterson. She changed it when we left Cornwall."

Louisa's hand trembled, and Bridget covered it with her own to reassure the maid that she wasn't in any trouble. "Why did she feel the need to change her name and run away from Cornwall?"

"When Sir Roald hired me, after his wife's maid had passed on, my instructions were to care for the lady and also to watch over her. She lived in the upper chambers of the estate—very comfortable chambers they were, but far away from Sir Roald's chambers. It was so they never saw each other, I think. He said she weren't well. She needed laudanum every day on account of her nervous disposition. She suffered from bouts of hysteria, so the laudanum kept her calm. She were only to leave the house once a day for a walk in the gated and high-walled gardens of the estate. And I were always to be by her side. I were never to leave her alone. When we walked into the garden, one of the footmen also followed us. She were never to be alone. That were his instructions."

"So, Sir Roald kept his wife prisoner in her own home?" Bridget said, and Nate heard the anger in her voice. "How awful. No wonder she ran at the first opportunity and declined to mourn him."

"He said it were for her protection, on account of her suffering from hysteria and a nervous disposition. But I came to find out later it was on account of her son."

"I thought you said she had no children," Nate said.

"She didn't—not anymore. But she would have terrible nightmares and talk in her sleep of a child drowning. She'd scream for Sir Roald to save him and bring him home to her."

"After George died, she told me that her babe had drowned in a pond on her estate," Bridget said. "Perhaps that's what the dreams were about."

"Maybe," Louisa said. "In her dreams, she'd cry out for her 'babe'—'don't take him from me,' she'd cry—'he's only an innocent child.'"

Nate frowned. He was at an utter loss. Then Bridget said, "How soon did you leave after Sir Roald died?"

"The very next day," Louisa said. "Lady Matheson wanted to leave before the burial because she feared the new baronet. So we packed her traveling chests and fled at night."

"How did you flee?"

"In one of Sir Roald's carriages—he had so many, and Lady Matheson said the new baronet owed her a carriage at least. But she also took a few other items—jewelry, some candlesticks, and silver. And all the banknotes and Sir Roald had stored away in his study. Gerald told her about those." Louisa clamped her hand over her mouth.

"Gerald? Her driver? He is here at Villa De Lacey, is he not?" Nate said.

Louisa nodded. "I didn't mean to...he didn't do anything wrong."

"Are you afraid of Gerald?" Bridget asked and then glanced at Nate.

"No, of course not. He were a great help to my lady, and I don't want him in trouble."

"Where did you go after leaving Cornwall? Did you come directly to Westmorland?" Nate asked. He would deal with Gerald later.

"We stopped many places along the way," Louisa said, "to change the horses and such. We stayed at many inns."

"Of course you did, but was your final destination Westmorland?"

"Not at first. We only came here after leaving Knaresborough."

"Knaresborough?" Nate straightened. "Why did she want to go there?"

"She never said—only that it were important. But in the end, we only stayed a few days. We visited a reverend and his wife. There was an awful row with the reverend. And then we left. But the next day, the reverend's wife came to our inn. She spoke with Lady Matheson again. And then we departed for Westmorland. I must say, I were mighty pleased when we came here. It's so peaceful, but I suppose now I shall have to leave." She burst into tears.

Bridget put her arm around the maid. "Don't worry about that now. We shall do all we can to help you stay if that's what you wish." She handed Louisa a handkerchief. "Now, dry your eyes and tell us—do you remember the name of the reverend's wife in Knaresborough?"

"I do." Louisa sniffled and nodded at the same time. "It were Mrs. Phillips."

Well, well! Nate thought. *And so the plot thickens.*

CHAPTER TWENTY

"So, Lady Matheson likely knew George Otis before they 'met' here in Westmorland," Bridget said in wonder, her brain still digesting the information after they'd dismissed Louisa and sent for Gerald.

"Yes, it seems that way." Nate ran a hand through his wavy black hair and went to pour himself a brandy. "I am forced to question myself at every turn now." He sat beside Bridget with his drink in hand. "I was utterly convinced that Collins had killed Otis. It made complete sense—what with their contentious history and the symbolism of leaving his desecrated body in the daffodils. And now it appears a jealous footman, turned driver, may have done it."

"What do you mean?"

"I mean, when Sir Roald died, his entire estate went to his heir, and Gerald helped Lady Matheson steal valuables from the house and then aided in her escape. So, he was likely in love with her. In which case, he'd have been jealous of her relationship with Otis. And if Lady Matheson rejected him after Otis's death—well, a spurned lover is a powerful motive."

"True, but let's not jump to conclusions again...." Seeing the sharp look on Nate's face, Bridget stopped her words. "I didn't mean to say that you were—"

"No, you're right. That's exactly what I've been doing." Nate drained his glass and set it on the desk. "First Collins, then Angert, now Gerald. We have no proof whatsoever."

"We are theorizing. It's a process of elimination. That's all. It's necessary."

"Except we have eliminated no one," Nate said dryly.

Just then, a knock sounded on the door, and Gerald entered. He was a strikingly tall and well-built young man, with a head of short dark curls, hazel eyes, and a sharp face.

Nate started with the questions the moment the young man sat down. "Can you tell us what position you held in Sir Roald's home?"

The young man's Adam's apple bobbed in his throat as he swallowed. "I were a footman, sir."

"For how long?"

"Just over three years, sir."

"And after Sir Roald died, you decided to leave with Lady Matheson. Why?"

"There were to be a new baronet coming, and none of us knew if we were to keep our positions. I thought it were best to go with the lady. She promised me permanent employment."

"So you left to secure your future?" Nate scoffed. "I think not. You would have been better off staying and getting a reference to find a new position had the new baronet decided not to keep you on. After all, you knew that Lady Matheson didn't have a lot of money—didn't you? She was reduced to stealing jewelry, candlesticks, and banknotes from her husband's estate before she left. So your reasons for giving up your position in the house don't make sense. It seems like you took a great risk."

Gerald shifted in his seat.

"I think your motives were somewhat different," Nate said. "By leaving with Lady Matheson, you were helping her escape, rather than helping yourself. The question is, why?"

"Louisa said the new baronet would have Lady Matheson locked away in one of those asylums. They are horrible places. She didn't deserve that. She always treated me well."

"But she was kept upstairs, away from the rest of the household. When did you have contact with Lady Matheson?"

"During her walks, mostly. I would follow behind Lady Matheson and Louisa to make sure everyone was safe."

"Hmm. So, I expect you got to know Lady Matheson well during those times."

Gerald shrugged.

"She was a very handsome woman," Nate said. Bridget watched for Gerald's reaction, but he appeared unmoved and simply shrugged again.

"Were you in love with her?" Nate said abruptly. Bridget held her breath. She could not help but feel sympathy for the driver.

"In *love* with her?" Gerald frowned. "She were the age of my mama, sir. How should I have been in love with a woman of those…years?"

"That is of no matter. She was beautiful and richer than you were. Why else would you risk helping her escape—with stolen goods, I might add?"

"I told you why," Gerald said, shifting in his seat again.

"Do you know what I think?" Nate crossed his arms. "I think you were infatuated with her, and you saw yourself as her 'white knight.' If you came to her rescue, perhaps she'd be so grateful that she would fall in love with you. You would be her savior, and she would owe you her life. But that's not what happened, is it? Instead, she fell in love with George Otis—a man even younger than you—and you couldn't stand it, could you? So you killed Otis and took his heart."

"What?" Gerald half rose out of his seat.

"But that didn't change anything, did it?" Nate raised his voice, and Gerald backed down into his chair again. "Lady Matheson didn't turn to you for comfort. She'd all but forgotten about you. After everything you did for her. That must have enraged you—perhaps enough to kill her?"

"You…you've got it all wrong," the driver said, and Bridget could see beads of sweat forming on his forehead.

"How so?" Nate leaned forward on his desk. "Tell me what I've got wrong."

Gerald inhaled and then closed his eyes for a few seconds before opening them again and looking directly at Nate. "I did indeed fall in love," he said, "but it wasn't with Lady Matheson. It was with Louisa."

Bridget covered her mouth to stifle her gasp.

Nate looked momentarily taken aback. "Louisa?" he said.

"Yes. We were…are in love. And with Sir Roald dead, Louisa was certain to lose her job when Lady Matheson was sent away by the new baronet. We didn't know what to do…and when Lady Matheson asked Louisa to come with her, well, I weren't going to let her go without me. So we helped her escape. But I didn't kill anyone. Why should I want my lady to die? She were good to us. Now, we are both without positions once again."

"Oh, you mustn't worry about that now," Bridget said, her heart going out to the young man. "I am certain we can find a…" she started, but stopped when she caught sight of Nate's frown. He was likely feeling frustrated and not in a generous mood right now, but that would change later. Then she'd be sure to secure positions for Louisa and Gerald at Villa De Lacey.

In the meantime, they had a killer to catch.

"WE SHALL NEED to take a trip to Knaresborough," Bridget said. "It's imperative we speak to George's parents and find out what their connection is to Lady Matheson."

"I cannot. How can I leave Villa De Lacey when there might be a killer among us?" Nate rubbed his forehead and then slammed his fist onto the desk.

Bridget jumped involuntarily.

"I'm sorry." Nate glanced at her. "It's just that…it's Henry I worry about. I don't think this is the best or safest place for a child. But Helen will not listen to me. She refuses to take Henry back to Scotland. I tried to explain things to her without revealing any of the details about the possible murder of Lady Matheson, but she accused me of not wanting her and Henry here because of…." He sighed.

"Because of what? How can she say such a thing? You love Henry. Doesn't she know that?" Bridget felt outrage on behalf of Nate rising in her chest.

"She's using him to blackmail me—emotionally, I mean. She accuses me of having feelings for you, and she thinks I want her and Henry out of the way."

"Accuses you?" Bridget felt as though she'd shrunk inside.

Nate came around the desk toward her. "That's the way it sounds when it comes from her—as if caring for you is a crime."

Heat spread across Bridget's cheeks, and she dropped her gaze, remembering their earlier almost-kiss in the garden. The conversation had now taken a turn into something else entirely. For almost a year, she and Nate had danced around their feelings for one another. And with her having been in mourning for all of that time, it hadn't seemed an appropriate subject. But now—no. They couldn't. There was Villa De Lacey to think of, not to mention Henry. He was a father! Whether he liked it or not, he'd have to do Helen's bidding for years to come. She looked up at him and met his midnight blue eyes. "I'm sorry," she said. "I don't wish to come between you and Henry. I know how—"

"You're not coming between us. His mother is doing all she can to use him to control me." Nate threw his hands up. "And what can I do about it? Nothing. I have no claim on Henry, so I am at her mercy." He pressed his eyes closed and took a deep breath. "If anything happens to Henry," he said, opening his eyes, "I shan't ever be able to forgive myself."

"Don't say such things. It's unnerving that a killer might be lurking among us, but we don't know that to be true. It seems that Lady Matheson was rather unstable. She may have been the one who killed George and then took her own life. We know she slashed Angert's paintings, so she wasn't behaving rationally—although I tend to think her awful husband drove her to madness by locking her up for years."

"You may be right. But until we know that for certain, I cannot leave our guests or my son alone."

"Of course not. Henry needs you here. I shall go," Bridget said.

"No." Nate shook his head. "I can't allow you to go. It's too dangerous."

"You cannot allow it?" Bridget raised her eyebrows.

Nate at least had the awareness to blush a little. "I mean, your aunt won't allow it. You know it would upset her greatly."

"Then she shall come with me."

"Who will run the inn? Mrs. Harley is with child. I cannot impose on her."

"Harriet is here, and she is more than capable. She can take care of Bijou and help manage the staff. Anything beyond her capabilities, you can surely see to," Bridget said.

"Harriet? She's a lady's maid. What does she know of running an inn? And won't you and your aunt need her with you?"

"We will take Louisa for a lady's maid and Gerald for a driver, seeing as they know where the Phillips family lives."

Nate hesitated.

"Are you still concerned about what people will think? What do they say about you to your brother?"

"Not in the least," Nate said. "My brother can go to the dev…"

Bridget suppressed a smile. "I shall leave tomorrow morning."

"Very well," Nate said, still looking perturbed. "But I insist that Bennett accompany you. I don't trust Gerald to drive you there alone."

"Bennett? How will you do without your valet?"

"I'll do better knowing he is protecting you in Harrogate than dressing me over here," Nate said.

Bridget smiled. She could not think of a sweeter gesture.

CHAPTER TWENTY-ONE

T HE REVEREND PHILLIPS lived in a thatched cottage across from the Chapel of St. Michael's in the peaceful, market town of Knaresborough.

"Well, this looks quite respectable," Aunt Marianne said as Bennett helped her from the carriage.

"Yes, it does," Bridget said, feeling reassured as she admired the darling cottage with its whitewashed exterior, mullioned windows, and pristine garden. She stepped forward, and Bennett followed.

"I think it will be best if the two of us go in together and the servants wait in the carriage," Aunt Marianne said, glancing at Bennett.

"I shall remain here," Bennett said. "But do not hesitate to holler if you need me."

"Oh, you're not to worry. It looks perfectly safe," Bridget said as she pushed open the small wooden gate in front of the cottage and admired the neat garden, studded with roses, pansies, bluebells, and…daffodils. She stopped. Nerves churned in her stomach. This was a time of deep mourning for George's poor family. How would they react to seeing her, of all people, at their doorstep? And how would they react to the news of Lady Matheson's death? She had the sudden urge to turn and race back to the safety of her carriage.

"Good grief, Bridget! Why have you come to a standstill? Go and knock on the door. I am parched. Let's hope the reverend and his wife will be kind enough to offer us a cup of tea." She gave Bridget a gentle shove, and Bridget had no choice but to move forward.

Bridget used the iron knocker to rap gently on the wooden door, and a few seconds later, a pale-faced young housekeeper answered.

"We are here to see the Reverend and Mrs. Phillips," Bridget said. "My name is Miss De Lacey from Westmorland. We are…were…friends of Mr. George Otis. Phillips," she added.

"Wait here," the housemaid said. "I shall inquire whether the reverend can receive you." She closed the door, leaving Bridget and her aunt on the doorstep. A minute later, she returned and invited them inside the impeccably neat and sparse cottage. After taking their coats and bonnets, she led them to the parlor where the reverend and his wife stood to greet them.

Bridget was immediately taken aback by Mrs. Phillips's tall, broad-shouldered physique, black hair, and dark gray eyes. Could this be fair George's mama? She turned to Mr. Phillips, who, like his wife and George, was tall. But that is where the resemblance with his son ended. He had sharp features with small brown eyes and neatly-combed brown hair. Bridget was completely taken aback. How was it that the blue-eyed, yellow-haired George looked nothing at all like his mama and papa?

🔎

"Reverend and Mrs. Phillips," Bridget said once she found her voice, "I am Miss De Lacey, and this is my aunt, Mrs. Brixton. We want to thank you for receiving us. I know this is a difficult time for you."

"Please, sit down," Reverend Phillips said, and Bridget could not help but notice how different his stiff mannerisms were from George's friendly and relaxed demeanor.

Bridget and her aunt sat. "Please accept our deepest condolences on the loss of your son," Bridget said.

"Indeed," Aunt Marianne murmured.

"Thank you," Reverend Phillips said. "But you needn't have come from Westmorland to extend your condolences. A letter would have sufficed."

Bridget nodded politely. "Unfortunately, that is not the only reason we are here. There's been another death, and we have reason to believe you are familiar with the deceased."

Just then, the housekeeper entered carrying a tea tray, and the conversation paused while she set down the tray and poured four cups of tea. Bridget added sugar and cream to both her cup and Aunt Marianne's. Then she waited for everyone to take sips of tea before continuing. "The deceased's name is Lady Matheson. Or shall I call her 'Lady Patterson'?"

Mrs. Phillips almost dropped her teacup, splashing tea onto her black mourning dress. She fumbled as she put the cup down, spilling more tea into the saucer.

"I'm sorry," Bridget said. "The news seems to have come as a shock. I take it you were close to the lady, then?"

"Not close," the Reverend said curtly. "But we are, of course, sorry to hear of her untimely demise."

"Can you tell me how you knew her? My understanding is that she had lived somewhat of a secluded life in Cornwell."

"Her husband, Sir Roald, may he rest in peace, was a distant cousin of mine," Reverend Phillips said.

"That's good news," Bridget said. "We are searching for her closest relatives to transport the body for burial. Can you help us with any information?"

"I am not aware of any living relatives on her part. My cousin is buried at his estate in Cornwall. Perhaps, the new baronet would care to bury the lady next to her husband."

"It would take several weeks to transport the body to Cornwall, and that might not be practical in the springtime."

"Of course." Reverend Phillips glanced at his wife, who sat stiff as a board and said nothing.

"May I ask how she died?" Reverend Phillips said.

Bridget shifted in her seat. Should she reveal that Lady Matheson may have died by her own hand and deny her a proper burial? "We are uncertain. At the moment, it appears to be a combination of accidental laudanum and arsenic poisoning," Bridget said hesitantly. "However, the magistrate has not ruled out foul play."

Mrs. Phillips's face paled.

"The doctor declined to perform an autopsy without the family's permission," Bridget continued.

"Tell him not to bother!" The reverend said. "She's a sinner. Always has been. Bury her at a crossroads and drive a stake in her heart."

The pain that shot through Bridget was like a poisoned arrow, spreading to every part of her body. She cleared her throat and worked hard to stay in control. "It was very likely an accidental overdose," she said, suddenly feeling the need to defend Lady Matheson from the cruelty of a murderer's burial. "Her maid, Louisa, said that she often took laudanum to help her sleep, and arsenic is used for many ailments, too. I am certain she did not…"

"Certain you say?" Mrs. Phillips shot out of her seat and gave Bridget a hard stare. "You know better than the reverend, then?"

"I-I-I…" Bridget stammered, so taken aback she did not know what to say.

Mrs. Phillips didn't wait for her response. She stalked to the window, turning her back to them in a silent dismissal.

"I'm sorry, but I must ask you to leave," Reverend Phillips said, getting to his feet. "This is a difficult time for us, you understand."

Bridget hesitated. She hadn't yet accomplished all she needed, which was to find out why Lady Matheson had hidden her true relationship with George. Why had she not simply said that he was related to her? Why had she pretended to have only known him for a few weeks? Bridget eyed the sharp-faced reverend, who looked nothing like George. Then she thought about Lady Matheson's love for George and how she'd lamented that he'd reminded her of her drowned child. Could it be that her son didn't drown at all? But that he was taken from her—maybe by a cruel husband who saw her as unfit and imprisoned her in her own home?

"May we come back tomorrow?" Bridget stood, and Aunt Marianne followed suit. "We are staying at the Olde Jerusalem Inn, not far from here; I'd like to ask you a few more questions."

"I don't think so, Miss De Lacey. As I said, this is a difficult time for us."

"It's just that…" She fought with the desire to give in to their wishes and the need to know the truth. So many things depended on it, and this was her only chance to investigate. "Well, there's a chance foul play may have been involved in Lady Matheson's death, and I wondered if you knew of anyone who would want to harm her?"

"No," the reverend said. "If you want to know the truth, my cousin's wife was unwell and she should not have been out in the world on her own. I should have apprehended her when she came here to inform us of my cousin's death, but sadly, I did not. Now it looks like she has committed the ultimate sin of taking her own life. There will be no hope for her soul now."

"That seems rather harsh," Bridget said as another painful arrow pierced her heart.

"Good day to you, Miss De Lacey, Mrs. Brixton," Reverend Phillips said firmly and gave a slight bow.

Bridget and Aunt Marianne had no choice but to bid the reverend goodbye. Mrs. Phillips kept her rigid back to them and continued to stare out of the window as they exited the parlor alone and without any escort.

"Well, that was odd," Bridget said to her aunt once they were safely ensconced in their carriage.

"Indeed," Aunt Marianne agreed. "The entire situation is very strange."

"There is something they are not telling us." Bridger gazed out of the carriage window at the Phillips's cottage. "And I think I know what it could be."

CHAPTER TWENTY-TWO

T HE NEXT MORNING, as Bridget and Aunt Marianne stepped outside in search of a teashop, the door to a black carriage parked in front of the Old Jerusalem Inn swung open, and someone beckoned to them from within.

Bridget froze and squinted at the carriage. Just then, the driver hopped down and approached them.

"Mrs. Phillips requests that you join her in her carriage. But you must make haste. She is short on time."

Bridget glanced at her aunt, whose look of surprise mirrored her own shock. Then the two of them hurried to the carriage and climbed inside. The driver shut the door, locking out the day's sunshine as the window shades in the carriage were drawn. Although they were on the street, they had complete privacy.

Mrs. Phillips looked exactly as she had the previous day, with her ink-black hair scooped in a tight bun and hidden under a large black bonnet, and her pale face pinched. She did not greet her guests but simply lifted her black umbrella and used it to tap the roof of her carriage, which then lurched forward.

"We shall take a turn around the block, so as not to raise suspicion," she said. "I only have a few minutes."

"Thank you for taking the time to talk to us," Bridget said, now extremely curious as to what information the woman had to divulge.

"I am only doing it to prevent you from asking questions around town. The minute I met you, I knew you were the sort who wouldn't be content until you got the answers you were seeking, and the last thing the esteemed reverend needs is people gossiping about his family."

"Oh," Bridget said, taken aback. She was certain Mrs. Phillips had not meant to compliment her but, all the same, she felt oddly pleased that the woman had noted her persistence.

Mrs. Phillips sighed. "The truth is that George is not our son. He came to us when he was a boy of nine."

"He's Lady Matheson's child, isn't he?" Bridget glanced at Aunt Marianne. It had not been difficult to put the pieces together after their meeting with the Reverend and his wife yesterday.

Mrs. Phillips pressed her thin lips together and nodded. "My husband's cousin, Sir Roald, married Lady Patter…Matheson when George was an infant—her first husband having died while out at sea. Even though she was below his station, Sir Roald was blinded by love, and so he made the mistake of marrying her. All was well for the first few years, but as George grew, his behavior became troublesome. He seemed like a very charming child on the surface, but there was something sinister about him. He'd lie and well…hurt people."

"Hurt people?" Bridget said. "That doesn't sound like George."

"I know it doesn't. That is because he could be very endearing, and his 'bad' deeds were conducted in secret. When caught, he was very good at playing innocent."

"But who did he hurt?" Bridget asked, still unable to believe that the winsome George, who loved poetry and nature, could hurt anyone.

"Mostly servants and other children. They'd accidentally trip in his presence, or he'd trick them into doing something dangerous, like retrieving an object from up high, and then he'd cause them to fall. One time, he sent his nanny tumbling down the stairs. Another time, he 'accidentally' bumped into one of the maids as she was stoking the fire. And her hand was severely burned."

"Oh my!" Aunt Marianne gasped.

"When George was eight, Sir Roald employed a new caretaker for his estate. The man arrived with his family—a wife and two sons. Right away, the two little boys, who often played with George, always seemed to be getting injured. On one occasion, the younger of the two boys almost lost an eye when George forced him into a fencing match using sticks. After the child accidentally poked George hard in the stomach, he lost his temper and thrust the sharp end of the stick at the child's face, just missing his eye."

Aunt Marianne gasped.

"I can hardly believe this," Bridget said.

"Neither could his mother. She wouldn't entertain any complaints about her son. And each time, the incident was blamed on the victim's clumsiness or simply dismissed as an unfortunate accident. No one wanted to believe that a small child was capable of inflicting harm on others, so they let him get away with it. He went through several nannies, not to mention governesses. Then one day, something truly terrible happened…" She paused.

"Go on," Bridget said, her nerves now on edge.

"The caretaker's wife gave birth to a third child—another little boy. Sir Roald doted on the infant—and I think you can guess why. His marriage to Lady Matheson had come under immense strain. Her mood declined, and she was often sullen and gloomy. Sir Roald sought comfort in the arms of another—the caretaker's wife, to be precise—and she had given him the son Lady Matheson had not. I am uncertain if Lady Matheson knew the child was his, but George noticed how Sir Roald doted on that baby, and it enraged him."

"Dear heavens!" Aunt Marianne said. "Don't say he did something to that poor infant…"

"Sadly, I cannot. The minute that poor helpless babe became the focus of George's anger, he was lost to the world."

"Are you saying that George hurt an infant?" Bridget asked fearfully.

"I'll tell you what happened, and you be the judge. One day, George took the child from the house with the help of his two older brothers, under the pretense of playing 'Moses and the Bulrushes'—as he'd recently been given a Bible lesson on that very subject. So, he put the child in a basket and set him sailing on the large, murky pond on Sir Roald's estate, telling his brothers that he would save the little lad and take him to live in the castle, which in that instance was Sir Roald's estate."

"Oh my, oh dear!" Aunt Marianne whimpered.

"Unfortunately, the basket he put the child in wasn't adequate, and it quickly filled with water." She fell silent. "It only took a few seconds before the infant disappeared under the murky waters of the pond."

"Good grief!" Bridget felt the sting of tears in her eyes.

"By the time his mama realized her babe was gone from his cradle, it was too late. George attempted to lay the blame on the infant's brothers, but there was no doubt in Sir Roald's mind about what had happened. There had been too many 'accidents' over the years to ignore the truth. That's when Sir Roald decided to banish George from his estate. He could no longer look at the boy. He paid my husband, a great deal of money to take care of the boy and instruct him in the Christian way of life. And I must say, it seemed to work. Reverend Phillips took a stern hand with George and instilled the fear of God in him. For the first four years that George was with us, the boy adhered to a strict schedule of Bible study, Latin and mathematics lessons, prayer, and chores. George had no time for mischief."

"But what about his mama? Did he not cry for her?" Bridget asked.

"No. He appeared to have scant feelings for her—for anyone, in fact. But he did rail against the rules he was forced to follow. He wasn't used to that, but once he realized that things were not going to be as they had been for him, he finally settled down. By the time he turned thirteen and went to boarding school at St. Joseph's, he was completely transformed. At least that's what we thought."

"Did he get up to mischief in school?"

"Oh, no. George loved school. It was a haven for him with its systematic bullying in place. They call it fagging, where younger boys do the bidding of older boys, who punish them in various cruel ways at their will. I fear it reignited George's appetite for cruelty. He thrived at boarding school, and afterwards, he went on to Cambridge. The reverend wanted him to follow in his footsteps. And for a time, it seemed he would."

Bridget pressed a hand to her pulsing throat as she waited to hear what happened next.

"About two years ago, a young woman came to see us, claiming George had courted her and promised to marry her but would not fulfill his obligation." Mrs. Phillips paused. "She was with child."

"My word!" Aunt Marianne said.

Bridget could hardly believe it. She hadn't known George for long, but was it possible that he could have hidden his true self so expertly? The George she knew had been a kind and sensitive young man.

"The reverend was furious and called him home from Cambridge," Mrs. Phillips continued, "but George denied ever having known the young lady. He was adamant. There was a big row, and George left us. He refused to return to university. Sir Roald cut him off. And we never heard from him again.

"But there was gossip—talk that he was in York. People said he claimed to be a poet and that he got money from…" She swallowed. "From women he entertained or charmed—widows and lonely wives." She covered her eyes and shook her head.

Bridget wanted to reach out to the woman and offer some comfort, but decorum held her back. She did not know Mrs. Phillips well enough to intrude on her personal space.

"Then I heard talk that he went to Westmorland. That was just before his mother arrived and gave us news of Sir Roald's passing. She wanted her son, of course. Even after all those years, she still thought of him as a little boy. It was as though time had stood still for her. The reverend threatened to have her locked away as her husband had done, but I was not so heartless. Men have all the power, you know. They can lock us away, deny us our freedom, our speech, and our children." She paused. "So, I told her that he was an aspiring poet and had gone to Westmorland to follow in Wordsworth's footsteps." She gave a half smile. "It seems I made the wrong decision because they are both now dead."

A cold chill ran down Bridget's spine. "You don't think Lady Matheson would have murdered her own son, do you?"

"I don't know." Mrs. Phillips said. "Perhaps I was misguided in sympathizing with her. It seems she was mad, after all. So, who knows what she might have done? It's quite possible she killed George and then killed herself. On the other hand, that butcher may in fact be the guilty one. I think George inherited a touch of his mother's madness, and it led him to wander dangerous paths. Indeed, I believe he would have ended up a victim of murder sooner or later." She shook her head. "Sir Roald tried to save them both, first by sending George away and then by keeping his wife under lock and key. Alas, it was not to be."

Bridget sighed. Despite everything she'd discovered, she was still no closer to knowing who killed George. And if she returned to Westmorland without answers, Groby would go to trial in York, where he was certain to be found guilty of murder.

CHAPTER TWENTY-THREE

IN BRIDGET'S ABSENCE, Helen had been more generous with Henry's time. She'd allowed Nate to spend a whole day with him—and herself—but it had not come without conditions.

"I cannot tell you what an awful bore my life has become," she'd said as they'd watched Henry play in the garden with Bijou. "You will never understand the sacrifices I made for our son."

Nate had bitten his tongue to keep silent. All he wanted was to be with Henry and arguing with his child's mother might cause her to take his access to his son.

"Lord Luxton is not well. He sleeps all day long."

"I am sorry to hear that," Nate had said.

"He's not even capable of..." She glanced sideways at Nate. He knew her tricks, and he felt immediately discomforted. Why could she not take 'no' for an answer? But he already knew the answer to that question. It wasn't about him at all. It was about getting what she wanted, at any cost. She could not tolerate rejection on any level, despite dishing it out whenever it suited her. He called to Henry and stepped forward, wanting to join his son in play, but she caught his arm. He stopped and turned to face her.

"I want another child," she said.

Nate was momentarily speechless. "Isn't that something you should be discussing with your husband?" he could not keep the iciness from his voice.

"My husband!" She laughed. "Didn't you hear what I just

said? He's not able to give me a child. He was barely able to consummate our marriage."

Nate turned away from her. He didn't want to talk about the intimacies of her marriage.

"You'd be doing it for Henry's sake." She stepped in front of Nate. "He deserves a brother."

Nate snorted. "I have a brother, and I can promise you that I wouldn't wish that upon anyone."

"Really, Nate. Are you still upset about…"

Nate stiffened. "About you having a liaison with my brother while we were betrothed? Not at all. I simply wouldn't wish something like that on my son. He is better off without a sibling."

"Well, perhaps I ought to ask your brother for help then. He was quite willing the first time. And who knows, he might even be Henry's father."

Nate clenched his fist behind his back. He'd never confronted Edward about his supposed liaison with Helen, nor would he, because he no longer cared. But still, the suggestion of Edward being Henry's father filled him with rage. "My brother's wife, the Countess of Westerly, is about to give him an heir, so I hardly think he will be interested in—"

"Lady Westerly is with child? Well, it's about time. Of course, she can't know it will be a boy. And if it is a girl, Edward is sure to be disappointed. And disappointed men always turn away from their wives to seek comfort in the arms of another."

Nate inhaled, trying to restore his calm and block out Helen's noise. He gazed at his son—for Henry *was* his son; he'd felt it instinctively and intuitively the first day he'd held him in his arms eight months ago. Oblivious to and unconcerned with the question of his paternity, Henry threw a stick for Bijou to fetch and giggled when the dog ran after it and snatched it up in his mouth. He was a happy little boy. At least Nate could take comfort in that.

"Are you truly content to be an innkeeper your entire life?" Helen was in front of him again. "Will you give up Henry and me for an infatuation you have with a woman far below your class?"

"I shall never give up Henry. Why do you say such a thing?"

"Think on it," she said. Then she called for Henry and took him inside.

Nate's heart drummed in his chest as he watched her go. She'd made her bid to control him through Henry crystal clear.

ᛩ

THE DAY AFTER she returned from Knaresborough, Bridget walked with Nate along the shores of Lake Windermere. It was a fine morning, and the sun warmed their backs as they strolled beside the sparkling lake, surrounded by lush green fells. Bridget inhaled, reveling in the fresh air. There was a noticeable difference in the air at home than in the bustling market towns of Yorkshire. She would never trade Westmorland for anything. This is where she grew up. *This* is where she belonged.

"Well, that's quite a turn of events," Nate said after Bridget had told him everything that had happened in Knaresborough.

"I know." Bridget sighed. "Yet still, we have nothing that will exonerate Groby. Despite everything we've learned about George, Collins, and Lady Matheson."

"At least we tried. If Groby does hang for this murder, at least we know that we did our best to ensure an innocent man was not wrongly accused. That is all we set out to do. Groby might well have done it after all."

"My instincts tell me he did not," Bridget said. "There are too many nefarious actors in this play. We are missing something…I just don't know what it is."

Nate stopped walking and took hold of Bridget's arm. A thrill passed through her at his touch. She stopped and turned to face him.

"Promise me you won't punish yourself forever if Groby hangs," he said.

Bridget lowered her gaze. How could she make such a promise? How could she live with herself if another innocent man lost his life and received a murderer's burial just like her papa? Groby had been her papa's friend. He'd been their butcher for over thirty years. And now, his body would be left to rot, hanging in a gibbet for all to see. The injustice of it was intolerable.

"Bridget," Nate said. "What happened to your papa…it was barbaric, fueled by superstitions. But Groby is different. A man was brutally murdered after Groby swore he would kill him. The court will find him guilty. You must prepare yourself for that. I think when the time comes for him to be hanged, we should leave Westmorland for a month. We will close Villa De Lacey and go somewhere far away. London or Paris. I don't care where. But I will take you away from here because…well, I cannot bear to see you suffer." He stroked Bridget's cheek and leaned forward.

He was going to kiss her again. She remembered the thrilling sensation of his lips brushing against hers, and her body tingled with anticipation. She closed her eyes and felt the softness of his lips on hers.

Then an animal-like shriek pierced the air, and Nate jerked away from her with a mild oath.

"What was that?" Bridget's heart raced as the screams continued.

"It's coming from down there." Nate took off running, and Bridget followed.

As the screamer came into focus, Bridget saw it was Lady Luxton. She stood on the shore, pounding her fists into Rupert's back. "Do something!" she screamed. "Help him! My son is drowning!"

Bridget looked out to the lake and saw Henry splashing wildly not far from the shore, his little head bobbing up and down.

"Dear God!" Nate said, kicking off his shoes and shrugging out of his tailcoat. He raced into the water.

Bridget held her breath as Nate, who was about shin-deep in

the water, pulled Henry out of the lake and lifted the child into his arms. Henry coughed and spluttered, and then started to wail, but appeared to be otherwise unharmed.

Bridget breathed a sigh of relief. Henry had been close enough to the shore that he'd likely lost his balance but had been able to hold his head up for most of his ordeal. He had, however, swallowed a lot of water from the sound of his coughing and gagging.

As Nate emerged from the water, Lady Luxton ran forward and held out her arms. "Give him to me!" she demanded. Nate reluctantly handed the child to her. She kissed Henry's face and squeezed him tightly. "Thank heavens you were here!" She reached to clutch at Nate's arm. "What would we have done? Henry would have drowned."

She turned to face Rupert, who still stood frozen. "*You* almost let him drown! What is wrong with you?"

Rupert blinked as if emerging from a trance. "I...I don't..." He stammered. Then he turned and fled.

"Why was Henry in the lake by himself?" Nate demanded.

"He wasn't...he was by my side. I only turned my back for a moment. Then, when I looked up, he was in the water. And that oaf did not help!"

"Never mind him. Where is Henry's nanny? Why wasn't she watching him?"

"I sent her to fetch his toy boat. He left it at the inn, and he was crying for it."

Bridget watched this exchange and wondered what she ought to do. She didn't want to walk away, and neither did she want to stay. "I'm going to check on Rupert. I think he's had an awful shock," she said finally.

Lady Luxton turned and glared at her. And it occurred to Bridget that she hadn't even noticed her standing there.

Nate took Henry from Lady Luxton's arms and said, "Let's get him inside. He's shivering."

"We both are." Lady Luxton continued to hold onto Nate's

arm, and Bridget watched as the three of them made their way back to Villa De Lacey. As she did, she realized with a sinking heart that Nate still and always would belong to Lady Luxton.

$$\mathcal{Q}$$

AFTER MUCH SEARCHING, Bridget found Rupert sitting under a large elm tree in the thicket, hugging his knees and rocking back and forth. He did not look at her as she approached him. Not knowing what else to do, Bridget sat down beside him and waited for him to speak. Perhaps all he needed was a comforting presence. But Rupert made no attempt to acknowledge her. He kept staring ahead, clutching his knees, and rocking back and forth. He seemed to be in a state of shock, and it frightened Bridget.

"Rupert," she finally said.

He gave no answer.

Bridget couldn't take the silence any longer. She felt the need to do something—*anything* to end the frightening rocking and staring. "You mustn't feel ashamed," she said. "You were in shock, and you froze. There's no shame in that. Lady Luxton was scared. That's why she said...well, you understand. She was frightened, that's all. Don't take it to heart."

Rupert turned to look at her, but his black eyes seemed blank as though he were staring right through her.

Bridget's heart quickened. Something felt wrong.

"Henry is going to be fine." She forced a smile. "He swallowed some water and got a terrible fright, but he is not hurt. You mustn't worry."

"He's drowned, you little twit!" Rupert's voice had deepened and become someone else's entirely. "You watched him die, and you did *nothing!*"

Bridget scrambled to her feet. "Stop," she said. "You're scaring me." She took a step back, but Rupert reached out and grabbed her ankle, sending her plummeting to the ground. She struggled to get free, but he held fast.

$$\mathcal{Q}$$

"RUPERT!" THE VOICE wasn't hers; it came from behind her. "Let her go!"

Charlie was at his brother's side. He crouched in front of him and shook him by the shoulders. "Let her go!"

Rupert released her, and she backed away from him. Rupert blinked, and then frowned at Bridget as if he had no idea what had just transpired.

"He didn't mean it," Charlie said, getting to his feet and helping Bridget up. "Please, it was the shock of seeing that little boy almost drown. I came as soon as I heard."

Bridget looked down at Rupert, who still sat on the ground, looking confused.

"Are you hurt?" Charlie stepped closer to her. "Did he…"

"No," Bridget said. "I'm fine. I was frightened, that's all. He frightened me."

"He didn't know what he was doing. He wouldn't have…it was the shock, you see." Charlie's pale face was creased with concern, and his dark brown eyes were soft and sympathetic, quite the opposite of Rupert's eyes moments earlier. Then she noticed it—a small, but deep scar at the corner of his left eye.

And suddenly, it all made sense.

"You're the caretaker's sons, aren't you?" she said.

⚜

CHAPTER TWENTY-FOUR

"**G**EORGE RUINED OUR lives," Charlie said. He and Rupert sat across from Nate and Bridget in the study, each with a brandy in hand. "But we didn't kill him."

Nate folded his arms. "You traveled from Dorset to Yorkshire with the express purpose of finding and befriending Mr. Otis so you could exact revenge, and you expect us to believe you *didn't* kill him?"

Bridget remembered the blank look in Rupert's eyes, and she shuddered. In that moment, she'd thought him capable of murder.

"That's right," Charlie said. It was odd for Rupert to be silent and for Charlie to be speaking when she was used to the opposite. But Rupert seemed to have lost the desire to communicate completely. "We knew he'd been sent to the north because our father told us when he was on his deathbed. He told us to avenge our brother's murder."

"So, you went to Knaresborough?" Nate asked.

"That was the plan, but we stopped in York first, and it was by sheer accident that we found him there—at a poetry reading. Of course, he was only playing at being a poet. Nothing he wrote belonged to him. He stole every line from the talented but struggling poets he met. He took their work and passed it along as his own."

Bridget swallowed. He'd been yet another person who'd gained her trust and then managed to fool her completely.

"All his talk of capturing nature's beauty and sublimity with his words. It was all a lie." Charlie snorted. "We knew who he was immediately. At least, Rupert did. He was seven when it happened. I was only five."

"You mean when your infant brother drowned?" Nate said.

"I mean, when George killed him," Charlie said, his voice bitter.

"And George didn't recognize you?" Bridget asked, wanting to break the tension.

"No. At least, if he did, he didn't say so. We used different names, of course. But to be honest, I don't think he'd bothered to give us a second thought in years. He was selfish, and, despite his persona, he only cared for one person—himself."

"Then your names aren't Rupert and Charlie?" Nate said.

Charlie shook his head.

"So, what was your plan? Befriend Otis, gain his trust, and then? How were you planning to extract revenge?" Nate asked.

Charlie opened his mouth to speak, but Rupert's words cut off his brother's speech.

"Kill him," Rupert said.

A chill ran down Bridget's spine.

"I was planning to kill him, and I would have done so if Groby hadn't got to him first."

"Did he? Or did you frame Groby?" Nate asked.

"I saw an opportunity," Rupert said. "Everyone was talking about Groby's pretty young wife, who always seemed to be in the company of George or Collins. It was easy to goad him. A man like that—all one needs to do is call him a cuckold in front of a room full of men, especially when he's far in his cups, and he is bound to threaten murder. A man must defend his pride, after all."

"And then you went and did the deed," Nate said.

Rupert shook his head. "That was my plan—to kill George and blame it on Groby. I wanted George dead, but I wasn't about to hang for murder and leave my brother on his own. I knew

Groby's threat was meaningless. He was too drunk to do anything but stumble home and crawl into bed next to his wife. So, I waited until he left The Black Horse, and then I went to find George. I knew he'd be with Lady Patterson—his mama. She'd been giving him money and hiding her real identity. But I recognized her immediately. I planned to conceal myself just inside the gates of Villa De Lacey and wait for them to return from their moonlit walk. If I thought I could have managed it, I would have planned to kill them both. But that was too large a task, so I planned to let George walk her to the door, and then I aimed to ambush him on his way out. I must have waited an hour. But they never arrived."

"Do you expect us to believe that story? You place yourself at the scene of the crime, and you admit that you were there to kill Otis. Not only did you have a motive to kill him, but his mother as well."

"It's true. I wanted them both dead, and I went there to kill George. I won't deny that. But in the end, there was no need for me to get my hands dirty. I was wrong about Groby. His threat wasn't meaningless. He killed George as promised. And as for Lady Matheson, she died by her own hand. I knew she would take her own life as soon as I told her who I was and that I was going to let the magistrate know she was a madwoman who had escaped captivity. They would have returned her to Cornwall and locked her away in an asylum forever. With George dead and her estate and freedom gone, she had nothing left to live for."

The malice in Rupert's voice broke Bridget's heart. She recognized his anger as masked pain. He had been steeped in that pain for so long that it had turned him into a person ready to kill.

"This is outrageous!" Nate fumed. "I'm calling the magistrate."

Charlie, who'd been sitting with his head in his hands, suddenly looked up and shouted, "No!"

"Call him if you wish," Rupert said. "But you will be letting a murderer go free and condemning an innocent man to death."

The words sent a chill down Bridget's spine.

"Like it or not, Groby killed George," Rupert said. "I know because I stumbled upon his body in the daffodils that night. I will admit to one thing, however." He smirked. "*I* am the one who took George's heart, and I am proud of it."

"What do you mean?" Nate said. He was certain Rupert was mad and playing games with him. He was the killer, but he wasn't going to admit it. "Do you expect us to believe you took a man's heart, but you didn't kill him?"

"I went to find George, like I said. But after waiting by the gates, I grew weary. Still, I wasn't ready to give up. The moon was out, and the stars were ablaze. It was a perfect night, and I knew George was meeting Lady Matheson because he'd bragged about it earlier. He never gave on that she was his mama. Instead, he boasted about how she was besotted with him and plied him with banknotes. It was sickening."

"Stick to the facts," Nate said irritably. He was still shaken by what had happened earlier with Henry and was in no mood for Rupert's unhinged rambling.

"Very well. As I said, I became weary of waiting, and once or twice, I dozed off behind the bush where I hid—but only for a little while."

Nate sighed.

"Then, I heard what sounded like a loud grunt followed by a short shriek. I'd been half asleep, and my eyes flew open. I sat up and listened but heard nothing further. So, I stood up and tried to keep myself hidden while I went to investigate. I peeked past the gates onto the grounds, and that's when I saw it."

"Saw what?" Nate could not keep the irritation from his voice. He was certain Rupert was inventing nonsense.

"Movement—someone running toward the villa. I couldn't say who it was because it was dark, and the figure was clad in black. I could barely make out the shape. I rubbed my eyes, which were heavy with weariness, to make sure I wasn't dreaming, and that's when I thought I saw the door to the villa close."

Nate glanced at Bridget, who looked as confused as he felt.

"I still thought I might be dreaming—or perhaps, I imagined it. So, I went to investigate. I walked across the garden through daffodils. And that's when I stumbled over George's body."

"How very convenient," Nate said dryly. "If Groby had killed Otis as you claim he did, why would he run into Villa De Lacey?"

"I don't think it was Groby I saw. I think it was Lady Matheson. I think she went out to meet George by the daffodils and came across his body. I heard her shriek and then saw her run back into the house."

"Surely, she would have screamed for help if she saw her son lying dead among the daffodils," Bridget said.

Rupert shrugged. "I don't have an answer for that. I can only tell you what I saw. And I can't tell you how happy I was to see George lying in the daffodils with a large knife sticking out of his chest."

"A knife?" Nate said.

"That's correct. A large one, just like I'd expect Groby would have in his collection. It was much bigger than the one I'd brought with me to slit George's throat. So I used it to cut him open and take his heart—just like he'd taken the hearts of my mama and papa."

Nate noticed that Rupert's fists were clenched. He glanced at Charlie, who sat pale-faced and silent.

"What did you do with it? The heart?" Nate asked.

"I tossed it in the lake and watched it drown. It seemed fitting after what George had done to my brother."

"And the knife?" Nate said. He wasn't believing a word of this story.

"Kept it. Until I came here."

"What do you mean?"

"I wanted to keep it as a trophy—a reminder of how I'd managed to avenge my brother. But after Lady Luxton brought me and Charlie here, I thought it would be too risky to keep. At first, I thought about burying it, but then I realized it would be much easier to put it in the kitchen among the other knives. So that is where it is."

Nate folded his arms. "I think you are wasting our time with this nonsense. I think you killed Otis because you were the one waiting for him, and you have already admitted to cutting out his heart. You framed Groby, and *you* shall take his place at the gallows."

"No!" Charlie stood up. "Please. I beg you. He's telling the truth."

"That will be something for the magistrate to decide," Nate said.

—⟡—

CHAPTER TWENTY-FIVE

Lady Luxton clutched Nate's arm as the magistrate led Rupert away. "I shudder to think how much danger I was in," she said. "He could have killed me and Henry."

"That's exactly why I told you to leave. Fortunately, he had no interest in hurting you or Henry. Still, you should have listened to me."

Bridget stood behind the pair but was too worried about Charlie to give them her full attention. He stood beside her, pale as a ghost and trembling from head to foot.

"You will stay at Villa De Lacey for a while, won't you, Charlie?" She hated to think of him alone after having lost the most important person in the world to him. She knew how painful that was.

"How can I? After you accused my brother? He told you he was innocent."

"Is that really what you believe? You know him better than anyone."

Charlie bit his lip, and his large, dark eyes filled with tears. "I don't know. He…he is a good person, but he…well, George and his mother ruined our lives."

"I understand how painful this is for you. That's why I hope you will stay—even if it's only for a few days."

"I shan't be paying for his bill anymore," Lady Luxton said, turning to face Bridget. "His brother almost killed my Henry."

Bridget's jaw ached with tension. *Can't she see that Charlie is in distress? Why does she have to be so cruel?*

"You are the one who sent Henry's nanny away," Nate said. "And you are the one who should have been watching him."

Lady Luxton released Nate's arm, and her lovely dark eyes flashed angrily at him. "I see you refuse to change," she said, and then stormed away, pushing past Bridget in the process.

"I think it's best I leave," Charlie said.

"Charlie," a voice sounded behind Bridget, and she turned to see Miss Jennings. "What's happening. Why did they take Rupert?"

"Perhaps you should ask Miss De Lacey. I'm going to pack my things."

"Wait," Bridget called after Charlie.

"Let him go." Nate put an arm on Bridget's shoulder. "It's for the best."

"What have you done?" Miss Jennings said in her usual whispery breath. "Rupert is innocent."

🔍

THE NEXT MORNING, Bridget awoke feeling refreshed but not entirely cheerful. With Rupert arrested, Groby had been released from prison in York and was on his way home to be reunited with his wife and children. Collins, who was still recovering from his injuries, had reportedly written home to his family in the hope they'd reconcile with him and allow him to convalesce there. And Lady Luxton was once again threatening to return to Scotland, although she had yet to make good on her threat.

Yet, despite justice being served, there would be no happy outcome. Poor Charlie would suffer greatly. If only he'd stayed on at Villa De Lacey. Perhaps then he'd have strengthened his bond with Miss Jennings. She reminded Bridget of Jane when she'd first arrived at Villa De Lacey—beaten down by her husband's cruel aunt, Lady Darby, for being unable to provide her with a grandnephew. And now, a year later, Jane was flourishing. Her womb, which she'd once thought barren, had opened, and her entire disposition had changed. Away from the oppressive Lady Darby, and despite her rather inattentive husband, she'd blossomed into a sociable and happy woman with a zest for life.

Bridget slipped out of bed, and Bijou, who sat in his basket, raised his head and wagged his tail. He watched expectantly as Bridget washed. He was ready for his walk.

By the time Harriet entered with Bridget's tea, she was sitting at her dresser brushing her hair.

"I'll take that, miss," Harriet said, setting down the tea and taking the silver brush from Bridget. She began to arrange Bridget's hair in a low bun. "Rose tells me that Miss Jane is ill this morning," Harriet said.

"Ill?" Bridget's stomach tightened. Illness was never a good thing, but it was especially alarming for women in Jane's condition. "What's wrong?"

"She didn't say, miss. But the doctor is being fetched."

"Good grief!" Bridget stood up, causing Harriet to stumble backwards.

"Your hair, miss."

"I must go to Jane. Will you see to Bijou?"

"Of course, miss. But your hair…it needs another clip…"

"Never mind that," Bridget said, picking up a hair clip and shoving it in place to secure her bun. "I must go to Jane now."

Guilt gnawed at Bridget as she made her way to Jane's room. With all the commotion the day before, she had neglected to check on her friend. She knocked softly on Jane's chamber door, and her lady's maid, Rose, answered.

"Oh, Miss De Lacey. I was hoping it were Mr. Harley with the doctor."

"How is she?" Bridget asked.

"Poorly, miss." Rose opened the door, and Bridget stepped inside. A stench of sickness assailed her nostrils. And she covered her nose with her hand. "Do open a window," she said.

"I'm afraid to, miss," the maid said, "lest the air do her harm."

"Harm? When did fresh air ever do anyone harm?" Bridget drew open the curtains and opened the windows, welcoming the blast of crisp air to her nostrils.

Then she turned and smiled, prepared to cheer Jane. But her smile quickly faded when she saw her friend's deathly pale face. A chamber pot sat next to her bed, filled with sick.

"Take that away," Bridget snapped, "and bring her a clean one."

Jane groaned. And Bridget went to her side.

"It started last night, miss," Rose said. "We thought it were just because of the babe. You know, some women can't hold their food when they are with child, like my cousin every morning for months, but this is different, miss. She looks…I don't know…I'm afraid for her babe."

"Yes, I know," Bridget said. "I am too. But we must do what we can, and the best thing you can do now is to take that away and get a clean, cool cloth for her forehead."

"Yes, miss," Rose said.

Bridget caressed her friend's forehead. It felt clammy and sticky. Then she noticed that Jane's fist was clenched shut. She was holding something in the palm of her hand. Bridget caressed Jane's fist, and Jane's fingers relaxed. Bridget eased them open. Inside Jane's palm lay the miniature portrait of George.

Bridget gasped.

Just then, Rose opened the chamber door and Jane heard her say, "Doctor, thank heavens."

Bridget snatched the miniature and stood up. Dr. Elias, Nate, and Jane's husband, Mr. Harley, entered the room.

"How is she?" Mr. Harley glanced down at the chamber pot Rose held and winced.

"Poorly, sir," Rose said. "She complains of horrible stomach pains. An' she hardly touched her tea. A few sips were all she could manage to wet her parched throat."

"I'd better take a look." Dr. Elias pushed past Rose, followed by Harley and Nate.

"Miss De Lacey," Harley said as Bridget scurried out of the way. "Good of you to come. You'll be a great comfort to Jane."

"I came as soon as I heard," Nate said to Bridget.

She squeezed the portrait in her fist as she watched Dr. Elias start to examine Jane. And although he was Jane's husband, Mr. Harley turned his back and went to gaze out the window with Nate by his side. That was a good thing, Bridget realized, because she almost bit her lip to shreds when Jane's body started to convulse. Thankfully, it only lasted seconds.

Why does Jane have George's portrait? What can it mean?

Dr. Elias finished examining Jane and looked up with a grave expression on his face. "Sometimes a woman with child suffers nausea and sickness, and in rare cases, it becomes so severe that it can kill her."

Harley gasped, and Bridget turned to see Nate put a comforting hand on his shoulder. Bridget forced herself to keep her composure, even though she wanted to collapse to the floor.

"I don't think that is the case here."

Bridget breathed a sigh of relief.

"I think she's been poisoned."

"What?" Harley strode forward. "Who would poison a woman…and one with child at that? Who would do such a thing?"

"I don't know. I'm not a magistrate. But the extent of the vomitus, convulsions, and severe stomach cramps coupled with the fact that someone in this villa has already been poisoned with arsenic, leads me to believe it's possible she was too."

Bridget squeezed the miniature so hard that the metal of the small oval frame that housed it bit into her palm. *Did Jane have a liaison with George? Had she been in love with him?* She glanced at Harley. *Did he know? And if so, did he kill George? Had they gotten everything wrong and sent another innocent man to his potential death?*

She recalled Miss Jennings's words, "'Rupert is innocent.'"

Rose reentered the room with a clean chamber pot and washcloth. She closed the door and froze, no doubt sensing the tension in the room. "Shall I…go?" she whispered to no one in particular.

"Stay," Doctor Elias said. "I have some questions for you."

Rose crept forward and placed the clean chamber pot and cloth on the small table next to Jane's bed.

"When was the last time your mistress ate?"

"She ate dinner last night."

He looked at Mr. Harley, Nate, and Bridget. "Did you all eat from the same dishes?"

They all nodded.

"And no one else is sick?"

"Not that we know of," Nate said.

"Did she consume anything else?" Dr. Elias turned back to Rose.

"Warm chocolate. She likes something sweet now that she's with child. Miss Jennings suggested the chocolate. She said when her dear sister were with child, nothing made her happier than a cup of warm chocolate before bed."

"Who prepared the chocolate?"

"Miss Jennings insisted on preparing it herself. It was ever so kind of her."

Miss Jennings! But why? Bridget opened her hand and glanced at the portrait.

"What's that?" Nate asked.

Bridget held out her palm, exposing the portrait. "Jane was clutching this in her fist."

Nate took the portrait and turned to Harley. "What do you know about this?"

Heat spread across Harley's pale, freckled skin. He turned to Rose. "Wait outside."

She left the room, and Harley said, "As it turns out, I am the one who is barren, not my wife."

"Didn't you learn anything from last summer?" Nate growled. "How many women must end up dead in your quest to have a child?"

"How many women die in childbirth every year?" Harley threw up his hands. "None of this was my fault. She fell in love with him. I didn't tell her to do it."

Bridget's gaze flew to Jane—her sweet, understanding friend—lying still and pale in the bed. All she'd wanted was to be a mother.

She'd been so good with the Groby's children, so loving. So made to be a mother. And she'd been so happy to finally learn she was with child. Her greatest wish had been granted, and her joy had been palpable.

And now…

"But you didn't care either."

"We didn't marry for love, as you well know. Our union is worth nothing without a child."

"Well, congratulations, because you are about to lose both wife and babe—"

No. It couldn't be. There had been too much death, and for her beloved Jane to be its next victim…the men's arguing became unbearable. "Stop!" Bridget yelled.

The two men turned and looked at her in stunned silence.

"Jane has been poisoned. She might *die!*" She glared at the men, who seemed unable to comprehend her feelings.

"I don't think she's been given a lethal dose," Dr. Elias said. "I believe she was given just enough to make her very ill—ill enough to end her pregnancy."

Oh no! Bridget covered her trembling lips with her hand. She wanted to cry out. Poor Jane! Who would do such a thing?

Nate appeared to have an inkling. He strode forward and pulled open the chamber door. "Rose," he said, "go and find Miss Jennings. Tell her Mrs. Harley is in desperate need of a cup of tea sweetened with plenty of sugar. Ask her if she'd be so kind to help you by preparing it herself and bringing it to Mrs. Harley's room." Then he shut the door and turned to Harley. "It's best you go back to Braithwaite and fetch the magistrate."

CHAPTER TWENTY-SIX

ROSE RETURNED TO the room several minutes later and reported that Miss Jennings would be up shortly with the tea. They all waited in silence for Miss Jennings to arrive. Bridget alternated between worrying about Jane, who lay groaning on the bed in apparent agony, and with her mind reeling about the possibility that shy, frail Miss Jennings could have committed these heinous killings.

It seemed incomprehensible.

Finally, a knock sounded on the door, and Rose went to open it.

"I have the tea." Miss Jennings stepped inside, carefully carrying a teacup. "Made with extra love and care for poor Mrs. Harley. I do hope—" She looked up from the cup and stopped when she saw everyone, including the doctor, waiting for her. "What's—oh, I didn't realize—should I fetch more tea?"

"That won't be necessary," Nate said. "In fact, Mrs. Harley is too ill for tea. So why don't you drink it instead?"

"Oh, no. I couldn't!" Miss Jennings looked alarmed. "I don't like sugar, you see. And I put three lumps in this cup," she babbled nervously, her usual shy tone sounding strident and almost hysterical to Bridget's ears. "It's…it's too sweet for me."

"Take a sip," Nate said. "Go on." He lowered his voice and raised his brows. "Unless there is something in there that would hurt you if you did."

Miss Jennings's hand appeared to shake as tea began to slosh over the edges of the cup. "What? No!"

"Very well. Then give it to Miss De Lacey," Nate said. "She'd like a cup of tea. Isn't that right, Miss De Lacey?" He turned to Bridget.

Well played, Nate. "Yes, thank you. I would. I am dearly thirsty." Bridget reached for the cup, but Miss Jennings stepped back.

"No, it's..." Her hands trembled, and she dropped the cup. Tea stained the plush pink carpet. "Oh dear, look what you made me do."

Dr. Elias stepped forward and picked up the cup. "There's still a little in here." He peered into the cup. "It'll be enough," he said.

"For what?" Miss Jennings asked.

"I have a solution in my bag to test for arsenic."

Bridget knew that Dr. Elias was lying. If he'd had a way to test for arsenic, he would have tested the contents of the snuff box after Lady Matheson died and Louisa got sick. But Miss Jennings evidently did not know as much.

She stood frozen as Dr. Elias rummaged in his bag and then took out a small bottle of liquid, shook it, and said, "Right, I'll simply pour a few drops of this tea in here and if it turns green, then..."

"Stop!" Nate lunged forward as Miss Jennings made a dash for the door. He caught her by the arm, and she squealed.

"I only gave her a pinch—just enough to make her sick. Not enough to kill her."

Everyone fell silent.

Fury rose in Bridget's chest, hot and searing. "Why?" She stepped forward. "Mrs. Harley is with child! You know that. And she has been nothing but good to you." Angry tears formed in her eyes. It wasn't fair!

"With child!" Miss Jennings spat the words. Her demeanor had entirely changed. "Do you know whose child she carries?"

"Yes." Bridget turned and held out her hand for Nate to give her the portrait. He put it in her palm, and then she offered it to

Miss Jennings.

Instead of snatching it up, Miss Jennings recoiled. "Get it away from me," she said. "I cannot stand to look upon his likeness."

"Why?" Bridget did not move her hand.

"Because he killed my sister!"

🔍

BRIDGET CURLED HER fist around the portrait, eliminating it from sight. Then they all waited for Miss Jennings to continue.

"Two and a half years ago, my younger sister was seventeen. She was very beautiful, and Papa had great hopes for her making a good marriage." She smirked. "I, however, had been a great disappointment. Six years of money spent on London Seasons and no proposals before he gave up on me completely. But Lilian, well, she was different. She was going to save my father's estate— our home in Cambridge. We were landed gentry, you see, but Papa was fast running out of money. He'd wasted far too much of it on me. Or so he said, though it was obvious he was losing it in other ways. Papa wasn't a businessman, and he wasn't skilled at growing an income. Lilian was all he had left. He had high hopes she'd marry a viscount or earl. He wanted both title and money for her. For us."

"That sounds rather awful," Bridget could not help saying.

"I thought so too," she said. "Consequently, I didn't agree with his plans. All I wanted was for Lilian to be happy. So, when she met George—a man my papa would never have approved of—I kept her secret safe. George was studying to be a clergyman at Cambridge. He seemed to me like a good sort. So, I helped their romance blossom by chaperoning their secret meetings. We both had to wear veils to disguise ourselves. If anyone recognized us and told our papa…well, at the time, I feared it greatly. Now, I wish someone had discovered our secret."

"You said George murdered your sister?" Nate said, and Bridget could feel his impatience wafting off of him in waves. She wondered if anyone else could sense it. "Why?"

"As time passed, George would request the meetings be in more secluded areas—the woodland and such. I would accompany her to the meeting place, but then they would go off on their own. By that time, I trusted George, so I'd sit among the trees and the bluebells and read my books while they enjoyed each other's company." She inhaled and smiled. "It was glorious for both of us to escape the oppressions of home. I love the peacefulness of the woodlands—the rippling brook and the sweet smell of the wildflowers." She swallowed. "I didn't think about what Lilian and George were doing. At that time, I didn't know about men and women…"

Bridget shifted her stance. The conversation had taken an uncomfortable turn.

"So, when Lilian came to me and told me she was with child, I simply couldn't understand how. But that didn't matter. She had to marry George, or she'd be ruined forever. I knew that much. George said he was thrilled about the babe, and I helped them plan their elopement. But on the night in question, he never materialized. At first, we thought something terrible had happened to him, but as the days passed, it became clear that he'd simply abandoned her." Miss Jennings paused, and when she spoke again, her voice had changed. It was guttural and filled with anger. "Lilian was broken. She couldn't take the shame. She took hemlock and died the most horrendous death."

Bridget stifled her gasp with her hand. Miss Jennings's anger now made complete sense to her. If she were mad, she'd been driven to it by George. He'd driven so many people to madness, it appeared. "Did your sister go looking for George? Did she go to George's family in Knaresborough and tell them what he'd done? That he'd abandoned her with child?" Bridget asked, recalling the story Mrs. Phillips had told her.

"Knaresborough? No. That's miles away from Cambridge.

She didn't even know George was from Knaresborough. He said his father had a grand estate in Cornwall."

So, Lilian Jennings wasn't the only young lady George had ruined.

"How did you come to find George here in Westmorland after all those years?" Nate asked.

"After Lilian died, Papa couldn't bear to look at me. I think he grew to hate me. So, he sent me away to be Lady Armstrong's companion. Suddenly, I'd lost my sister and my home, and I was imprisoned day and night in Lady Armstrong's cold, rambling mansion in Keighley. But all I could think about was George, and how I'd like to cut out his heart."

A chill ran through Bridget, not because of Miss Jennings's declaration, but because she understood it. She had felt the murderous desire of revenge that comes after a loved one is taken by someone else's callousness or cruelty.

"So, imagine my surprise when Lady Armstrong acquired a copy of Wordsworth's *Guide to the Lakes* and insisted on coming to Westmorland. Then imagine my surprise when, after our arrival at Villa De Lacey, I saw George playing the part of a poet without a care in the world." She smirked. "George was no poet. I know more about poetry than he ever did. Why do you think he took an interest in me? It wasn't because he had a kind heart and wanted to offer solace to a spinster. No, it was because I supplied him with the poems he claimed as his own."

"What?" Bridget exclaimed. "You wrote all those poems George read to the guests?"

"Indeed," Miss Jennings spat out the word.

"I don't understand," Nate said. "George didn't recognize you as Lilian's sister?"

"George never saw my face because I always wore a veil to protect my identity from prying eyes when chaperoning. Nor did he ever ask to see me. I was a spinster and of no interest to him. George only had eyes for my beautiful sister. And after he took what he wanted from her, he discarded her."

"How did you kill George?" Nate asked bluntly.

"I had a new poem for him, or so I told him. He arranged to meet me by the daffodils. I was to wait until he finished his walk with Lady Matheson and then slip outside and meet him. All went to plan. He was lying in the daffodils, gazing at the stars, waiting for me as he always did. But this time, when I left the villa, I picked up a rock I'd placed at the bottom of the stairs earlier that day. When I got to the daffodils, I whispered George's name, and he sat up. But before he had a chance to turn and greet me, I brought the rock down onto his skull. He didn't even cry out. He just groaned like a wounded animal. But he didn't go down, so I brought the rock down over and over again, until he stopped his awful moaning and slumped to the ground." A dreamy smile appeared on her face. "It was picture perfect. George's blood spilling on the golden daffodils under the moonlight. I think upon it often." She giggled and spun around in a sort of clumsy pirouette. "'And then my heart with pleasure fills, and dances with the daffodils.'"

Bridget swallowed. She wondered what Wordsworth would think when he learned that the meaning of his words had been skewed in such a murderous way.

"What about his heart?" Nate said.

"I tried to take it. I plunged my knife into his chest, and I tried to cut him open, but I didn't have the strength."

"What knife?" Nate said. "Where did you get a knife?"

"I took it from the kitchen earlier in the evening just in case the rock failed me. They were used to seeing me down there because Lady Armstrong is very specific about her chocolate and insists that I am the one who makes it for her. She instructed me on how to do it as soon as I became her companion, and she will turn anything back that is not according to her taste."

"Back to the knife?" Nate said. "Did you leave it in his chest?"

"Yes. Imagine my shock the next day when he was found with his heart cut out. It seems there was more than one person who wanted George Otis's heart." She giggled maniacally.

"So, Rupert was telling the truth," Nate said. "And what

about Lady Matheson? Did you kill her too?"

"Indeed, I did. I couldn't stomach the way she spoke about George to everyone, as though he were a hero. And then she talked of erecting a monument to him by the lake, so people would remember what a great poet he was. It made my stomach turn. That's when I decided to mix some arsenic into her nightly laudanum supply. I wanted to eliminate all trace of George from this world."

"All trace of him," Bridget said, looking sadly at Jane.

"That's right. All trace. And now that my work is done, I am ready to go to my sister."

Just as she said those words, the chamber door opened, and a breathless Mr. Harley entered with Magistrate Hunt.

"What is going on here?" the magistrate demanded.

Miss Jennings stepped forward. "I just confessed to killing Mr. Otis and Lady Matheson. Take me to the gallows and let me rot for all I care."

Magistrate Hunt looked from Nate to Dr. Elias. "Is this a game?"

"It's no game," Dr. Elias said. "We all heard her confession. She killed Mr. Otis. But it seems young Rupert was the one who took the man's heart, just as he said."

"Well, I never." Magistrate Hunt looked down at the petite Miss Jennings. Then he took her by the arm and led her out of the room.

As he did, she shrieked, "I killed George Otis, and I want all the world to know it."

The sounds of her crazed laughter echoed through the hall.

EPILOGUE

Summer 1821

NATE HELD EDMUND Groby close around the waist as he dipped the little boy's feet into Lake Windermere. The child giggled and screamed with delight each time his toes touched the water.

Bridget sat on a blanket next to Jane, now big with child, and Alice, who held her daughter on her lap and watched Nate with a smile on her face.

"I shall miss this place," Jane said mournfully.

"And I shall miss you," Bridget said, turning her attention to her friend. "I do wish you didn't have to go to London."

"I know. But Lady Darby insists. She says if we want her money, then we must return. She won't have her grandnephew growing up so far from proper society."

"What if you birth a girl?" Alice asked.

"I shouldn't mind a little girl." Jane smiled at Alice's cherub-faced daughter. "But I'm afraid it would mean that Lady Darby would cut us out of her will."

"How awful," Bridget said.

"Perhaps you will be like me and have one of each," Alice said.

Jane dropped her gaze and caressed her stomach, and Bridget knew what she was thinking. With a barren husband, this babe was likely to be her only child. Only Bridget, Nate, Mr. Harley, and Dr. Elias knew that George was the father of Jane's child—

aside from Miss Jennings, of course, and she'd been locked away in an asylum with no hope of ever being freed.

"Mr. Squires will make a good papa," Alice said. "I wonder why he does not marry."

The comment shot through Bridget's heart like an arrow. Despite being unmarried, Nate was not free. Lady Luxton had left him at the altar, but she had him in her control. Bridget watched Nate play with Edmund in the water, and she knew how painful it was for him now that Lady Luxton had taken Henry back to Scotland. There was no doubt in her mind that Nate cared for her as much as she cared for him, but if they were ever to marry, Lady Luxton would cut him off from Henry. She'd have no reason to ever visit Villa De Lacey again.

"You must come and visit me in London," Jane said, interrupting Bridget's thoughts. "It's a shame you never had a Season. You would have been—would be—hailed as the greatest beauty of London."

"Would be? What are you implying? I am two-and-twenty and too old to debut into society."

"Two-and-twenty is hardly an old maid," Jane scoffed. "You would be inundated with offers of marriage."

Bridget laughed, but inside her heart cracked. The truth was that if she ever wanted to marry and have a family, she would have to leave Villa De Lacey and Nate behind. But the alternative was to grow old while living in Lady Luxton's shadow.

Just then, Bennett appeared with a silver tray in his hand and stood on the shore a few feet from Nate. Nate stepped out of the water, put Edmund down, and took an envelope off the silver tray Bennett held. Bridget watched as he opened the envelope and read the letter enclosed within. She saw the color drain from his face as he finished reading, and her chest tightened. Had something happened to Henry?

She stood and went to him. "What is it? Is something the matter?"

Nate dismissed Bennett and then turned his attention to

Bridget. "It's my brother," he said. "He and the countess were both killed in a carriage accident."

Bridget gasped.

"I am summoned to London as the new Earl of Westerly."

Author's Note

In 1821, when this book takes place, the town known as Windermere today was called Braithwaite. It was a lot smaller than what I describe in this book, but I have taken license for the sake of my story. In 1821, Braithwaite and Lake Windermere were in the county of Westmorland (today called Cumbria). When I refer to Windermere in this book, I'm referring to Lake Windermere. Thank you for reading *Death Among the Daffodils*. I hope you enjoyed it.

About the Author

Aviva holds a master's degree in English and has a keen interest in British literature. She is an anglophile and Brontë enthusiast who is happiest when traveling to or writing about England. Inspiration for her first book, The Mist on Brontë Moor, came after she visited the Brontë Parsonage in Haworth.

Born and raised in Cape Town, South Africa, Aviva now lives in Southern California with her husband, two daughters, and rambunctious Yorkshire terrier—named for the oft-forgotten Brontë brother Branwell.

Website: www.avivaorrauthor.com
Twitter: twitter.com/aviva_orr
Facebook: facebook.com/AuthorAvivaOrr
Goodreads: goodreads.com/author/show/6464067.Aviva_Orr
Bookbub: bookbub.com/profile/aviva-orr